"S... its elegant writing, ex... xquisitely romantic lov... —*Chicago Tribune*

"Deft plotting and sparkling characters mark this superior debut historical . . . Thomas propels the plot forward with revealing repartee and gives the leads real nuance. . . . The results are steamy and smart."

—*Publishers Weekly* (starred review)

"Thomas tantalizes readers as she skillfully peels away the layers of Cam and Gigi's relationship in an enchanting, thought-provoking story of love lost and ultimately reclaimed. Lively banter, electric sexual tension, and an unusual premise make this stunning debut all the more refreshing." —*Library Journal* (starred review)

"Thomas's lyrical writing is really the star of the show. There are writers who can tell a great story, and writers who can tell a great story with beauty and artistry. Thomas is in the latter category, and her writing is, quite simply, a cut above." —*All About Romance*

"We readers of romance go through a lot of books. A few are wallbangers, more are okay but not great, even more are enjoyable, and some are more than that. When I'm reading a book that falls into that fourth and smallest category, I find myself saying, 'OMG, I can't believe how good this is' with one part of my brain, while the rest of it is saying, 'Shut up and keep reading.' . . . Needless to say, this is an A read for me." —*Dear Author*

continued . . .

Beguiling
the Beauty

SHERRY THOMAS

BERKLEY SENSATION, NEW YORK

THE BERKLEY PUBLISHING GROUP
Published by the Penguin Group
Penguin Group (USA) Inc.
375 Hudson Street, New York, New York 10014, USA

Penguin Group (Canada), 90 Eglinton Avenue East, Suite 700, Toronto, Ontario M4P 2Y3, Canada
(a division of Pearson Penguin Canada Inc.) • Penguin Books Ltd., 80 Strand, London WC2R 0RL,
England • Penguin Group Ireland, 25 St. Stephen's Green, Dublin 2, Ireland (a division of Penguin
Books Ltd.) • Penguin Group (Australia), 250 Camberwell Road, Camberwell, Victoria 3124, Australia
(a division of Pearson Australia Group Pty. Ltd.) • Penguin Books India Pvt. Ltd., 11 Community
Centre, Panchsheel Park, New Delhi—110 017, India • Penguin Group (NZ), 67 Apollo Drive,
Rosedale, Auckland 0632, New Zealand (a division of Pearson New Zealand Ltd.) • Penguin Books
(South Africa) (Pty.) Ltd., 24 Sturdee Avenue, Rosebank, Johannesburg 2196, South Africa

Penguin Books Ltd., Registered Offices: 80 Strand, London WC2R 0RL, England

This is a work of fiction. Names, characters, places, and incidents either are the product of the author's
imagination or are used fictitiously, and any resemblance to actual persons, living or dead, business
establishments, events, or locales is entirely coincidental. The publisher does not have any control over
and does not assume any responsibility for author or third-party websites or their content.

BEGUILING THE BEAUTY

A Berkley Sensation Book / published by arrangement with the author

PUBLISHING HISTORY
Berkley Sensation mass-market edition / May 2012

ISBN: 978-0-425-24696-2

BERKLEY SENSATION®
Berkley Sensation Books are published by The Berkley Publishing Group,
a division of Penguin Group (USA) Inc.,
375 Hudson Street, New York, New York 10014.
BERKLEY SENSATION® is a registered trademark of Penguin Group (USA) Inc.
The "B" design is a trademark of Penguin Group (USA) Inc.

PRINTED IN THE UNITED STATES OF AMERICA

10 9 8 7 6 5 4 3 2 1

ALWAYS LEARNING   **PEARSON**

For my agent, Kristin Nelson,
who makes everything possible

ACKNOWLEDGMENTS

Wendy McCurdy, for her exceptional instincts and abundant patience.

Kristin Nelson, for an invaluable last-minute consultation. And for her yummy crème brûlée.

Kris Alice Hohls, for correcting all the German phrases in the manuscript—and for being wonderful.

Maili Ryan, for being the bottomless fount of knowledge she is and for her help in eradicating Americanisms from my writing. Responsibility for those that remain is solely mine for not asking her.

Joanna Chambers, for stepping in to answer questions for Maili.

Judith Ivory, whose novel *Beast* inspired this novel.

Janine, for always being there, ready to help.

Ivy Adams, for being endlessly entertaining.

Tiffany Yates Martin of Fox Print Editorial, who was accidentally left out of the acknowledgment page of *His at Night*.

Google Books, the best friend I've ever had on the research front. How did I ever live without you? Google Maps, my other indispensable buddy. Together you make every day a fun threesome.

Acknowledgments

My readers, for their interest and support during my gap year from the shelves.

My truly wonderful family.

Deadlines being what they are, acknowledgments are always written when I'm bleary-eyed and underslept, my heart full of gratitude but my three remaining brain cells flopping about uselessly. If I've forgotten anyone, it is not from a lack of appreciation, but only a temporary absence of gray matter.

As always, if you are reading this, thank you. Thank you for everything.

PROLOGUE

*I*t happened one sunlit day in the summer of 1886.
Until then, Christian de Montfort, the young
Duke of Lexington, had led a charmed life.

His passion was the natural world. As a child, he was
never happier than when he could watch hatchling birds
peck through their delicate eggshells, or spend hours ob-
serving the turtles and the water striders that populated
the family trout stream. He kept caterpillars in terrariums
to discover the outcomes of their metamorphoses—
brilliant butterflies or humble moths, both thrilling him
equally. Come summer, when he was taken to the seashore,
he immersed himself in the tide pools and understood instinctively that he was witnessing a fierce struggle for sur-
vival, without losing his sense of wonder at the beauty and
intricacy of life.

After he learned to ride, he disappeared regularly into

the countryside surrounding his imposing home. Algernon House, the Lexington seat, occupied a corner of the Peak District. Upon the faces of its chert and limestone escarpments, Christian, a groom in tow, hunted for fossils of gastropods and mollusks.

He did run into opposition from time to time. His father, for one, did not approve of his scientific interests. But Christian was born with an innate assurance that took most men decades to develop, if at all. When the old duke thundered over his inelegant use of time, Christian coolly demanded whether he ought to practice his father's favorite occupation at the same age: chasing maids around the manor.

As if such nerve and aplomb weren't enough, he was also tall, well built, and classically handsome. He sailed through life with the power and imperviousness of an ironclad, sure of his bearing, convinced of his destination.

His first glimpse of Venetia Fitzhugh Townsend only further fueled that sense of certainty.

The annual Eton and Harrow cricket match, a highlight of the London Season, had just paused for the players' afternoon tea. Christian left the Harrow players' pavilion to speak to his stepmother—his former stepmother, as a matter of fact, as she had recently returned from her honeymoon with her new husband.

Christian's father, the late duke, had been a disappointment, as self-important as he'd been frivolous. He had, however, been fortunate in his choice of wives. Christian's mother, who'd died too young for him to remember, was generally praised as saintly. His stepmother, who came into his life not long thereafter, had proved a great friend and a staunch ally.

He'd seen the dowager duchess earlier, in the middle of the match. But now she no longer stood in the same spot. As Christian scanned the far edge of the field, the sight of a young woman momentarily halted his gaze.

She was casually perched on the back of an open phaeton, yawning behind her fan. Her posture was slouchy, as if she'd secretly rid herself of the whalebone undergarments that bludgeoned other ladies to sit as stiff as effigies. But what made her stand out from the crowd was her hat—a coronet of apricot-colored feathers that reminded him of the sea anemones that had fascinated him in childhood.

She snapped closed her fan and he forgot all about sea anemones.

Her face—he lost his breath. He'd never encountered beauty of such magnitude and intensity. It was not allure, but grace, like the sight of land to a shipwrecked man. And he, who hadn't been on a capsized vessel since he was six—and that had only been an overturned canoe—suddenly felt as if he'd been adrift in the open ocean his entire life.

Someone spoke to him. He couldn't make out a single word.

There was something elemental to her beauty, like a mile-high thunderhead, a gathering avalanche, or a Bengal tiger prowling the darkness of the jungle. A phenomenon of inherent danger and overwhelming perfection.

He felt a sharp, sweet ache in his chest: His life would never again be complete without her. But he felt no fear, only excitement, wonder, and desire.

"Who is that?" he asked no one in particular.

"That's Mrs. Townsend," answered no one in particular.

"She is a bit young to be a widow," he said.

The arrogance of that statement would amaze him in subsequent years—that he would hear her called a missus and immediately assume her husband to be dead. That he took it for granted nothing could possibly stand in the way of his will.

"She isn't a widow," he was informed. "She happens to be very much married."

He hadn't noticed anyone accompanying her. She appeared to him as if on a stage, alone and flooded by limelight. But now he saw that she was surrounded by people. Her hand rested casually on a man's forearm. Her face was turned toward this man. And when he spoke, she smiled.

Christian felt as if he were falling from a great height.

He'd always considered himself a breed apart. Now he was just another sod who might yearn and strive, but never achieve his heart's desire.

You made quite a display of yourself today," said Tony.

Venetia hung on to the carriage strap. The brougham plodded through London's congested streets; there really was no need to use the strap at all. But she could not seem to unclench her fingers from the strip of leather.

"One of the Harrow players couldn't stop staring at you," continued Tony. "If someone had handed him a fork he'd have devoured you in one sitting."

She didn't respond. When Tony fell into one of his moods, there was never a point in saying anything. Clouds gathered overhead. Beneath the spreading shadows, the summer leaves turned gray—nothing escaped London's reign of soot.

"Were I less discreet I'd tell him you can't breed. You are God's elaborate ruse, Venetia. All that prettiness on the surface, quite useless where it counts."

His words were drops of acid upon her heart, burning, corroding. On the sidewalk the pedestrians opened their umbrellas, held ever at the ready. Two fat plops of rain hit the carriage window. They slid down the glass pane in long, blurred streaks.

"It is not certain I can't have children," she said. She shouldn't. She knew he was goading her. But somehow, on this subject, she rose to the bait every time.

"How many physicians does it take to convince you? Besides, my friends marry and within a year they already have heirs. It's been two years for us and you show not the least sign of increasing."

She bit the inside of her lip. The blame for their failure to procreate could just as well lie with him, but he refused to even contemplate that possibility.

"But you will be glad to know that your looks aren't entirely useless. Howard agreed to join my rail venture—and I daresay he did so to have more opportunities to seduce you," said Tony.

At last she looked at him. The harshness of his voice was reflected in his countenance, his once winsome features now hard and brittle. During their courtship she'd thought him impossibly appealing—funny, smart, and lit from within by a thirst for life. Had he truly changed so much or had she been blinded by love?

And if he despised Howard for wanting her, then why

bring Howard deeper into their lives? They didn't need the rail venture. Nor another source of displeasure for him.

"Are you going to betray me?" he demanded suddenly.

"No," she said, weary almost beyond what she could bear. His contempt and dismissal of her had become a near-permanent condition of their marriage. The only thing he cared about—or so it seemed sometimes—was the matter of her fidelity.

"Good. After what you've made me become, being faithful is the least you can do for me."

"And what have I made you become?" She might not be a paragon but she had been a decent wife. She saw to his every comfort, never overspent her allowance, and gave no encouragement to men like Howard.

His voice was bitter. "Don't ask useless questions."

She turned her face back to the window. The pavement had disappeared under a horde of black umbrellas.

Even inside the carriage she felt the incipient chill. Summer would end early this year.

A short time later Christian finished his last term at Harrow and went on to read the Natural Science Tripos at Cambridge. The summer after his second year at Trinity College, he took part in a dig in Germany. On his way back to Algernon House, he stopped in London to inspect a new shipment of marine fossils at the British Museum's natural history division, fossils that would not be available for public viewing for some months.

The discussion engendered by the new fossils was most stimulating, so much so that instead of continuing on with his journey home, Christian accepted an invitation to dine with the curator and several of his colleagues. Afterward, rather than retiring immediately to his town residence, where a small staff kept the house ready for his use should he require it, he decided to while away an hour at his club. Society had departed London at the end of the Season; he could expect to be largely undisturbed.

The club was indeed quite empty. With a glass of brandy by his side, he settled in and tried to read the *Times*.

The days were easier. Between his course work, his estate, and his friends, Christian's hours were fully occupied. But at night, when the world quieted and he was alone with his thoughts, his mind turned all too often to the woman who'd pickpocketed his heart without so much as a glance.

He dreamed of her. Sometimes the dreams were lurid, her naked, lithe body under his, her lips whispering lecherous words of encouragement into his ears. Other times she remained resolutely out of reach, walking away while he was rooted to the ground, or coming to stand next to him just after he'd been turned into a stone statue. He would struggle and shout inside his marble confines, but she took no notice at all, as uncaring as she was lovely.

Someone entered the dark-paneled library. Christian recognized the man instantly: Anthony Townsend. Her husband.

The years since his encounter with Mrs. Townsend had been a long tutorial in the frailer aspects of humanity. Until he'd met her, he'd not known envy, misery, or despair. Nor guilt, which pulsed through his veins at the sight of Townsend.

He'd never wished the man ill—and rarely ever thought

of him as anything but an immovable object. But he'd lain with the man's wife countless times in his mind. And if something were to befall Townsend, he'd be the first in line for an introduction to his widow.

Those were cause enough for Christian to drain his brandy and lay aside the paper, still crisp from its ironing. He rose to leave.

"I've seen you before," Townsend said.

After a moment of paralysis, Christian said coldly, "I do not believe we have met."

He did not quite share his ancestors' reverence for the family heritage, but he was as unapproachable as any de Montfort who ever breathed.

Townsend, however, was undaunted. "I didn't say we've met, but I know your face from somewhere. Yes, I remember now. Lord's Cricket Ground, two years ago. You were in a Harrow striped cap, gawking at my wife."

Christian's reflection in a window, a stark etching of light against the dimness of the street beyond, showed a man stunned into stillness, as if he'd stared directly into Medusa's face.

"I can't remember what my maids look like, but I remember the faces of all the men who salivate after my wife." Townsend's tone was strangely listless, as if he was beyond caring.

Christian's face burned, but he remained silent: No matter how vulgar it was to discuss one's wife in this manner—and berate those who coveted her—Townsend was within his rights.

"You remind me of someone," Townsend went on. "Are you related to the late Duke of Lexington?"

If Christian admitted his identity, would Townsend

blacken his name before the missus? He watched his lips move in the window. "The late duke was my father."

"Yes, of course. You'd be Lexington, then. She'd be thrilled to know that someone with your exalted stature considers her a prize." Townsend chortled, a dry, humorless sound. "You may yet have your wish, Your Grace. But think twice. Or you may end up like me."

This time Christian could not help his scorn. "Speaking to strangers about my wife, you mean? I don't think so."

"I didn't think I'd be the sort, either," Townsend shrugged. "Forgive me, sir, for detaining you with my unmanly bleating."

He bowed. Christian returned a curt nod.

It was not until the next day that he wondered what Townsend had meant by "you may yet have your wish."

*T*ownsend's obituary was in the paper within the week. Shocked, Christian made inquiries and learned that Townsend had been on the verge of bankruptcy. Moreover, he owed massive amounts to jewelers both in London and on the Continent. Had he been driven to accumulate those debts to keep his wife happy, so that her gaze would not stray to overeager admirers ready to step in with lavish gifts for her favors?

A year and a day after his death, Mrs. Townsend married again—a scandalously early remarriage when the regulation mourning period was two years. Her new husband, a Mr. Easterbrook, was a wealthy man thirty years her senior. Soon came rumors of a rampant affair she conducted right under Mr. Easterbrook's nose, with one of his best friends, no less.

Evidently Christian's beloved was a shallow, greedy, selfish woman who injured and diminished those around her.

He forced himself to accept the truth.

It was not terribly difficult to avoid her. He did not move in the same circles as she, did not attend the London Season, and did not follow the fashionable calendar of events. Therefore he should not have run into her coming out of the Waterhouse Building on Cromwell Road, which housed the British Museum's natural history collections.

Almost five years had elapsed since he last saw her. The passage of time had only enhanced her beauty. She was more radiant, more magnetic, and more dangerous than ever.

A wildfire raged in his heart. It didn't matter what kind of woman she was; it only mattered that she become his.

He turned and walked away.

CHAPTER 1

Cambridge, Massachusetts
1896

*T*he ichthyosaur skeleton at Harvard's Museum of Comparative Zoology was incomplete. But the fish lizard was one of the first to be found on American soil, in the state of Wyoming, and the American university was understandably eager to put it on exhibit.

Venetia Fitzhugh Townsend Easterbrook stepped closer to look at its tiny teeth, resembling the blade of a serrated bread knife, which indicated a diet of soft-bodied marine organism. Squid, perhaps, which had been abundant in the Triassic seas. She examined the minuscule bones of its flappers, fitted together like rows of kernels on the cob. She counted its many rib bones, long and thin like the teeth of a curved comb.

Now that this semblance of scientific scrutiny had been performed, she allowed herself to step back and take in the creature's length, twelve feet from end to end, even

11

with much of its tail missing. She would not lie. It was always the size of these prehistoric beasts that most enthralled her.

"I told you she'd be here," said a familiar voice that belonged to Venetia's younger sister, Helena.

"And right you are," said Millie, the wife of their brother, Fitz.

Venetia turned around. Helena stood five feet eleven inches in her stockings. As if that weren't attention-grabbing enough, she also had red hair, the most magnificent head of it since Good Queen Bess, and malachite green eyes. Millie, at five feet three inches, with brown hair and brown eyes, disappeared easily into a crowd—though that was a mistake on the part of the crowd, as Millie was delicately pretty and much more interesting than she let on.

Venetia smiled. "Did you find interviewing the parents fruitful, my dears?"

"Somewhat," answered Helena.

The upcoming graduating class of Radcliffe, a women's college affiliated with Harvard University, would be the first to have the Harvard president's signature on their diplomas—a privilege roundly denied their English counterparts at Lady Margaret Hall and Girton. Helena was on hand to write about the young ladies of this historic batch for the *Queen* magazine. Venetia and Millie had come along as her chaperones.

On the surface, Helena, an accomplished young woman who had studied at Lady Margaret Hall and currently owned a small but thriving publishing firm, seemed the perfect author for such an article. In reality, she had vehemently resisted the assignment.

But her family had evidence that Helena, an unmarried woman, was conducting a potentially ruinous affair. This presented quite a quandary. Helena, at twenty-seven, had not only come of age long ago, but had also come into her inheritance—in other words, too old and too financially independent to be coerced into more decorous conduct.

Venetia, Fitz, and Millie had agonized over what to do to protect this beloved sister. In the end, they'd decided to remove Helena from the source of temptation without ever mentioning their reasons, in the hope that she'd come to her senses when she'd had some time to reflect upon her choices.

Venetia had all but bribed the editor of the *Queen* to offer the American assignment to Helena, then proceeded to wear down Helena's opposition to leaving England. They'd arrived in the Commonwealth of Massachusetts at the beginning of the spring term. Since then, Venetia and Millie had kept Helena busy with round after round of interviews, class visits, and curriculum studies.

But they wouldn't be able to keep Helena on this side of the Atlantic for much longer. Instead of forgetting, absence seemed to have made Helena's heart yearn ever more strenuously for the one she'd left behind.

As expected, Helena began to mount another protest. "Millie tells me you've even more interviews arranged. *Surely* I've collected more than enough material for an article. Any more and I'll be looking at a whole book on the subject."

Venetia and Millie exchanged a glance.

"It may not be a bad idea to have enough material for a monograph. You can be your own publisher," said Millie, in that quiet, gentle way of hers.

"True, but as outstanding as I find the ladies of the Radcliffe College, I do not intend to devote much more of my life to them," answered Helena, an edge to her voice.

Twenty-seven was a difficult age for an unmarried woman. Proposals became scarce, the London Season less a thrill than one long drudgery. Spinsterhood breathed down her neck, yet in spite of it, she must still be accompanied everywhere by either a servant or a chaperone.

Was that why Helena, whom Venetia had thought the most clear-eyed of them all, had rebelled and decided she no longer wished to be sensible? Venetia had yet to ask that question. None of them had. What they all wanted was to pretend that this misstep on Helena's part never happened. To acknowledge it was to acknowledge that Helena was careening toward ruin—and none of them could put a brake to the runaway carriage that was her affair.

Venetia linked arms with Helena. It was better for her to be kept away from England for as long as possible, but they must finesse the point, rather than force it.

"If you are sure you have enough material, then I'll write the rest of the parents we have contacted for interviews and tell them that their participation will no longer be required," she said, as they pushed open the doors of the museum.

A cold gust greeted them. Helena pulled her cloak tighter, looking at once relieved and suspicious. "I'm sure I have enough material."

"Then I will write those letters as soon as we've had our tea. To tell you the truth, I've been feeling a little restless myself. Now that you are finished with your work, we can take the opportunity to do some sightseeing."

"In this weather?" Helena said incredulously.

Spring in New England was gray and harsh. The wind blew like needles against Venetia's cheeks. The redbrick buildings all about them looked as dour and severe as the university's Puritan founders. "Surely you are not going to let a little chill dissuade you. We won't be coming back to America anytime soon. We should see as much of the continent as we can before we leave."

"But my firm—I can't keep neglecting it."

"You are not. You've kept fully abreast of all the developments." Venetia had seen how many letters Helena received from her publishing firm. "In any case, we are not keeping you away indefinitely. You know we must return you to London for the Season."

A huge blast of cold air almost made away with her hat. A man putting up handbills on the sidewalk had trouble holding on to his stack. One escaped his grasp and flew toward Venetia. She barely caught it before it pasted onto her face.

"But—" Helena began again.

"Oh come, Helena," said Venetia, her tone firm. "Are we to think you do not enjoy our company?"

Helena hesitated. Nothing had been said in the open, and perhaps nothing ever would be, but she had to suspect the reason for their precipitous departure from England. And she had to feel at least a little guilty for roundly abusing the trust her family had accorded her.

"Oh all right," she grumbled.

Millie, on Venetia's other side, mouthed, *Well done*. "And what does the handbill say?"

Venetia had entirely forgotten the piece of paper she'd caught. She tried to open it to its full dimensions but the wind kept flapping it back and forth—then ripped it from her hand altogether, leaving only a corner that said *American Society of Nat*.

"Is this the same one?" Millie pointed at a lamppost they'd just passed.

The handbill, glued to the lamppost, read,

American Society of Naturalists and Boston Society of Natural History jointly present

Lamarck and Darwin: Who was right?

His Grace the Duke of Lexington
Thursday, March 26, 3 PM
Sanders Theatre, Harvard University
Open to the Public

"My goodness, it's Lexington." Venetia gripped Millie's arm. "He's going to speak here next Thursday."

English peerage had suffered from a collective decline in prosperity, brought on by plunging agricultural income. Everywhere one turned, another lordship was brought to his knees by leaking roofs and blocked flues. Venetia's brother, Fitz, for instance, had had to marry for money at nineteen when he had unexpectedly inherited a crumbling earldom.

The Duke of Lexington, however, had no such troubles. He benefitted handsomely from owning nearly half of the best tracts in London, given to the family by the crown when much of the land had been mere grazing grounds.

He was rarely seen in Society—the joke often went that if a young lady wanted a chance at his hand, she had to have a map in one hand and a shovel in the other. He could afford to be elusive: He had no need to jostle before the heiresses du jour, hoping his lordliness would harpoon him a whale of a fortune. Instead, he traveled to remote places, excavated fossil sites, and published articles in scientific journals.

Which was too bad. In fact, when Venetia and Millie commiserated between themselves over yet another failed Season for Helena, they invariably dragged Lexington into the conversation.

She said Belfort wasn't serious enough.

I'll bet Lexington is made of solemnity and high-mindedness.

She thought Linwood smirked too much.

A quid says Lexington never experienced a lecherous thought in his life.

Widmore is too much of a fuddy-duddy. Helena is convinced he'd complain about her endeavors.

Lexington is modern and eccentric—a man who digs fossils wouldn't object to a woman who publishes books.

They were not quite serious. Lexington in reality was probably arrogant and awkward, as reclusive eccentrics often were. But as long as he remained beyond introduction, they could look to him as a faint beam of hope in their increasingly demoralized endeavor.

That it had been so difficult to find Helena a husband mystified everyone. Helena was lovely, intelligent, and personable. She'd never struck Venetia as unreasonable or particularly hard to please. And yet since her first Season, she'd dismissed perfectly likable, eligible gentlemen out of hand as if they were a passel of murdering outlaws who also defecated on the lawn.

"You've always wanted to meet Lexington, haven't you, Venetia?" asked Millie.

Interesting how Millie, with her quiet, trustworthy demeanor, made the most convincing liar of them all. Venetia took her cue. "He likes fossils. That's quite enough to endear a man to me."

They were cutting across the grounds of the law school. The bare trees shivered in the wind. The lawns were invisible beneath the previous day's blanket of snow. The main lecture hall, rotund and Romanesque, had probably been a revolt against the rest of the university's severely rectangular architectural uniformity.

A group of students coming toward them slowed to a halt, gaping at Venetia. She nodded absently in their direction.

"So you plan to attend the lecture?" asked Helena, looking over the flyer. "It's more than a week away."

"True, but he has been impossible to meet at home. Do you know, I hear he has his own private natural history museum at Algernon House? I should be like a cat in cream, were I the mistress of that manor."

Helena frowned slightly. "I've never heard you mention a particular interest in him."

Because she had none. But what kind of a sister would she be if she didn't make sure that the most eligible—and possibly the most suitable—bachelor in all of England was introduced to Helena? "Well, he *is* a good prospect. It would be a shame to not meet him when I can. And while we wait for him, we can begin our sightseeing. There are some lovely islands off Cape Cod, I hear. Connecticut is said to be very pretty, and Montreal is just a quick rail journey away."

"How exciting," seconded Millie.

"A little rest and relaxation before the Season begins in earnest," said Venetia.

Helena pressed her lips together. "The duke had better be worth the trouble."

"A man rich in both pound sterling and fossils?" Venetia pretended to fan herself. "He shall be worth every trouble. You'll see."

I have a letter from Fitz," said Millie.

Helena was in the bath, and Venetia and Millie were alone in the parlor of the cottage they'd leased for their time at Radcliffe College.

Venetia moved closer to Millie and lowered her voice. "What does he say?"

In January Helena had gone to Huntington, Lord Wrenworth's country seat, chaperoned by her friend Mrs. Denbigh. Fitz's best friend, Viscount Hastings, had also been in attendance. Hastings left the house party early and called on Fitz and Millie at their seat, where Venetia also happened to be visiting. He told them that while at Huntington, for three consecutive nights he'd seen Helena walking back to her room at four o'clock in the morning.

Venetia had immediately set out for Huntington, showing up brimming with smiling apologies for missing her sister too much. There were still rooms at Huntington, but she'd insisted on sharing one with Helena and made sure never to let Helena out of her sight.

Then they'd squirreled Helena out of the country as quickly as they could, and left Fitz to ascertain the identity of Helena's partner in sin.

"Including Huntington, she'd attended four house

parties since the end of the Season—five, if you count the one at Henley Park that Fitz and I hosted. Hastings was at four of them—but he is obviously not our suspect. Lady Avery and Lady Somersby were at four of them, including the one at Huntington."

Venetia shook her head. "I can't believe she'd carry on with those gossips under the same roof."

Millie went down the list. "The Rowleys were at three of the parties. So were the Jack Dormers."

But Mr. Rowley was fifty-five. And the Jack Dormers were newlyweds devoted to each other. Venetia drew a deep breath. "What about the Andrew Martins?"

A number of years ago, Helena had developed a tendresse for Mr. Martin. All evidence pointed to her sentiments being fervently reciprocated. But in time Mr. Martin had proposed to and married a young lady who had been intended for him since birth.

Millie smoothed the folds of Fitz's letter, her eyes worried. "Come to think of it, I have not seen the Andrew Martins together in a while. Mr. Martin came by himself to three parties. And at each house, he requested an out-of-the-way room, citing his need for peace and quiet in order to work on his next book."

All the more convenient for conducting an illicit affair. "Does Fitz suspect anyone else?" Venetia asked without much hope.

"Not among those at Huntington."

If Helena's lover was indeed Mr. Martin, this would not end well. Were they to be discovered, the Fitzhugh family wouldn't even be able to pressure him to do the honorable thing by Helena—for Mr. Martin remained very much married, his wife as robust as a vintage claret.

Venetia rubbed her temples. "What does Fitz think we should do?"

"Fitz is going to exercise restraint—for now. He is worried that he might do Helena more harm than good by confronting Mr. Martin. What if Mr. Martin is not the one? Then word might leak that Helena was out and about when she ought not to be."

A woman's reputation was as fragile as a dragonfly's wings. "Thank goodness Fitz is levelheaded."

"Yes, he is very good in a crisis," said Millie, slipping the letter into her pocket. "Do you think it will help to introduce the duke to Helena?"

"No, but we still must try."

"Let us hope the duke does not fall for the wrong sister," said Millie with a small smile.

"Pah," said Venetia. "I am nearly middle-aged and almost certainly older than he is."

"I'm sure His Grace will be more than willing to overlook a very minor age difference."

"I've had more than my share of husbands and plan to be happily unmarried for the rest of my—"

Footsteps. Helena's.

"Of course I shan't bestow my hand freely," Venetia said, raising her voice. "But if the duke woos me with a monster of a fossil, who knows how I might reward him."

*H*elena listened carefully. Venetia was in her bath. Millie had gone to change out of her walking gown. She should be safe enough.

She pulled aside the curtain and opened the window of the parlor. The boy she'd employed to take her letters to

Andrew directly to the post office was there, waiting. The boy had his hand extended. She set a letter and two shining copper pennies in his palm and quickly closed the window again.

Now on to the letters that had arrived for her in the afternoon. She looked for any that had come in Fitzhugh & Co.'s own envelopes. Before she'd left England, she'd given a supply of those to Andrew with the instruction to have her American address typed on the front once he had it. Then he was to draw a small asterisk under the postage stamp, so that she might know it was from him and not her secretary.

Except on this particular letter, he did not put an asterisk, but a tiny heart beneath the queen's likeness. She shook her head fondly. Oh, her sweet Andrew.

My Dearest,

What joy! What bliss! When I called at the poste restante office in St. Martin's le Grand this morning, there were not one, not two, but three letters from you. My pleasure is all the greater for the disappointment of the past two days, when my trips into London bore no fruits at the post office.

And as for your question, the work on volume three of A History of East Anglia *comes along slowly. King Æthelberht is about to be killed and Offa of Mercia soon to subjugate the kingdom. For some reason I rather dread this part of the history, but I believe my pace should pick up again when I reach the rebellion thirty years later that would restore independence to the Kingdom of the East Angles.*

I'd like to write more. But I must be on my way home—I am due to call on my mother at Lawton Priory and you know how much she deplores unpunctuality, especially mine.

So I will end with a fervent wish for your early return.

Your servant

Helena shook her head. She'd instructed Andrew never to sign his name on his letters. That precaution became moot when he referred to both his book and his mother's house by name. But this was not his fault. If he were capable of subterfuge, he wouldn't be the man she loved.

She was tucking the letter into the inside pocket of her jacket when Venetia returned to the room, smiling. "What do you say we make a foray to Boston tomorrow, my love, and see what their milliners have to offer? Those hats you've brought are perfectly serviceable for speaking to professors and lady students. But we must do better for meeting dukes."

"He will have eyes only for you."

"Balderdash," said Venetia firmly. "You are one of the loveliest women I know. Besides, if he has any sense, he will know that the best way to judge a woman is to observe how she treats other women. And when he sees you with your plain hat from two Seasons ago, he will immediately conclude that I am a selfish cow who ornaments myself like a Christmas tree and leaves you dressed in rags."

If Venetia wanted Helena to believe that she was interested in the duke, then she shouldn't have spent the four years since she became a widow for the second time cordially turning down every proposal that had come her way.

In fact, Helena was convinced Venetia would swim the English Channel before she took another husband.

But Helena would play along, as she'd played along since Venetia unexpectedly turned up at Huntington. "All right, then, but only for you, and only because you are getting on in years and soon will only have gentlemen callers when they mistake your door for their grandmother's."

Venetia laughed, spectacularly beautiful. "Piffle. Twenty-nine isn't that old—yet. But it's true I might not have another chance of becoming a duchess if this one goes by. So you'd better have a proper hat."

"I will allow you to select one for me that looks like a carnival."

Venetia placed her arm around Helena. "Wouldn't it be marvelous if you met the perfect man this Season and accepted his proposal? Then we could have a double wedding."

I've already met the perfect man. I won't marry anyone else.

Helena smiled. "Yes, wouldn't it?"

CHAPTER 2

$\mathscr{S}$he was dressing—buttoning her combination, pulling on her stockings, stepping into her petticoat, her motions unhurried, dancerlike. Her back was to him, but the vanity mirror provided an unobstructed view of the rest of her. He remained in bed, his head propped up on his palm, and watched the ripple and sway of her dark, unbound hair.

Outside, a woodpecker tapped diligently. Inside, the late afternoon sun receded from the room, the wedge of dappled, coppery light on the ceiling growing ever more indistinct. Her twilit beauty was less precise—as if she had been turned into an Impressionist painting, brush-strokes of color and shadow. He could look at her without feeling as if he must shield his eyes or risk damaging them.

He reached out, took a loose curl of her hair, and wound it about his fingers, bringing her closer to him.

She acquiesced easily, sitting down at the edge of the

bed and looping an arm around his shoulders. "Haven't you had enough of me?" she asked, smirking.

"Never."

"Well, no more for you now, sir—I must summon my maid. And why aren't you getting ready?"

He stroked the inside of her elbow. "I'll start in another quarter hour. Meanwhile I'll use you to help me pass the time."

She laughed and slipped away from his grasp. "Later. After the ball—maybe."

The woodpecker struck ever louder.

Christian bolted upright in his bed. The room was dim, its recesses murky; the fire in the grate had burned down to embers. There was no one with him, beautiful or otherwise. It was the morning of his Harvard lecture and someone was knocking at his door.

"Come in," he said.

Parks, his valet, entered. "Good morning, Your Grace."

"Morning," he said, flinging aside the covers and getting out of bed.

The dream, which he'd never experienced before, had been so real. He could have described the translucent muslin curtain on the window, the stylized vines of the Oriental carpet on which she'd stood, the exact length and texture of her hair.

But it was not the intensity of the details that had disoriented him—after some of his more prurient dreams, he could have drawn her with great anatomical precision. Rather, it was the affectionate domesticity, the easy intimacy and sweetness.

"Sir," said Parks. "Your water grows cold. Shall I fetch you another basin?"

How long had Christian been standing before the wash-stand, daydreaming, the way a petty thief might yearn toward the vault beneath the Bank of England?

Another five years had passed since he last saw Mrs. Easterbrook, outside the British Museum of Natural History. Some days he sincerely believed he'd outgrown his adolescent obsession. On one such day he'd promised his stepmother that after the lectures at Harvard and Princeton, he'd be in London for the entire Season—to do his duty and find a wife.

Mrs. Easterbrook, who had an unwed sister, was certain to be in London. As the latter's chaperone she'd frequent many of the same occasions he'd be expected to attend. They might be introduced. There could even be occasions when, for civility's sake, he must speak to her.

"Your Grace?" Parks asked again.

Christian stepped aside from the washbasin. "Do as you see fit."

*S*he looks stunning, does she not?" Venetia asked Millie.

For the occasion of the duke's lecture, Helena had donned a promenade gown of deep green velvet. Bridget, Millie's maid, hovered behind Helena, making sure the drapes of the skirt fell just right.

"She is a vision," Millie readily agreed. "I love a red-head in green."

Venetia turned to Millie. "And may I add that you, too, look very well." The mustard color of Millie's dress, problematic on most women, somehow worked to her advantage, making her look fresh and unexpected. "The duke will conclude I am a devoted sister and sister-in-law and an upstanding woman. Then he will promptly ask me to curate his private museum."

Helena shook her head. "Always the fossils."

Venetia grinned. "Always."

She felt more optimistic than she had reason to be. But they'd had a good time the past week, touring the back-country of Connecticut and the pretty islands of Martha's Vineyard and Nantucket. Helena had seemed more like her old self than she had in a while. And Venetia was hopeful that by the end of the trip, she would come to fully realize the error of her ways.

Helena was not flighty or thoughtless. In fact, she was usually an exceptionally astute judge of character.

After their first meeting with Millie, during which the latter had said not above ten words, Helena had told Venetia, *Fitz is lucky. She will be a good wife to him.* Millie had proved to be the best wife a man could hope for.

And, of course, there had been the memorable occasion, so many years ago, when Venetia, eagerly in love, had pressed Helena for what she thought of Tony. Helena had answered reluctantly that he seemed to "lack a certain inner strength."

How right she had been. Which had made it twice as shocking that she, of all people, would behave in a manner that would jeopardize her entire future.

Bridget, satisfied with Helena's dress, turned to Millie. "Will you be needing anything else, mum?"

"No, and you may have the rest of the day off."

"Thank you, mum."

On this trip, they'd brought only Bridget. Venetia's maid, Hattie, suffered from terrible seasickness and had stayed behind. Helena's maid had left service a year ago to marry and was never replaced.

Venetia had not thought much of it at that time—Helena stayed with either Venetia or Fitz and Millie and it was easy enough for Hattie or Bridget to see to her. Now she wondered whether the oversight had been deliberate on Helena's part. Without a maid whose duties revolved entirely around her, Helena had one fewer person to keep track of her movements.

Had Helena *planned* her affair, clearing the obstacles one by one? Venetia did not relish the possibility.

Well, Helena could still change her mind. Perhaps the sight of a very proper, very unmarried young man was just the nudge she needed. And surely it must be providence, or the duke, who'd been as elusive as the Holy Grail for so long, would not suddenly appear at this particular juncture in their lives.

Venetia reached for her gloves. "I am ready to cast my eyes upon Lexington. Anyone else?"

They arrived half an hour early, but Sanders Theatre, the Harvard auditorium, was already packed. Only in the last row did they manage to find three seats together.

Millie glanced about. "My goodness, look at all the women in attendance."

Helena adjusted the angle of her new, suitably opulent hat. "Not surprising when the lecturer is a young, rich duke. It looks like you will have competition, Venetia."

"Maybe they are just curious," said Venetia breezily. "With so many of their grand heiresses marrying our penniless lords, they must be dying to see what an Englishman who doesn't need money looks like."

"You've never seen one of those, either, right, Millie?" Helena teased.

"Not in my marriage I have not." Millie chortled.

"At least your poor English peer is handsome," said Venetia.

"That he is, handsomer than Apollo."

The compliment toward her husband was uttered with perfect matter-of-factness, not a single flutter to her voice or the slightest coloring of her cheeks.

Yet for years now Venetia had wondered whether Millie wasn't secretly in love with the man who'd married her solely for her fortune. He treated her with courtesy and—in recent years—affection. But his heart, Venetia feared, would always belong to the woman he'd given up for the sake of duty.

"Chances of you being as lucky, Venetia," said Helena, "are next to nil. A quid says the duke looks like the Hunchback of Notre-Dame."

"Hmm." Venetia mused. "Is there such a thing as a young, rich, ugly duke?"

And if there was, he was not the Duke of Lexington, whose appearance upon the dais brought forth a collective sigh of admiration. He was indeed handsome—not the gentle, boyish looks that appealed most strongly to Venetia, but lean and angular: deep-set eyes, straight nose, high cheekbones, and firm lips.

Millie approved. "He has the look of a Roman senator, very magisterial, very distinguished."

"How old is the family, exactly?" Venetia asked.

"Very old," affirmed Millie. "A de Montfort fought at William the Conqueror's side."

A Harvard professor launched into a long introduction that was more about himself than the duke. Lexington stayed true to his breeding and displayed neither boredom nor irritation, only a neutral awareness of his surroundings.

Venetia noted with relief that he was also tall enough for Helena, whose height sometimes deterred young men who did not find themselves sufficiently towering. She glanced at Helena, hoping to see a spark of interest on her sister's face. After all, the duke was everything Helena had always said she wanted. But Helena's countenance showed only a bland politeness.

"Are you satisfied, Venetia?" whispered Millie. "Will you make him the luckiest man alive?"

Venetia remembered that she ought to keep up her pretense of matrimonial interest in the duke. "It will depend on the size of his fossil," she whispered back.

Helena made a sound halfway between a snort and a suppressed burst of laughter.

Venetia's anxiety doubled. She'd rather hoped Helena was still a virgin. Not that one trickle of laughter would settle the question, but that Helena understood the joke so immediately, when some of their maiden aunts would need a diagram, perhaps several diagrams . . .

The introduction concluded. The duke took to the podium. He spoke with a measured cadence, a spare use of words, and, unlike the man who preceded him, the discipline to meander not an inch from his topic.

He was brilliant, which would no doubt please Helena. His ideas were controversial—chief among them that the driving force behind evolution was more likely to be natural selection, as Mr. Darwin had proposed, and not the more commonly accepted theories of neo-Lamarckism, orthogenesis, or saltationism. Yet his delivery was almost impersonal, as if he were merely relating the thoughts of a third party and not his own.

But there was a charisma to him that held the audience in his thrall, a pull greater than the sum of his cogency and his good looks. Perhaps it was his very civil haughtiness, the unmistakable authority to his voice, or the combination of his ancient title and his very modern endeavors.

At the end of the lecture, a series of questions came from the men in the audience, some of whom were members of the Harvard faculty, some, members of the press.

Venetia reached across Millie and handed Helena a piece of paper. "Ask him."

To be the first woman to ask him a question would leave an impression on the duke.

Helena looked down at the question Venetia had suggested: *What do you think of theistic evolution, sir?* "Why me? You should do it."

Venetia shook her head. "I don't want him to think I'm too forward."

But before she could further push Helena, an American young woman rose from the audience.

"Your Lordship."

Venetia winced at the incorrect use of the duke's title. A duke was never "my lord," but always "Your Grace."

"I read with great interest your article in *Harper's Magazine*," continued the young lady. "In the article you briefly tantalized readers with your view that human beauty is also a product of natural selection. Would you care to elaborate on that?"

"Certainly," said His Grace. "From an evolutionary point of view, beauty is nothing more than a signifier of one's fitness for reproduction. Our concept of beauty derives largely from symmetry and proportion, which in turn denote structural health. Those features we find most pleasing—clear eyes, strong teeth, unblemished skin—represent youth, vigor, and freedom from disease. A man who is attracted to young, healthy females is more likely to breed than one who is attracted to elderly, sickly ones. Therefore, our view of beauty has undoubtedly been influenced by millennia of successful selections in the past."

"So when you see a beautiful woman, sir, is that what you think, that she is fit for reproduction?"

Venetia's jaw slackened. Americans had such phenomenal cheek.

"No, I rather marvel at the homage we pay beauty—it is fascinating for a man of science."

"How so?"

"We have been taught from birth to judge one another on character. Yet when faced with beauty, everything goes out of the window. Beauty becomes the only thing that matters. This tells me that Mr. Darwin was exactly right. We are descended from animals. There are certain beastly instincts—the attraction to beauty, for example—that are primal to our makeup and override the markings of civilization. So we romanticize beauty, out of embarrassment that we should still be so susceptible to it in this day and age."

The audience murmured at his unconventional and very decided views.

"Does this mean you do not enjoy beauty, sir?"

"I do enjoy beauty, but I enjoy it the same way I enjoy a cigar, with the understanding that while it gives temporary pleasure, it is essentially meaningless, and perhaps might even be harmful in the long run."

"That is a very cynical view of beauty."

"That is all the consideration beauty deserves," said the duke coolly.

"You might have a slightly more difficult time than you first anticipated, Venetia," said Helena softly.

"The duke is clearly a troublemaker." In whom Venetia was developing a rather lively interest, an interest that was perhaps warmer than warranted for a potential brother-in-law.

A young man leaped to his feet. "Sir, if I understand you correctly, you have essentially declared all beautiful women untrustworthy."

Venetia tsked. The duke had said no such thing: He'd advised a neutral stance on the consideration of beauty. Beautiful women, like all other women, should be approached and judged on aspects beyond mere physical attributes. And what was wrong with that?

"But beautiful women *are* essentially untrustworthy," replied the duke.

Venetia frowned. Not that old chestnut. It was as bad as equating beauty with virtue. Worse, probably.

"A beautiful woman is desired for as long as her beauty holds, forgiven for all trespasses, and never asked to be anything other than beautiful."

Venetia snorted. If only.

"But surely, sir, the rest of us are not so blind as that," argued the young man.

"Allow me to present some anecdotal evidence, then. Anecdotal evidence does not constitute data. But where unbiased, unpolluted data is not possible—a given when it comes to the study of the human psyche—we will have to make do.

"Some years ago, I passed through London in the latter part of August, a time when English Society vacates the city entirely and repairs to the country. My club was empty, except for myself and another man.

"I knew this man because he'd once been pointed out to me as the husband of a very beautiful woman. He spoke briefly of his wife and warned that a man shouldn't covet her unless that man wanted to become like him.

"The conversation was distasteful to me. It also made no sense, until I read the man's obituary in the papers a few days later. I made some inquiries and learned that not only was he bankrupt, he had also run up exceedingly large accounts at several jewelers. The circumstances of his death had very nearly triggered an inquest."

Something clanged inside Venetia's head. This woman, whom the duke clearly blamed for her husband's death . . . Could he possibly be speaking of *her*?

"His widow remarried scarcely a year later, to a much older, very wealthy man. Rumors were rife that she conducted an affair with his good friend. And when he was on his deathbed, she did not even have the courtesy to attend him. He died alone."

He *was* speaking of her, only with the facts hideously distorted. She wanted to cover her ears, but she couldn't move. She couldn't even blink, but could only stare at him with the blind gaze of a statue.

The judgment on her second marriage stung, but that didn't quite matter as much—she'd helped spread some of those rumors herself. But what he'd implied about Tony, in Tony's own words, no less, insinuating that Tony wouldn't have killed himself had it not been for her . . .

"Exceptionally heartless, our beauty."

Had his speech slowed? Each damning syllable hung for an eternity in the air, an air brilliant with the projecting lantern's beam, a thousand specks of mote caught in a harsh white radiance.

"You'd think an odor of censure would hang about her," the duke continued inexorably. "But no, she is welcomed everywhere and constantly pelted with proposals of marriage. No one, it seems, can remember her past. So, yes, I do believe the rest of us are indeed that blind."

There were other questions. Venetia didn't hear them. Nor did she really hear the duke's answers, except his voice, that aloof, clear, inescapable voice.

She didn't know when the lecture ended. She didn't know when the duke left or when the rest of the audience filed out. The theater was dark and empty when she rose, politely removed her sister's hand from her arm, and marched out.

I still can't believe what happened," said Millie, pressing another cup of hot tea into Venetia's hands.

Venetia had no idea whether she'd finished the contents of the previous cup or whether it had turned cold and been taken away.

Helena paced the parlor, her shadow long and lean upon the wall. "There are a great many lies and liars involved here. Mr. Easterbrook's family is certainly a mendacious bunch. Mr. Townsend was capable of a great deal of it. And, Venetia, you, too, have contributed your share in covering for the two of them."

It was true. Venetia had lied her fair share. Sometimes people must be protected; sometimes appearances had to be kept; and sometimes her own pride needed preserving, so she could go about her business with her head held high, even when all she wanted was to cower in a corner.

"The duke, most likely, is not a liar," continued Helena. "But he has spoken with reprehensible recklessness, presenting a series of unsubstantiated rumors as if they were from the *Encyclopedia Britannica*. Unforgivable. We can only be grateful that while Americans might have heard of the Prince of Wales and the Duke of Marlborough, they don't know of Venetia and won't be able to guess her identity from what he's said."

"Thank goodness for small mercies," murmured Millie.

Helena stopped before Venetia's chair and lowered herself so that her eyes were level with Venetia's. "Avenge yourself, Venetia. Make him fall in love with you, then give him the cut."

Loud, dark thoughts had been crisscrossing Venetia's head like a murder of crows over the Tower of London. But now, as she gazed into her sister's cool, resolute eyes, the past dropped away, and the thought of Lexington likewise receded.

Helena. Helena was a woman who made her decisions with an almost frightful ruthlessness.

If Helena had truly decided that Andrew Martin was worth the trouble, then the die was cast, the board set, the bridge crossed and burned. Millie, Fitz, and Venetia could try all they want. They would not change her mind, not by any means in their possession.

Venetia could only be glad that her mind had gone largely numb. She could not feel any despair.

For now.

CHAPTER 3

When Venetia was ten, a train had derailed near her childhood home.

Her father had led the charge in pulling passengers out of the wreck. Venetia and her siblings had not been allowed to go near the scene, for fear it would upset them too much. But they were encouraged to attend to passengers, especially children who'd suffered only minor injuries.

There had been a boy about her age who bore no visible damages. When sandwiches were set down before him, he ate. When a cup of tea appeared, he drank. And when asked questions, he gave sensible enough answers. Yet it became apparent after some time that he wasn't entirely there, that he was still caught in the midst of the derailment.

In the days following Lexington's lecture, Venetia carried out a similar approximation of normalcy. At her insistence, they departed for their tour of Montreal as scheduled. Braving the cold—barely feeling the cold, in fact—she visited the Notre-Dame Basilica, smiled at the quaintly costumed country folk who thronged the Bonsecours on market days, and admired the panoramic views of the city from the belvedere atop Mount Royal.

All the while she relived Lexington's condemnation. And relived the awful days immediately following Tony's death. For longer than she thought possible, she was but a bystander in her own mind, witnessing the events as if they were happening to a stranger a continent away, and marveling that she should be so removed.

The first crack in her detachment came three days before they were to leave for New York. She woke up in the middle of that night, her heart pounding, wanting to destroy something. Everything.

By the time Helena and Millie awoke she was already packed and dressed, her portmanteau strapped to the boot of a hired carriage. If she were to scream and smash things, she didn't want her family to see her.

"I've decided to go ahead to New York and facilitate your arrival," she said.

Helena and Millie looked at each other. In this day and age, all one needed was a decent guidebook and access to a telegraph office to make travel arrangements. There was no need to send a scout ahead to thoroughly modern New York, especially as they'd already applied for and received reservations in one of the best hotels in town.

Helena began, "We can come with—"

"No!" Venetia winced at the harshness of her refusal. She took a deep breath. "I'd like to go by myself."

"Are you sure about this?" Millie asked hesitantly.

"Quite. And don't look so downcast—it will only be two days before you see me again."

But they did look downcast, dismayed, and anxious. They wanted to keep her near and protect her. Some hurts, however, were beyond the protection of sisterly love and some wounds better licked in dark, lonely caves.

"I'd better hurry," she said. "Or I'll miss my train."

*V*enetia had once thought she'd made peace with Tony's memories. She'd lied to herself. There had never been peace, only a tenuous truce with him forever silent and her studiously avoiding the subject.

And now even that truce had been undone. As her train sped south, she stared at the still-frozen landscape rushing by, while a bewildered, plaintive voice in her head kept repeating the same question. *Why had you said such things to Lexington, Tony, why?*

It's simple enough, you idiot. He wanted *someone to believe you were responsible for his death.*

Why this should come as such a bitter surprise, she didn't know. Perhaps with the passage of time, she'd allowed herself to romanticize the past, to believe that her marriage hadn't been so suffocating after all, that she'd been no more unhappy than anyone else, and that Tony hadn't really proved himself anywhere near as mean-spirited a man.

This, then, was his way to remind her, from beyond the grave, of her misery, heartbreak, and shame.

Of the truth.

* * *

*V*enetia's head pounded as she detrained at Grand Central Station. She almost walked past the sign held by her friend Lady Tremaine's driver. Lady Tremaine, her husband, and their two young daughters had already departed for England, but they'd put their automobile at Venetia's disposal.

The manservant, who told her his name was Barnes, guided Venetia outside, to where he'd parked the vehicle. Except for the lack of harnessed horses, the automobile exactly resembled a victoria—the open body, the raised driver's seat in the front, even the calash hood at the back.

"Driving hats for you, Mrs. Easterbrook, from Lady Tremaine." Barnes motioned toward the stack of hatboxes on the seat.

"Very considerate of her," Venetia murmured.

Most veiled hats employed ornamental lattices of fabric meant not to conceal, but to draw more attention to the face. The driving hats from Lady Tremaine, however, were not the least bit frivolous. Not that they were ugly, but their veils were proper veils, consisting of two layers of fine netting that wound all around the brim of the hat.

"We won't go very fast in the city," said Barnes, adjusting his driving goggles, "but you might find a hat useful driving out in the country, ma'am."

Venetia unpinned her own hat and set the driving hat on her head. The effect was that of being plunked down inside a fog—not a London pea souper, but the kind of fog she encountered on early morning walks in the country, like smoke flowing on the ground.

41

The bustle outside Grand Central Station receded. Barnes cranked the engine, climbed onto his seat, and released the brake. The now dreamlike streets of Manhattan glided by outside Venetia's translucent cocoon, the colors muted, the buildings smudged at the edges, the passersby blurred in ways that might intrigue modern artists.

Would that she traveled through her entire life at such a remove, protected from its pitfalls and upheavals.

They drove for a mile or so before the automobile came to a stop. "Here's your hotel, Mrs. Easterbrook. All seventeen stories of it," said Barnes proudly. "Ain't it grand? All electric, too—and a telephone in each room."

The hotel was indeed very tall, dwarfing its neighbors. "Very impr—"

Venetia froze. Striding down the street toward her, tall, haughty, and impeccably turned out, was none other than the Duke of Lexington. He cast a cursory glance at the automobile and headed inside the hotel.

Her hotel. What was he doing here?

Her first instinct was to run. She would lodge elsewhere—she didn't need seventeen stories or a telephone receiver in her room. She had not escaped to New York to be under the same roof as her nemesis.

But a perverse pride refused to let her make the request to Barnes. She squared her shoulders. "Very impressive. I'm sure I will enjoy my stay."

If anyone ought to run in the opposite direction, it was he, not she. She had not slandered anyone. She had not spread malicious rumors. She had not spoken without regard to consequences.

A doorman materialized to help her down. The hotel's porters came to receive her luggage. She declined Barnes's offer to speak for a room for her, tipped him, and bid him good day.

Not until she was crossing the onyx-and-marble rotunda of the hotel did she realize she was still fully veiled. The dim interior made it more difficult to see, but she was far from blind. She arrived at the hotel clerk's station without mishap.

The hotel clerk blinked once at her appearance. "Good afternoon, ma'am. May I help you?"

Before she could reply, another clerk several feet down the counter offered a greeting of his own. "Good afternoon, Your Grace."

She froze again.

"Any news on my passage?" came Lexington's cool voice.

"Indeed, sir. We have secured you a Victoria suite on the *Rhodesia*. There are only two such suites on the liner, and you will be assured of the greatest comfort, privacy, and luxury for your crossing."

"Departure time?"

"Tomorrow morning at ten, sir."

"Very good," said Lexington.

"Ma'am, may I help you?" Venetia's clerk asked again.

Unless she abruptly abandoned the counter, she must speak and, at some point, give her name. She cleared her throat—and out came a string of German. "Ich hätte gerne Ihre besten Zimmer."

She was running away after all. She balled her fingers, the chaos inside her igniting into anger.

"Beg your pardon, ma'am?"

Through gritted teeth, she repeated herself.

The clerk looked flustered. Without turning, without ever having appeared to pay attention, Lexington said, "The lady would like your best rooms."

"Ah yes, of course. Your name, please, ma'am."

She swallowed and reached randomly. "*Baronesse* von Seidlitz-Hardenberg."

"And how many nights will you be staying with us, ma'am?"

She held out two fingers. The clerk wrote something in his ledger. Venetia signed the register with her new alias.

"Here is your key, baroness. And a walking map of Central Park, which you will find just outside our doors. We hope you enjoy your stay."

A hotel attendant ushered her toward the lift, which came promptly, the metallic cage shunting into place with a soft ding. An accordion door folded into the wall; the inner door slid open.

"Good afternoon, ma'am," said the lift attendant. "Good afternoon, Your Grace."

Him again. She turned her head a few surreptitious degrees. Lexington stood to the side, slightly behind her, waiting for her to enter the lift. *Move*, she ordered herself. *Move*.

Somehow her feet carried her forward. Lexington followed her inside. He glanced her way, but did not acknowledge her. Instead, he turned his attention to the gilded panels that adorned the elevator's interior.

"Which floor, ma'am?" asked the lift attendant.

"Fünfzehnter Stock," she said.

"Pardon, ma'am?"

"The lady wishes to go to the fifteenth floor," said the duke.

"Ah, thank you, sir."

The lift was leisurely, almost sluggish, in its ascent. She began to suffocate under her veil. Yet she dared not breathe with any vigor, for fear she'd betray her agitation.

The duke, on the other hand, was at his ease. His jaw carried no tension. His posture was straight but not rigid. His hands, folded over the top of his walking stick, were perfectly relaxed.

Her anger blazed to a firestorm. It roared in her ears. Her fingertips were hot with a desire for violence.

How dare he? How dare he use her to illustrate his stupid, misogynistic points? How dare he destroy her hardwon peace of mind? And how dare he ooze such cool smugness, such insufferable satisfaction with his own life?

When the lift dinged into place on the fifteenth floor, she charged out.

"Gnädige Frau."

It took her a moment to recognize his voice, speaking in German.

She walked faster. She did not want to hear his voice. She did not want to further perceive his presence. She wanted only that he should fall into a pit of vipers on his next expedition and suffer the painful effects of their venom for the remainder of his life.

"Your map, madam," he said, still in German. "You left it in the lift."

"I don't need it anymore," she answered curtly in the same language, without turning around. "Keep it."

*C*hristian tossed the baroness's map on the console table just inside his suite. He pulled off his coat, dropped it on the back of a chair, and deposited himself in the chair opposite.

Ten days after the fact, he remained astonished by his own conduct. What had possessed him? As a man plagued by a chronic condition, he'd learned to live with it. He carried on. He kept busy. And he never spoke of it.

Until he did, luridly, at length, in a theater full of strangers.

He wanted to never think of this gross misstep again, but he kept revisiting his confession—the defiant pleasures of at last acknowledging, however obliquely, his fixation upon Mrs. Easterbrook, the bottomless mortification once he realized what he'd done.

Perhaps he'd made a strategic mistake by avoiding the London Season and the possibilities of running into her. By staying away, he also deprived himself of a large pool of young women. Who was to say he would not find among them someone who could take his mind permanently off her?

A knock came. Christian opened the door himself— he'd given his valet two weeks' leave to visit his brother, who'd immigrated to New York. A very young porter bowed and handed him a note from Mrs. Winthrop, a fellow guest at the hotel who had been throwing herself at him for the past three days.

Christian badly needed a distraction, but he liked to uphold a minimum of standards in his dalliances. Mrs. Winthrop, unfortunately, was not only excessively vain, but more than a little stupid. Judging by her newest invitation, she also could not take a hint.

"Send Mrs. Winthrop some flowers with my regrets," he said to the porter.

"Yes, sir."

His gaze landed on the Central Park map on the console table. "And return the map to the Baroness von Seidlitz-Hardenberg."

The porter bowed again and left.

Christian walked out onto the balcony of his suite and looked down. The height was perilous, the air abrupt and chill. The pedestrians were the size of drawing dolls, jointed mannequins milling about the pavement.

A woman emerged from the hotel: Baroness von Seidlitz-Hardenberg, as evidenced by her daft hat. The rest of her, however, was altogether shapely—a figure meant for reproduction. Product of evolution that he was, even though he had no intention of procreating with her, he was still coaxed out of his preoccupation to contemplate the obvious pleasures of her form.

In the confines of the lift, her attention had all but licked him from head to toe.

He was not unpopular either at home or abroad. Still, the baroness's interest had been extraordinarily intense, all the more so for the fact that she never once directly gazed at him.

Now, however, she did. From sixteen stories below, she looked up over her shoulder and unerringly located him, a glance that he felt through the cream netting that concealed her face. Then she crossed the street and disappeared under the trees of Central Park.

*V*enetia was vaguely aware of the trees, the ponds and bridges, the young men and women zipping by on their safety bicycles. The sea lions at the menagerie barked; the children clamored to see the polar bears; a violin wailed the mournful notes of *"Méditation"* from *Thaïs*—yet all she heard was the duke's inescapable voice.

The lady would like your best rooms.

The lady wishes to go to the fifteenth floor.

Your map, madam.

He had no right to appear helpful and gentlemanly, he who'd judged her as if he knew everything there was to know about her. When he knew nothing—nothing at all.

Yet she was the one who felt ashamed that her husband had despised her so much. She could have continued in her blissful ignorance had the duke had the decency to keep a private conversation private. But he hadn't, and his revelation would haunt her always.

She wanted—needed—to do something to knock him off his arrogant, comfortable perch. Actions carried consequences. He would not decimate her good name and not pay a price for it.

But what could she do? She could not sue him on grounds of defamation, as he'd never named her. She knew no dirty secrets of his that she could spill in return. And even if she warned every woman under the age of sixty-five of his savageness of spirit, his title and wealth would still ensure he'd have the wife of his choice.

It was dark by the time she returned to the hotel, her feet sore, her head throbbing. The lift was empty save for the lift attendant, but as it ascended, the duke might as well have been there, taunting her with his invulnerability.

She smelled the lilies as soon as she opened the doors to her suite. A large peach bloom vase that hadn't been there before occupied the center table of the sitting room. From the vase, aggressively tall stalks of white calla lilies and orange gladiolus shot toward the ceiling, their petals glaring in the electric light.

Her family would never send her calla lilies, a cascade of which she'd carried when she walked down the aisle to marry Tony. She plucked the card from the fronds that buttressed the flowers.

The Duke of Lexington regrets his departure from New York and hopes for the pleasure of your company another day, madam.

The gall of the man. The extravagant bouquet was nothing but an announcement that should they meet again, he'd like for her to be waiting in bed, already naked. So he despised Venetia Easterbrook's soul, but liked her backside well enough when he didn't know to whom it belonged.

She tore the card in two. In four. In eight. And kept tearing, choking on her impotence.

Helena's words leaped to mind. *Avenge yourself, Venetia. Make him fall in love with you, then give him the cut.*

Why not?

What would it be to him? Merely a dalliance gone wrong. He'd hurt for a few short weeks—a few months, if she was lucky. But she, she would go through the rest of her life oppressed by the weight of his disclosure.

She telephoned the concierge and asked for a first-class stateroom on the *Rhodesia*, as close to the Victoria suites as possible. And then she sat down to write Helena and Millie a note concerning her sudden exit.

It was only as she sealed the note that she thought of the specifics of her seduction. How would she manage to breach his defenses when he had such entrenched preconceptions about her? When he'd take one look at her face, otherwise her greatest asset in a quest of such nature, and turn away?

No matter. She'd have to be creative, that was all. Where there's a will, there's a way. And with every fiber of her being, she willed that the Duke of Lexington would regret the day he chose to stick a knife into her kidney.

CHAPTER 4

*L*exington stood at the rail and surveyed the hive of activity beneath him.

Carriages and heavy drays drove on and off the dock, their procession surprisingly speedy and orderly. Trunks and crates, hefted by stevedores with meaty shoulders and bulging upper arms, slid down open chutes into the cargo hold. Tugboats tooted at one another, readying themselves to nudge the great ocean liner's nose around—for her to head toward the open sea.

Up the gangplank came the ship's passengers: giggling young women who had never before crossed the pond; indifferent men of business on their third trip of the year; children pointing excitedly at the ship's smokestacks; immigrant workers—largely Irish—returning to the old country for a brief visit.

The man in a hat too fancy for his clothes was likely to

be a swindler, planning to "aggregate funds" from his fellow passengers for an "extraordinary, once-in-a-lifetime opportunity." The lady's companion, plainly dressed and seemingly demure, examined first-class gentlemen passengers with mercenary interest: She did not intend to remain a lady's companion forever—or even for much longer. The adolescent boy who stared contemptuously at the back of his puffy, sweaty father appeared ready to disown the unimpressive sire and invent an entirely new patrimony for himself.

But what hypothesis should he form concerning Baroness von Seidlitz-Hardenberg, for that was her coming up the gangplank, was it not? He recognized her hat, almost like that of a beekeeper's, but sleeker and more shimmery. The day before, the veil had been creamy in color. Today it was blue, to complement her blue traveling gown.

Logically, a woman shouldn't need to don a traveling gown for the two and a half miles between Hotel Netherlands and the Forty-second Street piers on the Hudson River, where the *Rhodesia* was docked. But he'd long ago given up trying to apply logic to fashion, the offspring of irrationality and inconstancy.

The degree of a woman's devotion to fashion frequently corresponded to her degree of silliness. He'd learned to pay no attention to any woman with a stuffed macaw in her hat and to expect shoddy food at the home of a hostess best known for her collection of ball gowns.

The baroness was certainly highly fashionable. And restless: The unusual parasol in her hand, white with a pattern of concentric blue octagons, twirled constantly. But she did not come across as silly.

She looked up. He could not quite tell whether she was

looking directly at him. But whatever she saw, she halted midstep. Her parasol stopped spinning; the tassels around the fringe swayed back and forth with the sudden loss of momentum.

But only for a second. She resumed her progress on the gangplank, her parasol again a hypnotic pinwheel.

He watched her until she disappeared into the first-class entrance.

Was she the distraction he badly needed?

A hush always descended in the final moments before departure, quiet enough to hear the commands issued from the bridge and passed along the length of the ship. The harbor slipped away. On the main deck below her, the crowd waved madly at the loved ones they were leaving behind. The throngs on the dock waved back, just as earnest and demonstrative.

Venetia's throat tightened. She couldn't remember the last time she'd felt such unbridled, unabashed emotions.

Or when she last dared to.

"Good morning, baroness."

She jerked. Lexington stood a few feet away, an ungloved hand on the railing, dressed casually in a gray lounge suit and a felt hat that had probably seen service on his expeditions. He regarded the waterfront of New York, its piers, cranes, and warehouses sliding past, and displayed no interest in her whatsoever.

It was as if an iceberg had come to call.

"Do I know you, sir?" He'd spoken in German; she replied in the same language, surprised to hear herself sound quite calm, almost unaffected.

He turned toward her. "Not yet, baroness. But I would like to make your acquaintance."

They'd been in greater proximity in the hotel lift. Yet whereas the day before his nearness only angered her, today she felt as if she were balanced on a high wire over Niagara Falls.

Was she ready to play the game?

"Why do you wish to know me, Your Grace?" No point pretending she didn't know his rank—the hotel staff had not been reticent about it in her hearing.

"You are different."

From the greedy whore you held up as an affront to decency?

She fought down her agitation. "Are you looking for a lover?"

Know the rules before you play the game, Mr. Easterbrook had always told her.

"Would that be agreeable to you?" His tone was utterly unexceptional, as if he'd expressed nothing more untoward than a desire for a dance.

After the flowers, she shouldn't be surprised. All the same, her skin prickled hotly. Thank God for her veil—or she would not have been able to hide her revulsion. "And if I say no?"

"I will not impose on you again."

She'd dealt with men wanting her favors her entire life. She could recognize feigned nonchalance from a furlong away. But there was no affectation to his dispassionate stance. Were she to turn down his overture, he would simply turn his attention elsewhere and not give her another thought.

"What—if I am not sure?"

"Then I'd like to persuade you."

Despite the brisk breeze on the river, the veil threatened to asphyxiate her. Or perhaps it wasn't the veil at all, but his words. His presence. "How would you do that?"

His lips lifted at the corners—he was amused. "Do you wish for a demonstration?"

She'd known only his sharp mind, his arctic demeanor, and his limitless capacity for slander. But now, with the almost playfulness of his tone, the lean strength of his build, and the sight of his fingers absently stroking the railing, she became conscious of his sensuality, her awareness dark and potent.

It was too much. She couldn't. Not in a million years. Not if he were the last man alive. Not even if he were the last man alive *and* the guardian of the last store of food-stuff left on Earth.

"No," she said, her voice seething. "I do not wish for a demonstration. And I would be grateful should I never see you again."

If her sudden rejection took him aback, he did not show it. He bowed slightly. "In that case, madam, I wish you a pleasant voyage."

*B*ridget, Millie's maid, came back from the hotel clerk's station with the news that Mrs. Easter-brook had not yet checked in.

"Do you think she might have gone to a different hotel?" Millie asked Helena.

Helena felt uneasy. "But Lady Tremaine's driver said he'd brought her here yesterday."

"I'll speak to the clerk myself," said Millie.

She approached the counter, Helena in tow, and made her request. The clerk checked the register again.

"I apologize, ma'am, but we do not have a guest by that name."

"What about a lady by the name of Fitzhugh or Townsend?"

Helena could not see Venetia ever using Tony's name again. On her calling cards she was simply Mrs. Arthur Easterbrook.

The clerk looked up apologetically. "Not those, either."

"Did anyone here see a singularly beautiful lady arriving by herself?" Helena asked.

"I'm afraid not, ma'am."

"Very well, then," said Millie. "Do you have the suite reserved for Lady Fitzhugh? I am a day early. I hope that will not present a problem."

"No, ma'am, not a problem at all. And we have a message for you and Miss Fitzhugh."

The handwriting on the envelope was Venetia's familiar scrawl—thank goodness. They opened the message as soon as they were inside their suite.

Dear Millie and Helena,

I have decided to take an earlier steamer out of New York. Please do not worry about me. Am in robust health and tolerable spirits.

I will be waiting for you in London.

Love,
V.

Helena bit her lower lip. If it hadn't been for her, Venetia would not have gone to his lecture.

Before she'd taken up with Andrew, she'd considered

all the possible outcomes of her action—or so she'd thought. But she had not remotely prepared for such unintended consequences.

Worry gnawed at her. Even for one who'd contemplated and accepted the likelihood of the worst, it was still unnerving just how quickly and unpredictably things could go so wrong.

*C*hristian worked steadily through the two packets of letters that had caught up with him in New York. The sea, smooth as a tablecloth when the *Rhodesia* passed Sandy Hook into the open Atlantic, grew noticeably less level as the day wore on. He stopped reading reports from his agents and solicitors when the rocking of the ship made it unprofitable to continue. A walk on the decks required frequent use of the handrails, as the ship rocked from side to side. In the smoking lounge, where the gentlemen made their customary bets on the ship's daily progress, he had to chase after his ashtray.

The rain began at tea, gently enough at first. But before long each drop slammed into the windows with the ferocity of a thrown rock. He watched the rain and thought again of the baroness.

It was possible that she still distracted him because she'd spurned him and he was not accustomed to rejection. But he did not believe so. He was concerned less with his own sentiments and more with the seething intensity of hers. She was ferociously aware of him, yet even more ferociously offended by his attention. And that intrigued him more than her identity or the reason she kept her face concealed.

A strange but not altogether unpleasant sensation, being preoccupied by a woman who was not Mrs. Easterbrook.

Too bad the baroness would have nothing to do with him.

*I*n theory, repudiating Lexington to his face should have afforded Venetia a modicum of satisfaction.

But the truth was she hadn't dismissed him. She'd fled from everything that was masculine, confident, and powerful in him, the way a very young girl might run away from the first boy who challenged her to do more than just flirt.

For the rest of the day, instead of congratulating herself on knowing when to cut her losses and abandon clearly demented goals, she stewed in frustration. Was she truly so useless a woman? Had Tony been correct when he'd told her that everything she was, she owed to her looks? Without the advantages conferred by her face, did she have no hope of holding her own with Lexington?

She stared at herself in the mirror. The stewardess she'd selected to help her dress for dinner, Miss Arnaud, had coiffed her hair into a sleek chignon that left her face quite bare. "It's better this way," the girl had said. "Madame is so beautiful; nothing must interfere."

Venetia could not judge. She saw an assembly of features that were often a little odd: Her eyes were *very* far apart; her jaw was rather too square for her own taste; her nose was neither diminutive nor pert—it went on and on, in fact.

But none of it mattered here. To conquer him, she would have to wage her campaign with an arsenal that did not include beauty.

If, that was, she had the guts to go back to him.

The thought of his hands on her—she shuddered. But not entirely from revulsion. As much as she despised him, he was a handsome man. And a part of her found his nerve and sangfroid utterly riveting.

She must come to a decision soon. She'd dismissed Miss Arnaud a long time ago. In the dining saloon they would be serving the final courses of dinner now. If she missed him tonight, quite likely by tomorrow he'd have found himself another lover.

She shuddered again, a mixture of fear, loathing, and a fierce, perverse need to bring this man to heel.

Her hand reached toward her veiled hat.

Her decision, it appeared, had been made.

*T*he going was more difficult than she'd anticipated. She knew, of course, that the *Rhodesia* had run into a fairly significant storm. But sitting in a bolted chair, alternately questioning her sanity and raging at her cowardice, had not given her a proper appreciation of how animated the Atlantic had become.

But out in the mahogany-paneled corridors, she tottered as if drunk, lurching from bulkhead to bulkhead. It wasn't so bad when the floor rose to meet her. But every time it dropped away, there was a moment of disconcerting weightlessness.

The ship's lights flickered. It plunged at an angle that would have served for a young children's slide. She gripped a nearby doorknob to keep her balance. The *Rhodesia*, reaching the trough of the wave, began to climb again. She grabbed onto a sconce so she wouldn't tumble backward.

The dining saloon was reached by a grand staircase adorned by a frieze of Japanese gold paper. There were also carved teak panels, but she could not see them very well, for the steps were packed with ladies in feathers and gentlemen in tails heading out, everyone hanging on to the banister.

Panic assailed her. Had dinner already concluded? Was she too late after all? But Lexington was not among the departing diners, so she pressed forward, descending the stairs against the exodus of passengers, ignoring their stares of curiosity and disapproval.

The dining saloon was a hundred feet long and sixty feet wide. The ceiling opened at the center into a rectangular wall that rose two decks to a glass-covered dome. On a clear day, sunlight would spill down this well and illuminate the rows of Corinthian columns and the four long tables that ran nearly the whole length of the room, each capable of accommodating more than a hundred diners.

On this stormy night, a bright if quivery light still cascaded from the well, its source the large, silver-branched electric chandelier that swung with the pitch and roll of the ocean liner. Had Venetia arrived an hour earlier, the sound of silverware and muted laughter would have greeted her, the familiar murmurs of privilege and satisfaction. But now the dining saloon was largely deserted. Two of the long tables were completely empty, all the dishes and cutlery cleared, all the bolted chairs turned out. A few hardy passengers still lingered, their plates and glasses held in place by a special wooden frame set on the table. A middle-aged, robust-looking woman loudly discussed her experiences with past nor'easters.

Lexington, in evening formals, sat by himself near the windows, a cup of coffee before him, his gaze on the storm outside. She prayed for no abrupt changes to the rhythm of the *Rhodesia*'s movement—she did not want to stumble along the way, but cut through like a shark, sleek and dangerous.

He glanced in her direction. With her veil on, it was difficult to judge his expression, but she thought she caught a flicker of surprise.

And anticipation.

Her stomach tightened. Her face heated. Her heart pounded loudly in her ears.

He rose as she approached the table, but offered no greeting. A waiter emerged from nowhere to help her with her chair, another presented her a cup of coffee.

Lexington retook his seat. Without taking his eyes off her, he lifted his coffee and drank. It would seem he had no intention of making this easy for her.

She spoke before she could change her mind again. "I have reconsidered your proposition, sir."

He made no response. The air between them all but crackled with charge.

She swallowed. "And I've come to the conclusion that I am open to persuasion."

The steamer heaved. Her hand shot out to protect her coffee cup; his did the same. His finger wrapped around hers. She felt the shock of it deep into her shoulder.

"I was about to go back to my rooms," he said. "Would you care to join me?"

For a long second, her voice refused to work. Her lips trembled. The thought of being alone with him squeezed the air from her lungs.

"Yes," she rasped.

He set down his cup and came to his feet. She bit her lip and did likewise. Their exit garnered inquisitive looks from the remaining diners. Lexington took no notice of them. Strange how on her way to him, she'd been equally heedless of the unwanted attention she'd attracted. But now she felt as if she were about to be pilloried.

She preceded him up the grand staircase. The ship listed sharply. His arm was instantly about her waist.

"I'm quite all right, thank you."

He let go of her. She grimaced at her tone—she sounded nothing like a woman with lovemaking on her mind. If she were any severer, she'd be leading the temperance movement.

The Victoria suite was several decks above the dining saloon. For the rest of the way, they said not a word to each other. At the door of the suite he glanced at her—an unreadable look—before he turned the key.

The parlor was dimly lit. She could only make out the location and general outline of the furnishing: a desk and a Windsor chair before the window, a chaise longue to her right, two padded chairs opposite, shelves that had been built into the bulkhead.

He shut the door.

A surge of panic made her blurt out, "You will not ask to see my face."

"Understood," he answered quietly. "Would you care for something to drink?"

"No." She inhaled hard. "No, thank you."

He walked past her, deeper into the room. It was not until he reached out a hand that she realized he was extinguishing the light. Shadows enfolded her, alleviated only by flashes of lightning.

He drew the curtain, the slide of rings on rod quick, metallic. The unbroken darkness pressed against her sternum. The din of the storm faded. Even the slant and toss of the *Rhodesia* seemed to happen elsewhere. Her body knew how to brace itself for the volatile swells of the sea, yet the very predictable course Lexington set was a maelstrom, threatening to tow her asunder.

"Would you agree that I can't see anything now?"

He was right in front of her, just on the other side of her veil. Her fingers clutched the folds of her skirts. "Yes."

He removed the veiled hat. Her breath caught. She had never felt more naked in her life.

He slid the back of his hand against her cheek. It was as if a torch caressed her. "The door is unlocked. You may leave at any point."

The scene crashed into her head: Lexington wedged inside her, and she, overcome at last, begging to be let go.

"I won't." Her voice was small but defiant.

He made no reply. Her shallow, erratic breaths drowned out the waves battering the *Rhodesia*. He touched her again—the pad of his thumb grazing her lower lip, leaving a burning trail in its wake.

"You don't want to sleep with me. Why are you here?"

She swallowed. "I am not unwilling, only afraid."

"What do you fear?"

He kissed her just below her jaw. She shuddered. "It—it has been a very long time."

His hands were on her arms, their heat scorching her through the satin of her sleeves. "How long?"

"Eight years."

He wrapped one hand around her nape and kissed her, parting her lips without hesitation. The kiss tasted of Arabian coffee, as pure and potent as his will. And she felt that will deep inside her, in places that had lain dormant for nearly a decade.

All too soon he pulled away. The ship staggered. But the violence of the sea was nothing compared to the turmoil inside her: She wished he hadn't stopped.

"Where is the door?" she asked, her voice uneven.

He did not answer immediately. Into the impenetrable night came the sound of his breathing, less quiet, less controlled. "Five paces behind you." He paused a second. "Would you like me to walk you there?"

"No," she said. "Take me in the opposite direction."

The bedroom was, if possible, even darker than the parlor. Christian stopped when he reached the bed. Under his thumb, the small vein at the baroness's wrist throbbed wildly, one beat indistinguishable from the next.

He spread open her tightly clenched hand. She was as tense as a full-blown war. Yet beneath all the rigidness, all the reluctance, pulsed an arousal made audible by every one of her ragged breaths. He couldn't remember the last time a woman so incited him.

Cupping her face, he kissed her again. She tasted impossibly clean, of rain and snow and spring water. The scent of her was equally spare, no sultry musk or sweet flowers, only the fragrance of freshly laundered hair and skin, underpinned by the warmth of her body.

She made small whimpers in her throat. Lust shot through him. His fingers were impatient, almost unsteady, as he undid the top of her bodice, peeling back the layers that imprisoned her.

He was more interested in her reactions than her flesh, yet the sheer smoothness of her skin made him light-headed with desire. He took her mouth once more, invading it thoroughly. His body pressed hers into the footboard of the bed.

She trembled. Did she feel him through everything they still wore? He was hot and hard, almost senselessly so. Then she did something that poured fresh fuel on the fire of his lust: She helped him with her corset, her hands and his working the busk closures together.

The corset was the castle gate. Once it had been undone, everything else was but formalities. He pulled the pins out of her hair and rid her of the rest of her clothes, touching her as little as possible in the process, not quite trusting his own usually ironclad control.

When she was naked, she asked, "Can I still leave?"

"Yes," he said, pressing her down onto his bed. "Anytime."

"What would you do, if I left now?"

"Sulk."

He kissed her chin, her throat. She was delicious everywhere. And still so wound up, her fingers gripping the bedspreads as if she might fall off the bed otherwise—a real possibility, with the *Rhodesia* reeling every which way. But he doubted she noticed. What she feared was not God, but man.

"Why don't you want to see my face?" she murmured.

"Did I ever say I do not want to see your face?" He palmed her breast, a most tactile handful, and grazed its underside. "But if you don't want me to, I will learn to recognize you by the texture of your skin." He rolled her already erect nipple between his fingers, eliciting a trembling exhalation from her lips. "By your voice," he said, taking the nipple into his mouth. "And by your taste."

She moaned and undulated beneath him. He'd always been a meticulous lover—it was only fair that he should repay the lady for his gratification. But her he wanted to overwhelm with pleasure, to have her bask in it, wallow in it, revel in it. He wanted to make her forget that she'd ever been anxious and afraid.

She'd never been more anxious, more afraid.

That he was the one to give her such pleasure frightened her. But she had no one to turn to, except him. The next time he kissed her, she gripped his shoulders and kissed him back, because she didn't know what else to do.

His response was fierce. He removed his own clothes, slid his hand under her bottom, and came fully inside her.

She sucked in a breath. Yes, she'd been another man's wife. Yes, Tony had been a competent lover in the early days of their marriage. But had the sensations ever been this sharp, this white-hot, as if lightning had struck?

"Can I—can I still leave?" she heard herself ask.

He withdrew and drove into her again. "Yes." Another long, infinitely pleasurable stroke. "Anytime."

She panted. "What would you do if I left?"

He ground into her. "Weep."

She could not help smiling—just a little.

He gripped her hair and kissed her. "But you are not going anywhere."

He did dirty, delicious things to her. Fanned the flames of her desires until she was nothing but fever and need. Her pleasure gathered into such an immense, pressure-filled mass that the only way to relieve the pent-up tension was to convulse and scream.

"It really *has* been eight years," he murmured.

His hand caressed her where their bodies were still joined. How good it felt, how exquisite. She writhed, whimpering.

"It's only been a few months for me, but I begin to be convinced I must also have gone years without."

He withdrew and pushed slowly, ever so slowly, back into her. Her breaths shuddered. It dawned on her that he had not yet reached his resolution.

His fingers stroked her again at the juncture of her thighs, arousing fresh, hot desires. But it was his lips at her ear that thoroughly reignited her. "You are so tightly strung," he whispered, with a bite to her earlobe that she felt all the way in her toes, "the least touch makes you vibrate."

After that, there were no more words. He calibrated and fine-tuned her until the merest contact between their bodies was a crescendo of sensations. When his control broke, he pushed her over the edge again. She was deafened and blinded by pleasure. Drowning in it, clutching onto him as her only salvation in the maelstrom.

They stilled. He was solid and heavy above her. She listened to his tattered breathing and felt strangely raw, the way a patch of skin that had been bandaged for a long time did when it was at last exposed to air, light, and touch.

Don't think, she told herself. *Don't think of anything. For as long as you can.*

CHAPTER 5

The rumbles of thunder had grown more distant. The pelting of rain was not as savage upon the deck. The *Rhodesia* still wobbled, but she no longer lurched in unpredictable directions.

Christian rolled onto his side, taking the baroness with him. Her hair, cool and silky, tickled his arm. Her breaths were little puffs of moist warmth at the crook of his neck. Her body, at last, was slack, almost limp.

He was pleased with himself—too much so, perhaps. To a naturalist, there was no act more mundane than the sexual one. Yet making love to Baroness von Seidlitz-Hardenberg had been anything but ordinary. To the contrary, it had felt momentous, far more significant than merely the beginning of a weeklong affair.

He'd been so caught up in the heady events of the evening he hadn't even given a thought to a sponge or a French letter until now, he who was usually far more scrupulous about such things. That she was in his bed was another aberration. In his liaisons, he preferred to set the itinerary, to leave or stay as he chose. But this time, he'd ceded the control to her: She wanted to conquer her fear, and that appealed to his sense of gallantry.

He lifted a strand of her hair and wound it about his fingers. "I'm glad you decided to reconsider my proposition."

Against his shoulder, she made a sound, something of a *humfft*.

He let go of her hair, turned her face, and kissed her on her mouth. "What made you change your mind?"

Her answer was the same *humfft*, but she tensed again—he felt it in the set of her jaw.

He had an idea why she might not be keen on speaking to him: She probably thought he'd propositioned her randomly and she still hadn't made peace with her eventual acceptance.

"There is an interesting contradiction to you. You hide your face, but your gait is anything but retiring."

Not only did he want her to stay, tonight he'd be the one to make conversation as well—quite a reversal for a man who was more accustomed to seeking his solitude afterward.

"Oh?" she murmured against his cheek.

"You walk with a certain swagger. Not a strut, mind you, but a confident, assertive gait. A woman out and about with her face covered can expect a great deal of attention, which can be daunting. But you carry on as if this attention is the least of your concerns, as if you daily part a sea of staring eyes."

She stirred. "And *that* interests you?"

"Your *reasons* interest me. I asked myself whether you might be a fugitive, and decided no, the veil makes you far too visible. There is also a small chance you are a Musulman, but no Musulman woman who takes the trouble to cover her face entirely would be caught dead traveling unaccompanied. Which leaves two possibilities. One, you simply do not wish to show anyone your face, and two, there is something highly irregular about your features."

She pulled away. "You've a taste for deformed women, sir? Is that why you asked me to be your lover?"

"Did I ever ask you to be my lover?"

"Of course you—" She stopped.

When he'd stated that he'd like to know her better, *she'd* been the one to ask whether he was looking for a lover.

"When you instantly jumped to the conclusion that I'd like to sleep with you, you answered my question. A woman of highly irregular features might be suspicious about my interest in her, but she is unlikely to immediately accuse me of a lascivious overture. You, on the other hand, take it for granted that a man's interest in you lies in that direction.

"Since there is nothing physically wrong with you, if I were to pretend I did not have some carnal curiosity about you, I'd be lying. So, yes, I acknowledged that component of my intent. But if you'd asked, I'd have told you that I was more interested in the why of you than the naked pleasures of your body." It was strangely easy to talk to this faceless woman in the dark, as if he were speaking to the sea or the sky. He brushed her hair back from her shoulder. "Although, had I known just how monumental were the naked pleasures you'd bring into the bargain, I'd have pursued you with much greater vigor."

He must have failed abysmally at explaining himself—
or offended her anew. For she pushed away from him and
sat up.

"I should go."

*W*ould you like me to help you find your clothes?
They might be scattered around—I'm afraid
I wasn't too careful about collecting them in a neat pile."

His German was quite nimble and there was a smile in
his voice. She bit her lower lip. Why hadn't she planned
things better? How would she be able to find everything
in the dark—and dress herself to a semblance of decency?

He left the bed the same time she did. "This is something of yours. This is mine. What is this? A corset cover?"

Her toes encountered her shoes and stockings. But
before she could pick them up, he was already upon her,
handing her a bundle of clothes. When she took the clothes
from him, his hand brushed her arm.

"Need some help dressing?"

"No, I—"

"We'll pretend this is an excavation site and work
methodically," he said, taking the clothes from her again.
"I'll lay out your clothes on the bed one by one, then we'll
know what is what and which pieces are still missing."

She had not expected this helpful alacrity. Her clothes
landed on the bed with a small *whomp*. He rounded to the
other side of the bed, presumably to begin the classifica-
tion of said garments.

She bent down and gathered her stockings. When she
straightened, she came up against what felt like a very soft

blanket at her back. "Put it on, or you'll be cold," said Lexington.

It was a dressing gown of merino wool. She tightened the sash at her waist. "What about you?"

"I have found my trousers. Now, let's see about your clothes. Your dress"—something rustled; his voice once again came from the far side of the bed—"will form the bottom of the heap, to be followed by everything else in reverse order. How many petticoats were you wearing?"

"One."

"Only one?"

"The skirt is split, so the dress comes with an embroidered inner skirt. And the cut is narrow. More than one petticoat and the fit will suffer."

Why had she explained in such detail? It was almost as if she was afraid he'd think the lack of multiple petticoats translated into moral laxity on her part. When she'd just slept with a man to whom she hadn't even been properly introduced!

"Wise choice," he murmured. Again that smile in his voice. "The fit most certainly did not suffer."

She felt as if she'd fallen down the rabbit hole. Or perhaps he was a strange incarnation of Dr. Jekyll and Mr. Hyde—but instead of turning evil in the dark, he became much nicer.

"Can you find your way here?" he asked. "I have your things in readiness."

She skirted the edge of the bed. "Where are you? I don't want to step on your foot."

"Hmm," he said, "there is an accent to your German."

She halted. She'd grown up with a German governess.

Native German speakers usually remarked on her *lack* of an English accent. "What kind of an accent?"

"I've spent some time in Berlin and you don't have the vowels of Prussia proper, either the German parts or the Polish parts. You sound as if your origins are farther south—Bavaria, I'd say."

Her German governess had indeed been from Munich and spoke the lilting *Bairisch* dialect. "Very good for an Englishman."

"Yet I'm not convinced you are German."

Too good for an Englishman. "Why not? You yourself identified my Bavarian accent."

"When I mentioned your accent, you stopped cold. You are still standing in place, by the way."

She remained where she was. "Does it matter whether I am German, Hungarian, or Polish?"

"No, I suppose it doesn't. Is your name really von Seidlitz-Hardenberg?"

"And what if I am not a baroness, either? Will that cause the *Rhodesia* to sink?"

"No, but I'm convinced it precipitated the storm."

Judging by his tone, he was smiling once more—and standing all too close.

His hand combed her hair. "What are you still afraid of?"

"I'm not afraid of anything." Yet she *sounded* as if she were cowering.

"Good, you shouldn't be. What can I do to you? Once we disembark, I wouldn't know you even if we came face-to-face."

But she'd planned differently, hadn't she? At Southampton, she meant to reveal herself and let him know he'd been had. She'd imagined this denouement in dozens of delicious variations, each leading to that inevitable point of rage and devastation on his part. Looking back, it was as if she'd planned a trip to the moon, with her only qualification an enthusiasm for Monsieur Verne's scientific romances.

He tucked back her hair and kissed her beneath her earlobe, the sensation so jagged it almost hurt. Nibbling a path down the column of her neck, he pushed aside the collar of her dressing gown and exposed her shoulder.

"You are so very tense again, my dear baroness who may or may not be a baroness."

"You make me feel nervous." And guilty, even though she'd yet to do anything more reprehensible than sleeping with a man she did not love—or like.

He lifted her and set her down at the edge of the bed. "Unforgivable on my part. Let me offer my recompenses."

He undid the sash on her dressing gown. She fought a renewed surge of panic. "Why are you nice to me?"

"I like you. I'm never unpleasant to people I like."

"You are a high-minded man, are you not?"

"I do have some exacting standards."

"As a man of exacting standards, can you justify to yourself why you like me, beyond that I am a source of naked pleasures?"

"You turned me down, and that speaks well of you—a man who went about it with as little finesse and forethought as I did deserved to be rebuffed. Other than that, you are right; I don't have any firm foundations for approving of you. All the same, when you changed your mind, I was terribly flattered. So I am going to be unscientific and call this simply an affinity."

Affinity. When in real life, he had the greatest antipathy for her.

"There is something else about you that I like," he continued. She didn't know when he'd pressed her into bed, but she lay with him beside her, her dressing gown completely open. Lightly he ran his hand over her breasts and her abdomen. "I like that I can make you forget, however briefly, everything that agitates you."

*H*e made love to her again. Afterward, when she began to deliberately bring her breathing under control, Christian knew that she'd left her sweet oblivion behind. This time, when she told him that she must go, he pulled on his trousers and helped her dress. Then he went out to the parlor and brought back her hat.

"What about your hair?" He'd discarded the pins and combs that had held together her coiffure. "I've scant knowledge on the repair of ladies' hair."

"I've the veil," she said. "I'll manage."

Once her face was safely obscured behind the veil, he turned on the lamps and shrugged into his shirt.

"It's late. I'll walk you back."

The light danced upon the warp and woof of her veil, which rippled just perceptibly as she exhaled. He had the feeling she was about to turn down his offer, but she said, "All right, thank you."

A sensible woman, for he'd have insisted.

He remained in the bedroom. She walked slowly about the parlor, taking in the coffered ceiling, the stack of books on the writing desk, and the vase of red and yellow tulips on the mantel. For some reason he'd thought her dinner gown cream-colored, but it was apricot, the skirt spangled with beads and crystal drops.

He snapped his braces over his shoulders and tossed on a waistcoat and an evening coat. His cuff links, emblazoned with the Lexington coat of arms, were on the floor. He bent down and retrieved them.

As he straightened, he felt pinpricks upon his skin—the weight of her gaze. He glanced at her. She looked away immediately, even though he could see nothing but her faintly glimmering veil.

She did not trust him—or like him entirely, for that matter. And yet she'd let him seduce her—or was it the other way around?—twice. He could flatter himself and attribute the discrepancy to an intense attraction on her part, but years of training in objectivity made such delusions impossible.

He put on the cuff links. He even went to the trouble of a fresh necktie. If they were seen together at this hour, it might lead to certain suspicions, but he was not about to give concrete evidence by looking disheveled.

"Shall we?" He offered his arm.

She hesitated before laying her hand on his elbow. Still jittery, his baroness, almost as much as she'd been when she'd arrived in his suite. But questions to that regard set her on edge, so he refrained.

Instead, as they walked out of the suite, he asked, "Why were you celibate for so long? Clinging faithfully to the late baron's memory?"

She made a sound that could only be termed snorting. "No."

The *Rhodesia* was quiet except for the thrum of the mighty engine deep in its hull. The first-class passengers, whether asleep, seasick, or vigorously plugging away at their spouses, kept up the courtesy of decorous silence. The lamplit corridors might well have been those of a ghost ship.

"If you weren't still mourning the baron, then I can't imagine going so long without."

"It is hardly unheard of."

"True, but you don't seem like someone who would want to be deprived for years upon years."

Her sigh was one of impatience. "As much as this might amaze you, sir, a woman doesn't always need a man to satisfy her. She can see to it herself with great competence."

He chortled, delighted. "And you are, no doubt, tremendously capable in this respect?"

"I daresay I am sufficiently skilled from all that practice," she said, rather grumpily.

He laughed again.

Even across the veil he could feel the glance she shot at him. "Are you always this cheerful afterward?"

"No, not at all." His mood usually turned somber, sometimes downright dark—the women he slept with were never the one he wanted, whose hold over him remained unbreakable. But tonight he'd thought not once of Mrs. Easterbrook. "Are you always this testy afterward?"

"Maybe. I can't remember."

"Was the late baron a clumsy lover?"

"You'd like him to be, wouldn't you?"

He'd never known himself to care whether a woman had had better or worse lovers than he. But in this instance, he found that, yes, he did have a preference. "Indeed. I'd like him to be thoroughly useless—impotent, if possible."

He wanted to be the only one who'd ever brought her to peak after peak of shocking pleasure.

"Sorry to disappoint you. He might not have been Eros reborn, but he acquitted himself quite well."

"How you thwart me, baroness." A thought occurred to him. "So what *was* wrong with him?"

"I beg your pardon?"

"He was a decent lover, yet after his death, you resorted to your own . . . manual dexterity. And you did *not* dedicate your chastity to him. Was he unfaithful?"

She stopped. Not for long—she resumed her progress almost immediately, and at a faster pace. But he had his answer.

"He was a fool," he declared.

She shrugged. "It was a long time ago."

"Not all men are philanderers."

"I know that. I have chosen to stay away from men not because I have lost faith in all of them, but because I am no longer confident of my ability to choose well."

"I'm sorry."

"Being unattached has its advantages." Her face turned toward him. "At least I have been married. What is your excuse? Shouldn't a man who holds a title as lofty as yours have produced an heir or two by now?"

He did not fail to notice she'd changed the subject. Deftly, too.

"Yes, he should. And I have no excuse, which is why I am on my way to a London Season, to do my duty."

"You don't sound very enthusiastic. You've no love for the idea of marriage?"

"I've nothing against the institution, but I suspect I shan't be happy in it."

"Why not?"

Again, her anonymity made him speak freely of things he would not even consider mentioning before others. "There is no question that I must marry—and soon. But I have little hope of finding a girl who will suit me."

"You mean, no woman is good enough for you."

"Quite the opposite. Other than my inheritance, I have very little to offer a woman. I'm hardly a dazzling conversationalist. I'd rather be in the field or locked in my study. And even when I am willing to linger in the drawing room and make small talk, I am not particularly easy to be around."

"These are faults many girls would be more than willing to overlook."

"I don't want my faults overlooked. Members of my staff are there to deal with my eccentricities whether they approve or not. My wife should have the mettle to tell me I'm behaving abominably—if that is the case."

"So you do know you behave abominably at times," she mused. "But if you've such stringent requirements for a wife, if she must possess intelligence, gravitas, and fearlessness in equal abundance, why did you not start your search sooner? Why limit yourself to one Season and one batch of debutantes? Hardly an astute way to go about it."

No, it was not. He'd gone about it in the stupidest manner possible, all but assuring that his marriage would be a formal, stilted affair. But this was not something he could admit, no matter how anonymous the baroness was.

"I shall pay for it, no doubt."

"You sound very British, full of manly forbearance and resignation."

He adored her acerbic tone. "We are quite bloodless

when it comes to such matters. The pursuit of happiness we leave to Americans; romance we consider the specialty of the Continentals."

She was quiet. The ship rose and fell gently, as if it lay upon the breast of a sleeping giant. The beads on her skirt slid and clicked against one another, like a distant rain of pearls.

They descended two flights of stairs and turned a corner. She stopped. "I'm home."

He noted the number of her stateroom. "Will I have the pleasure of your company at breakfast?"

"You want to be seen in public with me?" There was an echo of surprise in her voice.

"Should I object to it?"

"You will be known as the man who accompanies the veiled woman."

"That is more than acceptable to me."

She stood with her back to the door, her hand on the knob—as if protecting the entrance from him. "And if I say no?"

"You will not be rid of me so easily now, baroness. If you say no to breakfast, I will ask whether you'd like to join me for a stroll after breakfast."

"And if I say I will join you for breakfast, but won't ever sleep with you again?"

"You are determined to make me weep, madam."

He touched his fingers to the edge of her veil, which fell several inches past her chin. The netting slipped weightlessly upon his skin. She would probably have pulled away from him, but he already had her back against a wall—or a door, for that matter.

"You didn't answer my question," she said.

It was vain to enjoy the slight tremors he caused in her voice, but how he relished them. "The bargain is the same," he said. "I will do my best to seduce you, and you can walk away anytime you wish. Now, will you meet me for breakfast?"

"No." Then, after an interminable beat, "I can't eat with this veil on. I will meet you for a walk."

He hadn't really believed she would turn him down altogether. Why then did his heart pound with relief? "Name the time and the place."

"Nine in the morning. The promenade deck."

"Excellent." He leaned in and kissed her lips through the veil. "Good night."

She slipped inside her stateroom and closed the door gently but firmly in his face.

*Ve*netia leaned her back against the door, unable to take another step.

What had she done?

And what, in God's name, had been done to *her*?

Revenge had seemed so simple. Lexington had injured her maliciously and unrepentantly. Therefore Lexington must pay. He dealt with fossils. She dealt with men. Ergo, she must have the upper hand in this very human struggle of theirs, even with her face covered.

Yet here she was, gingerly touching her lips, which still tingled from his chaste parting kiss.

She'd boarded the *Rhodesia* to punish a man, but he was not that man. He was someone else altogether.

After her marriage to Tony, it was not only her ability to choose a good man she doubted, it was also her ability to make a man—any man—happy. But Lexington, that most severe judge of character, had been almost buoyant in her company. And he now numbered among the few men to whom her appearance truly did not matter.

It was as if she'd set off across the Atlantic to find a route to India, only to encounter a whole new continent.

Had she accosted him in New York, she could have disappeared into the city. But on the *Rhodesia* she could not hide. And . . . she did not want to. The duke was affirmation that there *was* more to her than the shape of her face and the juxtaposition of her features.

Slowly she discarded her clothes, feeling her way to her berth. Under the covers she said her prayers, exhorting the Almighty to watch over Helena and bring the girl back to her senses. She also prayed that on the far side of the Atlantic, Fitz would continue to be patient and discreet, and that back in America, when they found out, Millie and Helena would not worry too much over her second abrupt departure in as many days.

For herself she did not pray—even if she thought her troubles important enough to bother the Good Lord, the fact remained that she no longer had any idea what outcome she wanted from her muddled revenge. So she lay for a long time, her hands over her abdomen, and thought of the spate of incidents and coincidences—beginning with Hastings coming upon Helena three nights in a row—that had brought her to this time, this place, this quandary.

And wished she had a crystal ball to see where it all would lead.

CHAPTER 6

*T*he sea had calmed, but the *Rhodesia* plowed through steady rain and frigid air. Few souls were out and about on the promenade deck. The Atlantic was a vast expanse of cold, misty gray, its dreariness only occasionally leavened by the zestful leap of a dolphin.

Lexington stared at his pocket watch. She was fifteen minutes late for their stroll. He summoned a steward. The man was to convey Lexington's compliments to the baroness. Not exactly a subtle reminder, but then she already knew he was not a man who greatly valued subtlety.

As he was giving instructions to the steward, she rounded the corner, clad in a sturdy, black gabardine. The wind expressed a great interest in her umbrella, jerking it about every which direction. Another woman would have looked frantic and clumsy, but she moved with the command and drama of a prima ballerina taking center stage.

He waved the steward away. "You are late, madam."

"Of course," she said firmly. Her veil, tied at the base of her throat to counter the wind, blew against her face, hinting at rich lips and high cheekbones. "Ladies are not carriages. We cannot be expected to pull up at the exact appointed hour."

It was the most charmingly ridiculous excuse he'd ever heard. "What is the appointed hour for, then?"

"You've been invited to dinner, have you not, even though you shun Society?"

"I have not thrown myself at the mercy of a London Season, but I do not shun Society when I'm at home. I dine at my neighbors' houses. I've even been known to give dinners."

A stiff squall nearly made away with her umbrella. He clasped a hand over hers to help her hold on to it. But after the wind had dissipated, he did not let go.

She gave him a look—a hard look, he imagined. But when she spoke again, her voice was not at all severe. "What were we speaking of?"

For some reason, his heart skipped a beat. "Dinners."

"That's right." She pulled the umbrella—and her gloved hand—out of his. "You do not sit down to dinner the moment you walk into the host's house. Instead, you circulate about and engage in pleasantries with the other guests. And so it is when you rendezvous with a lady. You wait, you pace, and you think of her—it makes her arrival all the more momentous."

He was a stickler for punctuality. Such tardiness he

would not have tolerated in another woman. Yet he found himself smiling. "Are you serious?"

She tilted her head. "My goodness, you've never waited for a woman in your life?"

"No."

"Hmm. Let's not stand here." She set out at a brisk pace. "I suppose it makes sense that kept mistresses would wait on you, instead of the other way around. But I can't believe you've never enjoyed a liaison with a lady."

"I have, but those who didn't arrive on time found I'd left already."

He wondered whether he sounded too harsh. He hadn't meant to reproach her, only to answer her question truthfully.

"You are still here," she murmured.

"I very much wished to see you again."

He'd said nothing new. But she dipped her head slightly, then glanced toward him at an angle, almost as if she were feeling shy.

"Did you fret that I wasn't going to come?"

He hesitated. Honesty was easy when one's answer was simply an opinion that revealed little of one's inner thoughts. But the honest answer to this particular question involved not only an acknowledgment of desire, but a confession of greater attachment.

"Yes. I was about to send a steward to remind you that I was waiting."

"And what were you going to do if that did not bring me rushing into your arms?" She paused. "Send flowers?"

There was a subtle but unmistakable edge to her voice.

He shook his head. "I never send flowers to anyone I wish to know."

Behind the veil, she might have frowned; certainly she had her face turned toward him, as if expecting him to read her expression. Only a moment later—realizing that he could not see anything, perhaps—did she ask, "What does that mean?"

"My father was a great philanderer who gave innumerable bouquets in his lifetime. I view flowers as false gifts. I would not give you flowers."

"But you did. You sent a huge vase of them to my suite at the New Netherlands Hotel."

His confusion did not last long. "I see what must have happened. I did order some flowers sent, to a woman whose acquaintance I did not wish to further. But I gave that task and the map you dropped to the same hotel attendant—so your map went to her and her flowers came to you."

The baroness did not reply.

"Have I offended you by not sending the flowers?"

She laughed, a dry, rueful sound. "Quite the contrary. You offended me deeply when I thought you *had* sent the flowers. I did not like such a bald expression of interest."

"A huge vase of flowers, you said?"

"Enormous. Pushy. And rather ghastly."

"I am doubly amazed now that you changed your mind."

She was silent for a while. "This wind is quite defeating me. Shall we go into one of the lounges?"

*T*he flowers had tipped her from rage into action. Had they not been delivered when she'd returned to her suite two nights ago, she'd have continued to stew in her fury, imagining his head on a platter, but she would not have set them on a collision course.

And now to find out that the flowers hadn't been for her. At all.

Did that still make him a hypocrite, condemning her and wanting her at the same time? Or had he only been stupid, sharing in public opinions that were better kept private?

The heated lounge was a shock of warmth after the damp cold of the promenade deck. She untied her veil—the air was becoming too still inside. He led her to a table at the corner, between two potted fronds.

"You are very quiet," he observed.

"I'm a little distracted."

"A terrible thing to say to your lover, who is letting nothing distract him from you."

Her heart thumped at the word *lover*. "What would you have done had I bought a ticket on a different steamer?"

"I would have had a much less enjoyable crossing."

"There are many other ladies aboard."

"They don't interest me as you do."

"How can you say that? You know nothing about them."

He turned and looked around the room. "Other than you, there are eleven women in this lounge, two are old enough to be my grandmother, three more old enough to be my mother, and one is barely fifteen, if that. Of the other five, one is recently engaged—she keeps looking at her ring while she writes her letter. The one in the pink frock is thinking only of chocolate—I can see her trying to sneak a piece from the secret stash in her pocket. The one in the redingote is rude to waiters—she sat not too far from me at dinner last night. The one in yellow, Redingote's sister, dissects every lady's dress down to the last detail—see, she is whispering to Redingote now, probably about *your* dress. And the woman in brown is a lady's companion who does not want to be a lady's companion anymore. But she is very practical. She does not take note of me because I have you by my side; she is looking for a lonely, unattached gentleman who might overlook her humble origins and make her his wife."

He turned back toward her. "See, they don't interest me as you do."

The veil obscured the color of his eyes, but there was no mistaking the pleasure in his countenance as he looked upon her. Her pulse turned erratic—more erratic, that was. She had yet to know a steady heartbeat in his presence.

Belatedly it occurred to her that he was a great deal more observant than she'd given him credit for. And with that realization came a frisson of alarm. "What do you know about me?"

"You probably married quite young. Your husband exerted tremendous influence over you—because you loved him very much, because he was a good few years older than you, possibly both. Even to this day you still haven't quite escaped the shadow he cast. But you do not think of your solitude as a sign that you remain bound to him. If anything, you have been glad to be alone—and safe."

She felt the blood drain from her face. He ought not to know this much about her. "I probably should have remained alone. I'm not sure I am safe with you."

"Tell me what you think of the men in this room."

She glanced at him, not sure what he wanted.

"Humor me," he said.

Other than him, there were only three other men. "One of them is glancing toward the girl who loves chocolate with exasperation. He is most likely her brother. Perhaps their mother is suffering from seasickness and he is forced to play chaperone. The young man who is actually talking to our chocolate lover reminds me a little of my brother: He has that aura of dutifulness to him—someone who takes his responsibilities seriously. I'd say Our Girl of the Hidden Chocolate and her brother have been ordered here by their mother to make a good impression on Responsible Young Man. Except Responsible Young Man is distracted. He keeps looking toward one of the women old enough to be your mother—and who might in fact *be his* mother.

"That woman is speaking to a man in his thirties. And I can see why Responsible Young Man might be wary. He taps his foot incessantly and blinks too much. His smiles don't quite reach his eyes. And his accent shifts: He is trying to pass himself off as an English gentleman, but I can hear traces of American vowels, especially in the diphthongs."

"Aha," said Lexington, evidently satisfied.

"What does that mean?"

"You said last night that you mistrust your ability to judge a man. My dear, you can judge a man just fine."

She fidgeted. She was not used to being complimented on her abilities.

"Being an astute judge of man, have you witnessed anything in my character or conduct that would lead you to conclude you won't be safe with me?"

"No," she had to admit.

"In that case, would you allow me to offer you a cup of hot cocoa in my rooms?"

"It would be very messy, drinking hot cocoa with this veil on."

"I'll blindfold myself. You can take off the veil."

"That is a very kind offer, but going into your rooms, sir, would encourage you when I have no intention of doing so."

"How can I change your mind?"

"I don't plan to change my mind."

"There must be something I can do. Or give."

She bit the inside of her cheek. "Do you think my favors can be purchased?"

"The point is not to purchase your favors, but to prove my sincerity. The knights-errant of old went on their impossible quests to prove that they were worthy of serving their lady. I will do the same here. Name something— anything—and I will find it for you."

"On the *Rhodesia*?"

"She is a great ocean liner carrying a thousand passengers, if not more. Chances are, whatever you want, someone has it, or a close enough approximation of it."

But if the duke woos me with a monster of a fossil, who knows how I might reward him.

She ought not. He was right. No matter how rare or exceptional an object, there was a chance that someone on board might have it.

"You are a naturalist," she heard herself say.

"How do you know?"

She swore inwardly: They'd never discussed why he'd been away from England. "I saw the books in your room; I inferred."

"Mysterious *and* sharp." He smiled at her.

Perhaps he'd smiled at her before, but never in the light, with her looking directly at him. The transformation was astonishing. Gone was the last vestige of the iceberg. In its place, the tropics, all warmth and graciousness.

Her heart stuttered, to her chagrin. Was it not enough that he had already turned her plan on its head?

"Now how is it significant that I am a naturalist?" he asked.

She was almost absolutely certain neither he nor anyone else aboard had access to what she had in mind, yet she felt a sting of nerves in her soles. "I want a dinosaur skeleton."

He raised a brow. "You jest."

"Not at all. Do you have one?"

"No, I don't. My specialty is not Dinosauria."

Her disappointment was disorientingly fierce. She did want to go to the duke's rooms, she now realized. But she wanted her decision to be made for her, for the Fates to compel her action.

"I do, however, have something that might pass as a suitable equivalent."

She shouldn't let him do this to her—dashing her barely understood hopes one second and reviving them the next. Especially now that she knew she shouldn't be entertaining such hopes in the first place. "I don't want to see the remains of little amphibians or trilobites."

"Nothing of the sort." He rose. "Come by my suite in an hour, will you? I will have it ready for you."

"If it is less than magnificent, I shall turn around and walk out of the door."

He smiled down at her. "And if it is everything I promised, what will you do?"

That smile was going to be her undoing. "I might stay and admire it for a while. But you still should not expect anything else."

"I don't *expect*. But I always go after what I want."

She wanted him to. Fate or him, as long as *someone* took the decision out of her hands. "I should like to see you do that blindfolded," she said, as haughtily as she could.

"Then I will make you come to me. Now if you will excuse me—I must see to the removal of a heavy object from the cargo hold."

*C*hristian had anticipated difficulties, but the bribe had proved even more uncooperative than he'd thought. By the time it was set down in his room and uncrated, more than an hour had passed. However, thanks to the baroness's practice of being fifteen minutes late, the stewards had just enough time to take away the crate and sweep up the clumps of straw that had scattered on the carpet.

She arrived as they were leaving. The men cast curious and appreciative looks at her—she'd shed the gabardine and was clad in a lilac walking gown that showed her figure to every advantage. She, on the other hand, barely noticed their attention and headed directly for the very large object at the corner of the parlor.

Christian closed the door. "Go ahead, unveil it."

It did not escape him that the bribe was probably the only thing they'd unveil on this trip.

She flicked aside the canvas that covered what he hoped would prove the best acquisition he'd ever made. The sandstone slab was six feet tall and four feet wide. Imprinted on it, going toward opposite directions, were two three-toed footprints, each measuring twenty-four inches long and eighteen inches across. In between marched a diagonal line of much smaller footprints, barely a quarter the size of the bigger ones.

"Oh my." She sucked in a breath. "Tetrapodichnites."

Tetrapodichnite was the scientific term for the fossil footprint of a saurian. It would appear she was quite familiar with paleontological argot.

"May I touch it?"

"Of course. There are paper and charcoal on my desk if you wish to take impressions. And here's a blindfold you can put on me, if you'd like to take off your veil."

He held out his white silk scarf. She turned around. "Your word that the blindfold would remain on."

"You have my word."

She took the scarf from him, tied it around his head, and guided him to the chaise longue. It was not easy, but he refrained from pulling her down onto the chaise with him. He wanted to inhale her again, that infinitely clean scent of her.

Her footsteps quickly crossed the parlor, back to the tetrapodichnites.

Her interest intrigued him. "Are you a naturalist yourself?"

"No, but I make an exception for dinosaurs."

He imagined her pressed rapturously against the slab and smiled at his puerile turn of mind. More likely she was tracing the imprints with reverence and awe. "They were marvelous creatures."

"Yes, they were. I dug one up myself."

That was something he didn't hear every day. "When? Where?"

"I came across a near-complete skeleton when I was

sixteen, on holiday with my family. It was a massive beast. Of course I didn't know when I saw part of the rib cage poking out of the ground that it would be quite that big, but I spent the rest of my holidays happily finding out."

"You did all the digging all by yourself?"

"No, of course not. My siblings helped, as did children from a nearby village, and some young men who wanted to see what the fuss was about."

"What species was it?"

A long beat of silence. "A—um—a Swabian dragon."

"A *Plateosaurus*? I like those—handsome beasts. What did you do with the skeleton?"

"I wanted to display it at home, of course, but no one would let me."

He laughed softly. "I can see why."

An adult *Plateosaurus* could reach more than thirty feet in length. Even in a palatial home like Algernon House, such a display would dominate the tone and tenor of the entire place.

"I came to my senses after a while and donated it to a museum instead."

The sound of charcoal scratching upon paper—she'd started to make an impression of a footprint. "Which museum?"

"It shall remain anonymous."

"Are you afraid I'd go and find out your identity?"

"I'm sure you have far more important things to occupy your time, but I'm not taking chances."

"Why not, when you are already taking the biggest chance you have in a long time?"

The scratching of the charcoal ceased—then resumed

more furiously. "It's precisely because I can disappear into the ether that I have taken a chance. What do you think this is?"

It took him a second to realize she was speaking of the fossilized footprints. She'd changed the subject on him again. "A juvenile iguanodon, possibly. Or perhaps a predator of some description."

"How old do you think it is?"

"My guess is late Jurassic to early Cretaceous."

"Amazing," she murmured, "that something as fragile and ephemeral as a set of footprints can be preserved for a hundred fifty million years."

"Anything can happen under the right conditions." He touched the blindfold with his fingertips. She had tied it securely. But it was not black behind the lids of his eyes— more a dark ocher crisscrossed with beams of bronze. "Have you done any other sort of fossil hunting?"

"No."

"Why not, if it delights you so?"

She gave no answer.

"Please remember, my dear, I cannot see you. So shrugging and rolling your eyes are not answers enough."

"I didn't roll my eyes."

"But you did shrug?"

He took her silence to mean yes. "You said you were sixteen when you came upon your Swabian dragon. How old were you when you married?"

"Seventeen."

"Did your late husband believe mucking about with sharp implements and old bones to be an improper pastime for a woman?"

Another silence—another silent assent, then.

94

"If memory serves," he said, "some of the most significant finds in British paleontological history must be credited to a woman."

"Yes, Mary Anning, I've read about her. My husband said her finds were due to blind luck."

He snorted. "If God saw fit to give a woman that much blind luck, he can't possibly object to such endeavors on a woman's part."

The scratching of the charcoal stopped. Her footsteps headed toward the desk—for another sheaf of paper? "You are trying to seduce me with words," she said, her voice arch.

"That doesn't mean I'm insincere. Come along with me the next time I go on a dig, if you don't believe me."

"I thought it was understood I would disappear into thin air the moment we sight land."

"But there is nothing preventing you from coming back to me, is there? You know who I am. You know where to find me."

"You will be married soon, and that will be obstacle enough for me."

"I can delay my marriage." His stepmother would have his head, but for the baroness, he'd willingly endure one of the dowager duchess's rare bouts of umbrage.

"It will make no difference."

He shook his head. "You are heartless, baroness."

She did not miss a beat. "And you, duke, want too much."

He left her in peace after that, but Venetia's concentration was already ruined.

Why must he of all people prove himself so open-minded?

And to invite her on an organized expedition! She'd day-dreamed of one for years. Anytime she'd heard of a significant new discovery, she'd wished that she had been the one gifted with a rich vein of sedimentary layers and the privilege of unveiling the hidden history of the geological past.

After a quarter of an hour, she gathered the impressions she'd taken and set her hat back on her head. It would be discourteous to make him wear the blindfold for much longer. "Thank you, sir. It has been quite a pleasure. I will show myself out."

Did she intentionally pass by too close to the chaise longue? She certainly felt all too giddy when he pulled her down on top of himself. Knocking away her veiled hat, he kissed her ravenously. Her blood simmered. Certain unmentionable regions of her body throbbed with need.

"I don't want too much," he whispered against her lips. "If you are going to vanish at the end of the crossing, it's only fair that you do not leave my sight for the remainder of it."

He should look helpless in his blindfold. But he was all purpose and confidence. Her heart thudded. "I need to go."

"When will I see you again?"

"You don't need to see me again."

"I do, most assuredly—I haven't enjoyed anything half as much as your presence in a very, very long time."

Then why did he not ravish her on the spot? She could feel his arousal pressed against her. She wanted him to carry her off like a plundering Visigoth and overpower her will.

"I am immune to sweet nothings," she declared—an avowal full of shaky syllables.

"I have never uttered a sweet nothing in my life," he said solemnly. "When I'm with other women, it's as if only part of me is there and the rest of me wants to be elsewhere, elsewhen. But with you I'm not split in two. I am not plagued by other thoughts and other wishes. You cannot begin to guess how gratifying that is—to be altogether here, altogether present."

And he could not begin to guess how gratifying it was to have such magical properties attributed to her person. She had nothing to do with the alignment of her features, but she could take some credit, couldn't she, when it was her presence, rather than her face, that held a man riveted?

"You don't need to go anywhere," he murmured.

"I do." She was afraid to take responsibility for the choice. The last time she'd plunged ahead with such a decision, she'd opened herself to years of anguish and misery.

"But you will be back," he said, autocratic at last. "That is not negotiable. You will have dinner here, with me."

She gazed at the fine shape of his lips, the clean, chiseled line of his jaw, and the perfectly undisturbed blindfold. Beneath her palm, his chest rose and fell. She had to clench her hand to not begin to undo the buttons of his shirt at once.

"All right," she said. "But only dinner."

CHAPTER 7

I feel deprived," said Christian.

She had honored her word and come for dinner. He'd dined beforehand so she wouldn't feel obliged to feed him while he remained blindfolded. Afterward, she'd walked him to the chaise longue for him to enjoy another glass of wine and withdrawn to the opposite corner of the parlor to further admire the fossilized footprints.

"I'm in your rooms—you should be ecstatic." She gave no quarter.

"I *am* ecstatic. But that does not change the fact that I am deprived. If I can't see your face, then I should be able to see the rest of you. And if I can't see anything of you at all, I should be able to touch you at will."

She snorted, not at all sympathetic toward his plight. He smiled. With his title and his often unapproachable demeanor, he intimidated most women—and a large swath of men. She, however, had no compunction about putting him in his place.

His fingers encountered something, her hat. He picked it up and turned it around in his hand. "Tell me what you are doing."

"Ogling the footprints, of course. Why else would I be here?"

He amused himself by imagining her licking the slab. "Same reason you came here last night—to get to know me better."

"I had enough last night to last me a few years."

He chortled, setting her hat on the far end of the chaise. "I can't decide whether that is a compliment or an insult."

"When I compliment you, sir, you will know."

"Ha. You have stiffened my resolve, madam. You *will* compliment me before the night is out."

"You have very nice fossils, sir—and that's all the compliment you are getting."

He smiled again and took a sip of his wine. "I do love a challenge."

Such easy, lucid confidence. And nothing of Tony's brittle braggadocio, which she did not recognize for what it was until it had been too late.

"Tell me, do you come from an enlightened clan?" she asked.

He, comfortably reclined on the chaise, his face raised toward the ceiling, moved not a finger. Yet somehow she had the impression that he'd become more alert, more . . . predatory. He'd scented the interest she shouldn't have displayed.

"No," he said, his voice perfectly calm and friendly, giving not the least indication that he might be on the prowl. "If anything, the de Montforts have always been hidebound. We didn't deign to speak English until Shakespeare's time."

She rubbed a gloved hand across one of the smaller footprints. "Did you not encounter any objection from your family when you took up the life of a naturalist?"

"My father disapproved intensely."

His tipped back his glass. She could not look away from the line of his throat. "Did that cause any unpleasantness?"

He set the glass down on the carpet. Was it a signal that he was ready to pounce? "He put in a few tirades here and there, but it is not easy to turn me aside from a path I wish to pursue. I ignored him by and large."

His fingers lightly traced the rim of the glass. She could not help remembering how he'd played with her tight-strung body the night before with such deft touches. "Most young men find it difficult to put aside paternal edicts."

He sat up, his long arms braced along the back of the chaise, an expansive, assertive gesture. "My father had tremendous regard for himself, but he was frivolous, which made it easy for me to turn a deaf ear to him. Besides, I knew where the kitchen was, so sending me to bed without supper was not something I feared."

She had all but pressed her back into the slab. "My family was always particular that I not become a self-indulgent person. That and my husband's views were enough to convince me that if I deliberately sought out fossils to excavate, I would be yielding to a flighty and selfish impulse."

He smiled very slightly. "Are you so easy to daunt?"

Were they still speaking of fossils? "I did not altogether

approve of my own interest. I want to find fossil skeletons that are bigger, better, and more unexpected than anything that has been discovered to date, not because I am a serious naturalist trying to make sense of the world."

He rose to his feet. "There is nothing wrong with wanting bigger, better, and more unexpected. The thrill of the hunt is what drives all of us, whether we are seeking the next planet, a new principle of physics, or that elusive fossil that would shed light on exactly how life left the ocean and walked on land."

He was still all the way across the room, still blindfolded. Already she couldn't breathe. "I should go," she blurted out.

He tilted his head a few degrees to one side. "You are safe with me. You know that."

He was wrong. She hadn't been in this much peril in a long, long time. How stupid she'd been, hoping he would tip the decision for her. She wasn't playing with fire; she was juggling sticks of dynamite with their fuses already lit. For every grain of pleasure she dared now, she would later pay with a pound of grief.

"Thank you for dinner. And thank you for the pleasure of the tetrapodichnites." Her words stumbled over one another in her hurry to leave.

"You will make this a very long night for me."

"I'm sorry, but I truly can't stay any longer."

He faced her squarely. "Good night, then. I will see you same time, same place tomorrow morning for our walk."

She shook her head. "There is no point to our meeting again."

"I thought I'd made it abundantly clear that I relish your company even when you are not naked beneath me."

Her mouth went dry. Memories of her wantonness the night before, of the pleasures he'd heaped upon her—she had to clear her throat before she could speak again. "Since we will go our separate ways, we might as well do it sooner rather than later."

He sat down again, his hand closing unerringly atop her hat. "I'm sorry our sentiments do not coincide," he said slowly, his fingers rubbing the edge of her veil.

She wanted his hands on her, touching her at will. "If you will hand me my hat, I will see myself out."

"If I am never to see you again, I deserve a good-bye kiss," he said. He shifted with such fluidity from easygoing agreeableness to implacable demands.

"That is unwise," she said weakly.

"I will have both hands firmly on your hat. Besides, you owe me that much."

Why couldn't she want only one thing? Why must she yearn for electrifying danger even as she clung desperately to safety—a lonely safety, but the only sanctuary she'd ever known?

She pushed away from the slab, marched across the room, sat down at the edge of the chaise, and touched her lips to his for a fraction of a second.

"Don't cheat me—that was not a kiss."

The Duke of Lexington had spoken; he would not be denied.

She braced her hand on the scroll arm of the chaise and leaned in again. Her lips brushed his. She took a deep breath and dove in.

He tasted of wine—a powerful claret older than their combined age—and desire. She was accustomed to being lusted after. Yet as she traced the edge of his teeth with her tongue, the tension of his body, as if he had to restrain himself from overpowering her, intoxicated her.

No one had ever wanted her as much as he did. Not even close.

She ended the kiss but did not move, her lips hovering bare inches from his. Their breaths mingled, agitated, uneven. Hunger emanated from him; her heart slammed with it, her cheeks hot as if she'd been standing too close to the fireplace.

Without thinking, she put her lips to his again. He yanked her to him. The force of his action thrilled her. Suddenly she could not wait. Her hands groped at the fastening of his trousers. He pushed her narrow skirts up and out of the way. She moaned as his fingers touched her through the seam of her combination.

He broke off their kiss. "I've a sponge somewhere." He sounded as if he'd been climbing stairs for an hour.

"No need. I can't conceive." She gripped his hair and kissed him harder, overcome by a lust as potent as his.

After that there were no more words, only heat, urgency, and pleasure upon pleasure.

*C*hristian played with the baroness's slender, pliant fingers.

He'd brought himself to peak three times. Her, he'd lost count—she'd begun to climax almost as soon as he'd driven into her. And remained voluptuously ravished for a long time afterward.

He smiled. She'd made him impressed with himself. This was unlike him. His belief was that a gentleman *should* be competent in bed, an elementary skill akin to the handling of horses and firearms: nothing to brag about. Yet now he felt like a rooster who had just rampaged through the entire henhouse: ready to jump upon a roof and crow.

He couldn't quite remember the details, but at some point, he'd extinguished the lights, ripped off his blindfold, and carried her to his bed. And now they were warmly ensconced beneath the covers, her head on his shoulder.

"I don't think I've ever been this proud of myself, not even when I read my first paper at the Royal Society."

"Humfft," she mumbled. For a moment he wondered whether she'd withdraw into herself again. But she said, "You value odd things, duke."

"You are an odd thing, to be sure, baroness, but you are also a beautiful thing."

She stirred. "You don't know what I look like."

"And that makes you less beautiful? I think not."

"We've known each other two and a half, three days? I spent most of those hours either refusing to sleep with you or changing my mind and sleeping with you. Is there something particularly lovely in that?"

He cupped her face. "Do you remember our conversation from this morning and your assessment of the gentlemen passengers in the lounge? There was a young man with an elder female relative enchanted by a confidence artist. I spoke with our young man in the afternoon. He told me you'd already warned him of Mr. Egbert."

"Anyone would do that."

"Everyone should, but not everyone takes the trouble." He smoothed a strand of her hair that had become tangled. "And do you know why you gave up pursuit of the next great fossil discovery? Because you valued your husband's happiness above your own. He did not deserve it, but that does not change the fact that *you* were giving and considerate."

"Or just a very young girl, very unsure of herself."

He turned her face and kissed her chin. "Are you *trying* to make me think less well of you?"

"No, but I don't want you to think better of me than I deserve."

She'd pulled her hand from his. He found out, as his fingers moved away from her face, that she'd crossed her hands at the base of her throat, her forearms shielding her breasts. As if she must defend herself anew now that her passion had been spent.

He kissed her shoulder, the skin beneath his lips decadently smooth. "So how *do* you deserve to be thought of?"

She didn't reply.

"You are dealing with a man of science, my dear. To change my mind, you must not give only generalizations, but concrete evidence. Or I shall go on thinking that you are a saint in a courtesan's body."

She sighed, a reluctant sound. "I've already told you I can't conceive, haven't I? Eighteen months into our marriage, my husband decided to consult a physician. We would consult a slew of them over the next two years. I'll"—her voice faltered—"I'll spare you a detailed description. But you are mistaken if you think he insisted on all the physicians. No, after the first one said I would not conceive, I was the one who went to physician after physician, subjected myself to examination after examination, all because I wanted to prove that *he* was the one responsible for our childlessness. Would you call that giving and considerate?"

"Maybe not, but you will never convince me to take his side against yours." In fact, he wanted to disinter the man's remains to give him a good kick. What kind of bastard would put his wife through such distress? And after only a year and a half, when many marital unions did not produce children for far longer durations. "So, what finally made you give up?"

Her hands clasped tightly onto each other. "One of our maids came to me. My husband had enjoyed her favors in the past. She told me she was increasing, that she had another follower who might be willing to marry her if I provided her with a small dowry. I gave her the money, she left, and I consulted no more physicians."

He turned her toward him and held her tight. "I'm so sorry."

"I was terribly young then. I didn't even want a child. All I wanted was to show my husband how wrong he was about my infertility. I must have believed that if I could do that, then I could prove him wrong in everything else, and that is not how a loving, generous person ought to think."

"You are wrong," he said firmly. "Let me tell you something about my stepmother, one of the most loving, generous persons I've had the good fortune of knowing. My father, on the other hand, was not. You know what she did? Whenever he brought a new mistress under our roof, she'd throw darts at the portrait of him he gave her for their wedding. We both did, passing some of the most pleasant hours of my youth desecrating his likeness.

"I did not think less of her. Quite to the contrary, I appreciated that she did not make excuses for him. He was an ass; why should she pretend that he wasn't? And why shouldn't you want to prove your husband wrong?

Unfortunately even a broken clock is correct twice a day, but that doesn't mean he wasn't wrong the rest of the time."

Beneath his, her hands unclenched. She gave him a quick kiss on his cheek. "Thank you. I've rarely heard sweeter music and certainly never sweeter words."

He returned a peck on her forehead. "So you will stay the night?"

Her voice was pained. "I might turn into a pumpkin at dawn."

"I'll sleep with my blindfold on. No fear of any gourd sighting."

She giggled. "You'd do that for me?"

"Of course. It's the least I would do for you."

She rested her palm against his cheek. "You don't have to do that—I'll stay."

They made love one more time. Afterward, she dozed off easily. He listened to her breaths deepen with sleep, the rhythm and comfort of it a greater intimacy than any he'd ever known.

*C*hristian was the first to awaken—he'd always been an early riser.

He did not find a pumpkin in his bed. Nestled in the crook of his elbow, she remained very much a woman, soft skin, warm arms, smooth hair. She'd kicked off part of the bedcover. In the semidarkness, her feet and calves were shapely, tempting.

If he turned his head, he'd be able to make out her features.

He'd promised her he wouldn't. But something beyond his honor held him back. It was . . . freeing to not see her face, to be beyond his own prejudices where a woman's appearance was concerned.

He lifted the bedcover, walked out of the bedroom, and did not return until he had his blindfold firmly in place.

$\mathcal{T}$he woman in the mirror was beautiful.

Venetia stared at herself. Her familiar features had been transformed. By excitement, elation, and caution thrown to the wind. She looked like a woman for whom life was only beginning, rather than one weighed down and calcified by disappointed dreams.

She was not the only one to notice. "Madame est très, très belle ce matin—même plus que d'habitude," said Miss Arnaud.

Madame is very, very beautiful this morning, even more so than usual.

"Merci," she murmured.

"On dit que Monsieur le duc est beau."

One hears that the duke is handsome.

So the rumor of their affair had already spread. It was only to be expected, the *Rhodesia* being such an idle, contained world.

A knock came at the door. Her pulse rate hastened. Had the duke come to call? She thought it was implicitly understood that her lair—like her identity—was her own.

"'Oo is it?" asked Miss Arnaud.

"Deck stewards," answered a man with an Irish brogue. "We've something for the baroness."

Stewards. What was this something that required more than one man to deliver?

Three stewards, with the help of a handcart, brought

into her stateroom a large, rectangular object wrapped in a tarpaulin.

"From His Grace the Duke of Lexington," said one of the stewards.

Venetia's hand went over her mouth. She could not believe it. She directed the men to remove the tarpaulin cover and another cover of canvas.

The duke had indeed given her the fossilized footprints.

"It's very grand. But me, I prefer *chocolat*," said Miss Arnaud.

Chocolate, pah. Venetia would gladly give up chocolate altogether if she could have such a magnificent record of prehistoric life once in a while. She tipped everyone handsomely—Miss Arnaud included. "Buy yourself some chocolate from me."

When she was alone again, she knelt before the stone slab and, with her cleanest pair of gloves on, traced her fingers over the imprints. "Me," she murmured, "this is exactly what *I* prefer."

Before she left the stateroom to meet with the duke, she looked at herself once more in the mirror. The woman who looked back at her was dazzling, for there was nothing more beautiful than happiness.

CHAPTER 8

$\mathscr{T}$he baroness was right: Anticipating her arrival was pleasant, even enjoyable. Christian felt young and excited, a boy who'd been let out of school early.

The day was cold but bright. Passengers thronged the promenade deck, watching pods of dolphins leap and cavort. Lacy parasols bobbed; walking sticks swished and pointed; the mood was as buoyant as the sea.

She appeared like the embodiment of spring in a walking dress of green silk overlaid with a diaphanous film of gauze. The gauze, light and fluttery, caught sunlight much as the sea did, in tremors and bobs, an ever-changing pattern of light and color.

Everyone turned to look: It was easy to see that they had become the juiciest item of gossip on board. He had always been a man of discretion. Now, however, he was conducting an affair in plain view. And not only did he not mind it in the slightest, he felt absurdly cocky that this gorgeously dressed woman was headed for him and him alone.

"I would have come sooner," she said as she drew up beside him, "but I was delayed."

"Oh?"

"Thank you for your present. It is far too generous."

"Not at all. It had never given me as much pleasure as it did when I sent it to you."

"You have thrilled me thoroughly, Your Grace."

He smiled at her. "Call me Christian."

He'd never offered any other lover the familiarity of his given name. She tilted her head. "Are you?"

"Christian? Sometimes. And what should I call you?"

"Hmm. I believe you may call me darling."

"My darling." *Mein Liebling.* "I like it. Adorable."

She leaned back. He had the distinct impression that behind her veil, she was grinning. "*Adorable*? I'm shocked the word made it past your lips, sir. I thought you were a stern man."

He returned her grin. "So did I."

She tsked. "How the mighty has fallen."

"When I was little, I sea-bathed off the coast of the Isle of Wight, the Bristol Channel, and sometimes Biarritz, depending on where my father wanted to sail in August. The year I turned sixteen, however, I swam in the Mediterranean for the first time. I spent a week in that gloriously warm water and it spoiled me for the Atlantic forever." He kissed the back of her gloved hand. "And you, baroness, have ruined for me whatever charms being a stern man once held."

"My, a lavishly generous gift *and* a comparison to the

charms of the Mediterranean—are you sure you were ever a stern man?"

"I am quite sure. I didn't know what I was missing."

She kissed him on the cheek through her veil and said the words he'd been longing to hear. "Well, let me spoil you some more."

*N*o!" Venetia giggled, both shocked and delighted.

"It was true. I hit him—and not a slap with my glove, either. I thought he was forcing himself on her. So I pulled him off the bed, slammed him into a wall, and nearly broke my hand punching his face."

She snuggled closer to him. They were back in his bed, spending the afternoon doing what lovers did best. "Then what happened?"

"Chaos. My stepmother pulling me off Mr. Kingston, me frantically throwing sheets to cover her, Mr. Kingston bleeding and swearing. It was a proper fiasco."

"I love fiascos, especially when there is a happy ending attached." She ought to be more worried for herself—a fiasco was headed her way without a happy ending attached. But if she were to pay for her lack of sense later, she might as well wring every drop of lightness and joy from the scant days that remained on the voyage. "Were you properly embarrassed when you found out you were not the hero you thought you had been?"

"Deeply mortified. I offered Her Grace a portrait of mine for the two of us to throw darts at."

She placed her hand over her heart. "That is so very sweet."

He smiled. So young and winsome, her blindfolded duke. How she wished she could see his eyes, too, at moments like this.

"I didn't know what else to do," he said. "But she absolutely refused. We threw darts at a tree instead."

"And what of poor Mr. Kingston?"

"I sent him a foal from my prized mare. We had a very civil conversation that did not involve either my stepmother or the incident. And that was my apology offered and accepted. They married a month later."

She sighed. "A most satisfying story."

He turned more fully toward her. "You should marry again."

"You should be glad I haven't—or I wouldn't be having affairs on ocean liners." Perhaps because he was so candid, she felt the need to tell the whole truth. "Besides, I *was* married again—a *mariage blanc*."

"Really?"

She nodded. "His lover was another man and he was afraid there were those who would use that to destroy him."

"And why did you enter into it?"

"The usual reasons. My first husband had left me quite destitute and I didn't want to be a burden to my brother."

He raised his head on his hand. "You have a brother?"

"A brother and a sister—twins—both two years younger than I am."

"And how old are *you, my darling*?"

She huffed exaggeratedly. "Now that is a question I refuse to answer."

"I am going to be twenty-nine in two weeks," he said.

"My, you are practically an infant." She was relieved: He was only a few months younger than she was.

"You'll give me a present, won't you? Children adore presents."

"I suppose I can find it in my heart to send you an engraved pen."

"I'd dearly enjoy an engraved pen, provided that you present it to me in person."

He was never afraid to express his desire to further their acquaintance beyond the confines of the *Rhodesia*. She marveled at his willingness to lay himself bare. Tony, in hindsight, had held back from the very beginning, content to let her love him more and to wield that power over her.

She traced the lower edge of his blindfold, across the ridge of his nose, across his cheek. The next thing she knew, she'd yanked him to her, her leg over his waist, her tongue in his mouth. She wanted this. She wanted him. She wanted to absorb his fearlessness through touch, until she, too, was open and brave and worthy of this closeness that lifted her like a tide.

It was the third night aboard the *Rhodesia*. Christian felt like Ali Baba, standing in the mouth of the Forty Thieves' cave, agog at riches beyond his imagination. *She* was riches beyond his imagination.

He was almost unnerved to be this happy. To listen to the beat of her heart and hear the meters of a sonnet. To hold her hand and know he would never again want for anything. To look upon an impenetrable darkness and see a future of unlimited possibilities.

Was he sitting atop a house of cards? A castle made of air and foolish wishes? Was this happiness but the gluttony that invariably preceded a bout of violent regret?

Her fingers combed through his hair.

"I thought you were asleep," he said, kissing the palm of her other hand.

"I've decided to not waste any more time sleeping."

The *Rhodesia* rocked gently, like a lullaby. But he, too, was wide awake, all too acutely aware of time slipping away. Usually a few days into a crossing he'd have become insensible to the rumble of the ship's engine. This time, however, he was ever mindful of its restless thrum. Each turn of the twin propellers brought him closer to the other shore.

"Tell me what was it like, being in a *mariage blanc*."

"Nothing like this, to be sure—no young, hard-bodied lover to pleasure me nightly."

He couldn't help smiling. "Right. You must have sprained your own wrist to make up for the lack."

She laughed and punched him on the arm. "I should be ashamed to confess this but oddly I'm not," she said, rubbing the spot she'd hit. "I did come close to spraining my wrist a time or two."

"My God, what a waste of such a juicy—"

She clamped her hand over his mouth, giggling.

He removed her hand, laughing. "What? I've said much worse and you've liked it."

"It's different when we are midcoitus."

He rolled atop her. "Then I'll say it midcoitus."

He said that—and much worse. Judging by her reactions, she liked it all.

* * *

*W*as your second husband good to you other-wise?" he asked afterward, his head in her lap, her fingers again combing through his hair.

"Oh yes. He was a longtime family friend—a very distant cousin on my mother's side, in fact. Someone I'd known all my life. My father passed away early, so he was the one who taught me how to use a shotgun and how to play cards."

"An older man?"

"Older than my parents and quite wealthy. When he proposed, it was the best of all possible worlds. I would be solvent. I would be the mistress of my own household again. And I would not have to deal with a man who might make my life miserable. We drew up our plans—"

"Plans?"

"Yes, it would have looked odd if his lover were constantly at our house. So we decided to pretend that *I* was the one having an affair with him. We shook hands on the plans and took ourselves to the altar."

"And lived hand-sprainingly ever after?"

She chortled. "Not for him—he had his lover, remember?"

"You envied them." He realized.

"And how. They were so engrossed in each other. At times I felt quite unnecessary, like a chaperone who didn't know when to leave—even though I was in my own home, so to speak."

He understood her exactly. When he visited his stepmother and Mr. Kingston, their fulfillment made his lack of hopes for the future all the more acute.

"Have you become less lonely in the years since?"

"My brother gave up the love of his life to marry an heiress. His wife, I suspect, has been in unrequited love with him all along. And my sister, God help us all, loves a married man. Compared to them, my loneliness seems terribly tame, something to be borne cheerfully." She drew little circles on his arm—or were those hearts? "What of you? Have you ever been lonely? Or have you been too self-sufficient to notice?"

He reached up and played with the lobe of her ear. "I don't think anyone has ever asked me such questions."

She stilled. "I beg your pardon. I did not mean to pry. Sometimes I forget that of the two of us, only I enjoy the luxury of anonymity."

It was easy to forget a great many things in the intensity of their affair. Sometimes he felt as if he'd never known anything but the sea, the *Rhodesia*, and her. "Please don't apologize for taking a personal interest in me—it reassures me you are not merely exploiting me in bed."

The sound of her laughter registered as a burst of brightness in the night. It still amazed him that she not only laughed, but laughed often. It amazed him even more that he'd been the one to elicit the laughter. When she laughed, nothing was impossible. He could climb Mount Everest, cross the Sahara, and raise the lost realm of Atlantis all in a day.

"The English aren't in the habit of inquiring into one another's happiness," he said. "Not that we do not know what is going on; we simply do not speak of it. My stepmother, for example, has never asked why I am sometimes in a black mood. But she makes sure to invite the best company for dinner and uncork Mr. Kingston's finest bottles from the cellar. Or we go for a long walk and she tells me all the latest gossip among her circle of friends."

"You like gossip?"

"Half of the time I have no idea who she is talking about, and most of the time her stories go in one of my ears and out the other. But I like being made to feel that she's been waiting for my return so she can tell me everything. I like remembering that even though I can't have everything I want, I'm still an extraordinarily fortunate man."

"Would you mind if I asked what it is that you can't have?"

He couldn't tell her before, but now that barrier had come down. "When I was nineteen, I fell in love with a married woman."

"Oh," she murmured. "So . . . when you said being with other women made you wish you were elsewhere, she was that elsewhere?"

"Yes." Mrs. Easterbrook had been the miasma of an opium den, calling out to an old addict.

"Do you still love her?"

"I haven't thought of her once since I met you."

In the silence there was only the soughing of the sea and her quickened breaths.

He put the question to her once more. "Are you sure you must disappear when we touch land?"

And she, bless her, at last spoke the words he'd been longing to hear. "Let me—let me think about it."

*M*illie, Countess Fitzhugh, stared at the disappearing American continent.

Once she reached England, hardly any time remained before she was at last to become Fitz's wife. In truth.

How had the years gone by so fast? Eight years. To a

sixteen-year-old girl, eight years comprised half a lifetime, a stupendously long span that would end in a future as distant as the stars. And yet here it was, close enough to breathe on her.

She did not regret the pact: Theirs had been a complicated and unhappy situation; postponing the consummation of their marriage had simplified their lives and allowed them to deal with each other on practical, friendly terms.

What she did regret was the length of their agreement. Had it been seven years, the bedding—and whatever its aftermath—would have been behind her. Had it been nine years, she'd still have more time to become accustomed to the idea.

But they'd shaken hands on eight years, and eight years was expiring fast.

Fitz trusted her. He liked and respected her. On some days, she'd even venture to say that he admired her. But he did not love her. If a man hadn't fallen in love with a woman after almost eight years together, was there any chance that he ever would?

"You must be cold," said Helena, coming to stand next to Millie on the aft rail of the promenade deck. "You've been out here a long time."

"Can't be that long—I've not frozen solid yet," said Millie, with a smile for her sister-in-law. "How are you, my dear? How is the article coming along?"

"Not too well," said Helena.

Would Fitz forget about their pact altogether if the situation with Helena proved too trying? He had no calendar on which he'd marked the date. He had plenty of women to keep his carnal urges satisfied. And by and large he treated her as if she were another one of his sisters. What if the day came and went and she remained alone in her bed?

Would that please her or would that break her?

Millie laid a hand on Helena's arm. "Don't worry too much about Venetia."

"I can't help it. I hope she is not all alone, hiding in her stateroom."

"She could be having a torrid affair, for all we know," said Millie.

That was perhaps not the right thing to say—not when she had no intention of insinuating anything about Helena.

Helena's face took on an obdurate cast. "I hope she is. She is a grown woman who has made too little use of her freedom."

And are you a grown woman who has made too much use of her freedom?

But what did Millie know of love that was ardently returned, love that yearned with a burning intensity across space and time, she who'd only ever been the destroyer of such love?

What she did know was that Fitz would never have compromised an unmarried lady, as Mr. Martin had. Helena was galloping unchecked toward a precipice, from which none of them could pull her out, if she were to fall.

She did not want anything to happen to Helena, who like Venetia had only ever been kind and accepting of Millie, especially in those days when Fitz could barely bring himself to speak to her. She wanted Helena to be happy. And if not that, at least safe from ruin and ostracism.

She took Helena's arm. "If you can't concentrate on your article, what say you we take a long, bracing constitutional?"

CHAPTER 9

*T*he western sky glowed. Fire burnished the edge of the sea. The last fingers of daylight caressed the long, feathery clouds and gilded them the golden peach of fine Calvados.

Christian had never seen a more perfect sunset. The baroness, however, was not on hand to share this incandescent view—instead, she was in her room, attending to her toilette.

It was their sixth day at sea. The ship was expected to call on Queenstown the next morning. The morning after that, Southampton. He had, therefore, gone to considerable trouble to convince her to attend the captain's dinner this evening. She'd thought him mad, but he was very persistent. He wanted to show her that it was quite feasible for them to appear in public while her veil remained firmly in place. That the rest of Society would defer to his wish and accept her as she was.

He would clear all obstacles. He would pave the way. And he would strew the path with the rarest fossils, for her to claim the place in his life that belonged to her and her alone.

*V*enetia had begun to consider possible strategies.

Perhaps the baroness would mention in a letter that her friend Mrs. Easterbrook lived in London. Perhaps Venetia, upon meeting Christian at some point during the Season, would let it slip that her delightful chum Baroness von Seidlitz-Hardenberg had mentioned that she, too, had recently traveled on the *Rhodesia*. And perhaps, before anything else, she ought to achieve calling terms with the dowager duchess—to such a degree that the latter would be willing to vouch for Venetia's character.

This was why, she thought ruefully as she tugged on her dinner gloves, sensible people did not lead double lives: There was no graceful way to collapse a bifurcated existence back into a single, uncomplicated one.

Miss Arnaud had taken the sparkling paillettes from another one of Venetia's dinner gowns and turned her veil into an accessory that, while still highly odd, exuded a certain glamour. Venetia stepped back from the mirror and turned in a circle. She wanted her presence to add to his stature, not detract from it. The cobalt blue dinner gown was certainly everything a frock ought to be—and would have matched her eyes if one could see them—

She shook her head. The irregularity of the proceedings

could not be helped; she could only follow his lead and hope to be remembered as agreeable.

$\mathcal{H}$e awaited her at the newel post of the stairs leading down into the dining saloon, highly delectable in his evening formals.

"You are the most sensational-looking lady tonight, darling," he said as he offered her his arm.

It always made her heart pound to hear him call her by that endearment.

"Oh, I don't doubt that. You do realize we are being very brazen, do you not?"

"Brazenness is for lesser mortals," he said. "The Duke of Lexington defines good form—or redefines it, if need be."

"At least you are diverting to be around."

He leaned close. "I'll tell you a not-quite-secret: No one else says that, not even my stepmother."

She turned her face. They were very nearly nose to nose—brazenness indeed. "Good, keep it that way. I want to see you at your loftiest and most glacial tonight."

"For you, I will. But if I fail miserably—if I act with insufficient condescension or, God forbid, put anyone at ease—know that you and you alone are responsible."

"What a heavy charge: hundreds of years of unbroken hauteur at stake."

He squeezed her hand briefly. "At last you understand what you have done."

They were seated together, with a young American embarking upon his grand tour of the Old World to Venetia's right. Someone had obviously informed him that she did not—or would not—speak English, for the young American, Mr. Cameron, greeted her with a "Guten Abend, Gnädige Frau."

His German had more courage than skill, but he was unconcerned about mistakes and game for conversation. They spoke of his planned itinerary. Rather than the relics of the classical age, Mr. Cameron was most excited to visit the Eiffel Tower and bestride that modern marvel. He informed Venetia, with charming frankness, that he hoped the top of the tower would sway majestically in a gust and that he, strong, sturdy man he was, would be just the person to catch a beautiful young lady fainting of fright.

Christian, who had been engaged in conversation with Mrs. Vanderwoude, a Manhattan matriarch, turned and said, "Good luck, Mr. Cameron. I was there during the Exposition Universelle and the top of the tower was so crowded that an unconscious young lady would have remained upright until she came to on her own."

Mr. Cameron had a hearty guffaw at this. Venetia couldn't help but smile at her lover. Of course he couldn't see it, but he had an uncanny sense for when she smiled beneath her veil—and he smiled back at her.

She felt as if she'd been hugging puppies all day.

"Excuse me, sir," said a young lady from across the table. She'd been introduced to Venetia as Miss Vanderwoude. "Are you by some chance the same duke who gave a lecture at Harvard?"

Venetia stilled.

"Gloria, must you speak in such stentorian tones?" Mrs. Vanderwoude was not pleased.

"Sorry, Grandmamma," said Miss Vanderwoude. The

volume of her voice, however, did not reduce at all. "But are you, sir?"

"I am," said Christian, taking a sip of his wine.

"What a coincidence!" Miss Vanderwoude all but clapped. "My cousin and his wife, who came to see me last week, had been at your lecture."

"I'm glad to hear they hadn't expired of boredom."

It was a droll comment, and Venetia meant to smile again. But she couldn't. A chill spread between her shoulder blades.

"They enjoyed your lecture very much. My cousin's wife especially relished your anecdote concerning the beautiful lady who has the heart of a Lady Macbeth."

Venetia's hand went to her throat. She couldn't seem to pull in any air.

"That would be taking it quite too far," said Christian. "I've never accused the lady of either murder or accessory to murder."

That was hardly a defense, was it?

"But if she drove her husband to an early grave—"

"Miss Vanderwoude, events that happen in a sequential manner do not necessarily imply causation. The lady might have made her husband miserable, but it is the nature of marriage for its inmates to devastate each other at times— or so I have been given to understand. Neither you nor I know the details of said marriage. Let us refrain from ill-founded speculations."

Venetia exhaled.

"But we are among friends here, aren't we?" said the girl conspiratorially. "What say you, sir, that you tell us who the lady is. And my friends and I, *we* will find out exactly how culpable—or not, as it may be—the lady was in her husband's early passing."

"Gloria!" protested her grandmother. "Your Grace, allow me to apologize for the child's impudence."

Christian inclined his head, accepting the apology. Now he turned his gaze on Miss Vanderwoude. Her cheeky grin faded. She began to look left and right, as if hoping someone might shield her from his attention. When no one said or did anything, she tried to meet his eye, with a sheepish smile that died awkwardly.

The nearby diners held their collective breath, waiting. They all believed he would mete out some terrible denunciation. But what if he did not find the idea lacking in merit, Venetia thought wildly. What if he only objected to the public nature of Miss Vanderwoude's overture?

"No," he said. "That is not a good idea."

Venetia's heart managed a weak beat. The occupants of the table exhaled at the propriety and restraint of his rebuke. Miss Vanderwoude's lips quivered before she smiled tentatively. "I do believe you are right, sir."

Indicating that nothing more was to be said on the subject, he turned toward Venetia, "You don't seem to have touched your prawns, baroness."

It was a little joke meant for her, as she never ate anything while she had on her veil. "I shall presently remedy this oversight," she said, through numb lips.

Mrs. Vanderwoude wanted his opinion on something. Venetia leaned in Mr. Cameron's direction.

"Miss Vanderwoude, is she headed to London?"

"No, to the Continent, like myself. We disembark at Hamburg, head for Paris, and from there, for points east and south."

"And is she in any way serious about pursuing the identity of the lady she mentioned?"

Mr. Cameron laughed softly. "I'd be surprised if by tomorrow morning she even remembers she'd ever had the idea. She is as impulsive and forgetful as a grasshopper, that one."

All the same, Venetia's evening was ruined. The incursion of reality had been too strong. If Miss Vanderwoude, who had never attended the lecture, now knew of the scandalous story the duke had related, there might be others who would hear of it and would not need a detective to realize of whom he'd been speaking.

On the other hand, what if he were to learn that Venetia—not the baroness, but Mrs. Easterbrook—had not only been in America, but had been in Cambridge, Massachusetts, at the exact same time as his Harvard lecture?

One could only juggle sticks of dynamite for so long before they exploded one by one.

I'm sorry, darling," said Christian, as soon as he and the baroness were inside his rooms.

She glanced back at him, the paillettes on her veil catching light like so many tiny mirrors. But the sparkle had gone from her voice. "Why do you apologize to me?"

"I have upset you."

He'd upset himself—Miss Vanderwoude's impertinence had been a grave reminder that his mistake had compounded far beyond its original dimensions. But the baroness's distress was, if possible, more acute than his own. Afterward, though she'd gamely kept up a constant stream of friendly banter with Mr. Cameron, he'd barely tasted anything, knowing he'd sunken far in her esteem.

She sat down on the chaise, the set of her shoulders both tense and weary. And something in the way her fingers clung to one another spoke more than just disappointment: She was afraid.

"Please say something."

She tilted her head back, as if looking heavenward for help. "Miss Vanderwoude was willing to devote her own time and funds to muck about the private affairs of someone she'd never met and only heard of secondhand. It astounds me what you must have said to arouse such unseemly interest."

Her dispirited words were nails pounded into his heart. "I'm sorry. I shouldn't have."

"Indeed you shouldn't. Your comments caused someone to be spoken of as undiluted evil."

He sat down next to her and took her hand in his. "I did not do it out of malice, if that is what concerns you. I relayed my anecdote less as an objective lesson for my audience than as a reminder to myself."

"I don't understand."

He would have to explain, to expose himself as he never had. But he cared little for his mortification. The only thing that mattered was that she must not turn away from him.

"The woman I used as an example at Harvard—she was my elsewhere."

She yanked her hand from his. He gripped her arm before she could leap away. "Please, listen."

"My God," she said, looking everywhere but at him. "My God."

If he could only pull out his heart to show her. But he had only words, slow, laborious, useless words. "The lady in question is bewitchingly beautiful. And for a decade, I was fixated by her beauty. I wrote an entire article on the evolutionary significance of beauty as a rebuke to myself, that I, who understood the concepts so well, nevertheless could not escape the magnetic pull of one particular woman's beauty."

Her veil rippled with her agitated breathing. "And that was not enough, the article? You had to speak of it in public?"

"My obsession was mindless. I had to stay away from places she frequented. If I saw her, it wouldn't have mattered whether she hastened her husband's journey to the grave. I'd have willingly married her just to possess her."

In her lap, her hands shook visibly. He, too, shook—but inside, where fear and regret threatened to drown the hopes that had been leaping and frolicking like pods of dolphins alongside the *Rhodesia*.

"I've long been ashamed of this fixation, but it clung to me like a leech. And this time, I wouldn't be able to stay away from her—she is a fixture at the London Season. I was troubled that I might give in and approach her, propriety and pride notwithstanding." The dream, damn the dream. "Believe me, I'd never intended such a catastrophic lapse of judgment."

She yanked free her arm, rose, and walked away.

*V*enetia felt blown to pieces, all the dynamite sticks she'd been juggling having detonated at once.

She hadn't been a random example, something casually plucked out of all his accumulated experiences to illustrate a passing point. Rather, she had been the bane of his existence.

She could not grasp it. The reach of her mind had been diminished by her shock. She could only gape at the idea, as if it were a tentacled sea monster come to sink the *Rhodesia*.

He said he'd been nineteen. She would have also been nineteen—very much still married, but with her erstwhile romantic illusions already dashed upon the hard rock of Tony's indestructible self-love.

One of the Harrow players couldn't stop staring at you. If someone had handed him a fork he'd have devoured you in one sitting.

He'd been that Harrow player. She'd been his despised obsession. And she was also his salvation—from *herself.*

Panic swept in like a cyclone.

Until now, it was possible to imagine her ruse being forgiven. Not anymore, not after he had exposed his Achilles' heel to the last person he'd willingly give that knowledge.

For that, he would not forgive her. Ever.

He rose to his feet. "Please say something."

But she couldn't speak. All she understood was a rising desperation: Their affair must end now, before things could get any worse.

*S*he turned her back to him. Her hands, braced apart, gripped the edge of the writing desk, as if she couldn't quite support her own weight. He couldn't breathe—to have caused pain to the woman who'd only ever brought him warmth and joy.

He turned off the lamp, approached her, and removed her veil.

She inhaled unsteadily. He set his hands on either side of hers and kissed her hair, holding the pristine, sweet scent of her deep in his lungs.

"I love you." The words had arrived on their own, like butterflies emerging from cocoons when their time had come. He, too, felt transformed, from a boy who mistook compulsion for love to a man who at last understood his own heart.

She shuddered.

"You are the one I've been waiting for all my life."

She spun around and covered his mouth with her hand.

He moved her hand aside. "From the beginning—do you not remember the lift? You overtook my entire—"

She kissed him, a rampage of lips and tongue. Relief flooded him—she would still have him. And such ardor, as if she could not bear the least distance between them. Her fever burned in him. He lifted her bottom onto the desk and pushed up her skirts. She tugged impatiently at her drawers. He would have gone down on his knees to worship her, but she refused to let their lips part.

Instead, she unfastened his trousers and, without further preliminaries, took him inside her. He was unspeakably aroused—the feel of her, the rain-clean taste of her, the urgency of her. She panted and trembled with her need, ravishing him, urging him to ravish her in return.

No more words were needed. She was the only thing that mattered. *They* were the only thing that mattered. The avalanche of pleasure to come would meld them into one seamless union.

There were no secrets left.

Nothing separated them now.

*C*hristian awakened to an eerie stillness, as if the *Rhodesia*'s heart had stopped beating. It took him a disoriented second to realize that the engines had stopped humming.

The liner had dropped anchor in Queenstown.

Instinctively he reached for her, but she was not in his bed, to which they'd repaired for more lovemaking, forging ever greater pleasure and closeness for the better part of the night. He called to her, thinking perhaps she was in the parlor or the water closet. Silence answered him.

Alarm prickled his spine—she'd never left without a word. He grabbed his pocket watch from the nightstand. Five minutes to nine—quite late for him. Maybe she had not wished to disturb his slumber. He pulled on some clothes, dashed off a note explaining his possible late arrival for their walk, and rang for the suite steward to take it to her.

The suite steward returned as he was applying shaving soap to his face. "Sir, the baroness's room steward told me that she has disembarked."

Christian turned around. "For a tour?"

Ocean liners replenished their supplies at Queenstown. It was not uncommon for passengers to use the time for an excursion into the Irish countryside.

"No, sir. She asked for her luggage to be sent ashore."

She was leaving. And last night, which he'd believed to herald a new era for them, had been but a long, wordless good-bye for her. She did not believe in his love. She did not trust that he'd left his former obsession behind. And she could not imagine any likely future for them.

All the possibilities that had come to life with her presence began to shatter, and his heart with them.

"She might still be in the disembarkation queue, sir," said the steward. "Shall I go down for a look?"

The disembarkation queue. Of course, the *Rhodesia* had not docked. She was somewhere in the harbor.

Passengers and their luggage must wait to be ferried in tenders.

Christian washed the soap from his face, threw on a day coat, grabbed his hat, and rushed down to the main deck. The sky was gray. The Atlantic was gray. Even Ireland, otherwise green and beautiful, was an unremitting spread of dreariness.

He pushed through the crowd, frantically searching for her familiar silhouette. The entire population of the ship seemed to have congregated near the tenders. Old ladies tottered about in pairs. Children were held aloft to see over the rails. Young Americans chattered about Buckingham Palace and Shakespeare's cottage, while waving at a tender rowing toward the *Rhodesia*.

At last he spotted her standing at the rail. Relief swallowed him whole. As if sensing his urgency, the crowd parted, and those near her scooted away to make room for him. But she did not acknowledge his presence as he came to stand beside her. Her face remained bent to the waves that lapped at the riveted steel plates of the ship's hull.

"Why? Why are you leaving?"

"I've reached my destination."

"Is it because you think I still love Mrs. Elsewhere?"

"It is not that."

"Look at me when you say that."

Her face turned toward him. Her hand tightened on the railing, as if she were surprised by his appearance. He'd been perspiring earlier. But standing on the open deck without his overcoat—the cold was sudden and intense.

"It is not that," she repeated. "You've always said that I could leave anytime. I am leaving now. I don't need another reason."

133

He shivered. From the cold or her words he did not know. "Does it mean nothing that I love you?"

"You don't love me. You are in love with a creature of your own imagination."

"That is not true. I don't need to know your face to know you."

"I am a fraud, remember? There is no Baroness von Seidlitz-Hardenberg."

"You think I have forgotten that? I don't need you to be a baroness. Who you are is more than good enough for me."

Her laughter sounded bitter. "Let's not argue a moot point."

He placed his hand on her arm. "I won't, if you stay."

She shook her head. "My luggage is already on the dock."

"It can easily be brought back on board."

She shook her head more vigorously. "Let it be. Some things are lovely precisely because they are brief."

"And other things are lovely because they are rare and beautiful—and should be given a chance to stand the test of time."

She was silent. His heart thumped wildly. Then she reached up and kissed him on the cheek through her veil. "Good-bye."

It was the end of the world, nothing but wreckage where entire cities of hope once stood, their spires shining in the sun. Disbelief and despair gripped him turn by turn. Chaos reigned. He was cold, so very cold, the wind like knives upon his skin.

Then, just as suddenly, the confidence he'd taken for granted in his youth reasserted itself. Or perhaps it was only a gambler's acceptance of all possible outcomes, as he laid his cards on the table.

"Marry me," he said.

*S*he swayed. She'd swindled a declaration of love, and now a proposal of marriage. He would despise her so much it would make Sodom and Gomorrah's fate seem like a fairy tale.

Irony—for it was exactly what she had wanted in the first place.

"I can't," she said weakly. "No marriage between us would be considered valid."

"Let's meet again and discuss what we need to do to make it valid."

She'd been shocked, when he first found her, to see him unshaven, without his collar, his necktie, his waistcoat, or his overcoat. And his agitation had, if anything, exceeded his dishevelment. But now he radiated mastery and purpose. He'd made up his mind, and nothing was going to dissuade him from his choice.

She, on the other hand, had become all jitters. "What can we possibly discuss?"

"Your circumstances, obviously. Some dilemma prevents you from using your own name. When we meet again you will do me the courtesy of giving me a frank account, nothing held back."

He might as well hand her a bucket of tar and the innards of a duvet. "It will be no use. Nothing will change."

"You forget who I am. Whatever your difficulties, I can help you."

"Even the Duke of Lexington cannot wave away every impediment in his path."

"Not when you won't tell me anything, I cannot. But we will meet. And you will tell me what is holding you back—you owe me as much."

She could see the headline: THE DUKE OF LEXINGTON STRANGLES SOCIETY BEAUTY.

"You want to come with me on my expeditions, don't you?" he said softly. "Have I ever told you that I've a small museum at home? And drawers upon drawers of enormous fossilized teeth that I'm sure will interest you greatly?"

Why must he do this to her?

"There is also an abandoned quarry on my estate, with beautifully differentiated geological strata and an abundance of fossils. Marry me and it's all yours."

Throw aside you veil, shouted a voice inside her. *Throw aside the stupid veil. End this right now.*

She couldn't. She couldn't face his wrath. Nor the very large likelihood that his love would not survive his first look at her face. Was it wrong to preserve their affair as it was, to let nothing blemish its perfect memories?

"Lady, are you ready?" one of the tender's crewmen called.

The tender that had been rowing toward the *Rhodesia* had disgorged the newcomers and was loading the final batch of passengers to be taken ashore.

"I must go," she murmured.

"The lady will need one more minute," said Christian.

His tone allowed no dispute. The crewman touched brim of his cap. "Aye, sir."

Her lover took her hands in his. "I will say good-bye

now, but I expect to see you in London. At the Savoy Hotel, ten days from today. Bring the engraved pen for my birthday and we'll drink to our future."

She expelled a long, long breath. She'd say yes to anything now, to get away. "All right."

But he didn't let her go so easily. "Your word, do I have it?"

Perhaps no one else cared whether a beautiful woman was also honorable, but she had never gone back on her word. She shut her eyes tight. "You have it."

He leaned in and kissed her cheek through the veil. "I love you. And I will wait for you."

*W*ell after the great ocean liner had disappeared beyond the narrow mouth of Cork Harbour, Venetia still remained on the pier.

She needed to locate a ticket agent to secure passage to England, cable Fitz to inform him of her time of arrival, not to mention find porters to haul the quarter-ton slab of stone that was Christian's gift to her. But to tackle any of those tasks was to signal the end of her last hour as Baroness von Seidlitz-Hardenberg.

The end of the happiest week of her life.

She didn't know how long she stayed in place. She didn't even notice that it had started to rain until a porter came to offer her an umbrella. She thanked him and allowed herself to be escorted away from the pier, toward shelter, toward the perfect life of the beautiful Mrs. Easterbrook.

CHAPTER 10

My Darling,

The Rhodesia *is a wasteland without you.*

I spent most of the day at the aft rail, though Queenstown long ago receded from the horizon. My corporeal self is here before the writing desk—upon which we made such memories last night—but the rest of me is in Ireland, with you.

It will be a long night ahead, in these rooms that have known you so well. The very air sags from your absence; my blindfold is a tired scrap of silk that has lost its purpose in life.

Has Queenstown been hospitable? Have you been provided with a hot supper and a warm bed? Men have laid cables and connected continents separated by vast

seas; would that the engineers discover a way to con-
nect two people thus. I'd empty my coffers—and borrow extravagantly besides—to be never again without
your news.

Your servant,
C.

~

My Darling,

I have arrived at my house in the country, the home
I hope to share with you in the not-too-distant
future.

Be advised that the manor had been conceived pri-
marily as a showpiece, to awe and overwhelm. It is
not and will never be a cozy, intimate residence. The
height of the ceilings is such that no matter how diligently the coal scuttles are replenished, many of the
public rooms remain unremittingly frigid in winter.
Thankfully the family wing provides better warmth
and comfort, and thus far no one has suffered
chilblain—yet.

The grounds are large and very English in the
arrangements of woods and gardens. Have you ever
visited the Englischer Garten in Munich? If that is to
your taste, then you will derive much pleasure from
the estate.

But of course it is the quarry that you will enjoy the
most. I paid a visit to it this afternoon, checked the
digging implements stored in a nearby shed, and

ordered a sharpening of the chisels. They will be ready for you when you come.

Your servant,
C.

P.S. I'd thought our separation would be easier to bear on the second day. I could not have been more wrong.

~

My Darling,

I write to you from my stepmother's house in Cheshire. I find the dowager duchess and Mr. Kingston in admirable health and spirits. My own flagging spirits revived somewhat in their excellent company. Would that I had you with me: They are the most sensible, amiable, and agreeable of friends.

And you'd have thoroughly impressed them with your presence, your warmth, and your wit. I would have been the proudest man alive.

Your servant,
C.

P.S. I grow accustomed to the ache in my chest.

~

My Darling,

The dowager duchess asked earlier this evening to whom I was writing. Fortunately Mr. Kingston spoke to her at the same time. I switched to a new sheaf of paper, and by the time she remembered to ask me again, I was able to answer truthfully that I was replying to a German geologist by the name of Otto von Schetterling.

I wonder, had Mr. Kingston not said anything, whether I'd have confessed. Very likely so: I have a terrible, almost irrepressible urge to speak of you. To boast of my remarkable luck in happening upon the same ocean liner as you.

So far I have restrained myself. For how much longer, I do not know.

I have never known such happiness, shot through with such misery. Only four days have passed, they tell me. But that is not true. It has been decades since I saw you last.

You will find me a stooped old man when we meet again. Perhaps I might even need a pair of spectacles to recognize your veil.

But I remain always,

Your servant,
C.

~

My Darling,

Today the dowager duchess gave me a list of young ladies she considered suitable to be my duchess. I very nearly informed her that I've already pledged my hand, but, with much difficulty and regret, refrained: She might worry that I am chasing a mirage.

But you are not a mirage. You are a true oasis, worth this wandering in the desert, this anxiety of never finding you again.

Tomorrow I depart for London, to arrange for our dinner at the Savoy Hotel. At last, something for you—for us.

I have an odd, giddy sensation that I will run into you. If you should see me, please come and introduce yourself, so that I may at least give you my letters. And if you will also take my name, I will be the happiest man who ever lived.

Your servant,
C.

P.S. It has been, admittedly, peculiar to be in a one-sided correspondence, but I feel closer to you when I put pen to paper. Needless to say, I will do anything to be closer to you.

CHAPTER 11

*W*ho is he, Venetia?"

Venetia started. She turned toward her brother. "Why are you shouting in my ear?"

An approaching train—likely the one carrying Millie and Helena home—whistled in the distance. The rail guards moved the crowd on the platform away from the tracks, to make room for those who would soon disembark.

"Because, my dear," said Fitz, in a more normal voice, "I've asked you the same question three times and you have not heard me."

She smiled weakly. "Sorry. What were you saying?"

"Who is he, the man you are thinking of? I've watched you since you came back. You hardly eat. You never put more than two stitches in your embroidery. One minute you smile into your lap; the next you are trying not to cry.

143

And let's not forget, this morning I stood by your chair for a good five minutes—and you hadn't the faintest idea I was there."

He'd eventually tapped her on the shoulder, yanking her out of an extraordinarily vivid daydream in which the first course of Christian's birthday dinner grew cold while they devoured each other on the table.

Had Claridge's not been demolished for renovation, she'd have hired a residential suite there for the Season, and Fitz wouldn't have been privy to the symptoms of her heartsickness. But with the hotel still building—and the need for an extra pair of eyes on Helena—she'd accepted Fitz's invitation to stay at his town house.

"It's all this trouble with Helena. I'm distracted," she said thickly.

Fitz was right about one thing: Every other minute she was close to tears.

Sometimes the crossing on the *Rhodesia* seemed as distant as the antiquities—when the great lighthouse at Alexandria still guided sailors. Sometimes she wondered if she hadn't imagined the man who adored her for who she was, instead of what she looked like.

Nightly memories of his every kiss burned within her. Each morning she'd reach for him, only to remember that he would never be hers again. Solitude, so long a tolerable state of being, had begun to smother her like a fast-growing vine that strangled its host.

As if he hadn't heard her, Fitz said, "I know he is not American—you've been looking at Millie's old copy of Debrett's."

She could recite from memory the long entry on the Duke of Lexington.

"So who is he? And why hasn't he broken down my door to offer for you?"

She did not want to lie to Fitz. But neither could she reveal what had happened on the *Rhodesia*.

"Millie and Helena will tell you soon enough what is the matter with me. It is not what you think."

She had suspected that Millie would have already said something to Fitz in their nearly daily exchange of letters, as Fitz had not once asked Venetia why she'd abandoned the rest of his womenfolk and returned solo.

Fitz placed his hand on her shoulder. "I'm sorry it is not what I think. I like the idea of you in love. You've shut yourself off for far too long."

Her eyes prickled. She blinked back the tears. "Oh look. I believe that's their train."

*I*t was Venetia's idea for them to all take luncheon at the Savoy Hotel. A sadistic notion: Now she'd be able to re-create in excruciating detail the dinner she'd never share with Christian.

And since there were a number of private dining rooms at the hotel, someday she'd ask for a tour of the one he'd specifically chosen for her, so the setting of her imaginary repast would not only be precise, but historically accurate.

The family luncheon went off well enough. Millie and Helena gave an account of their weeks in America. Fitz offered a compendium of news concerning their friends and acquaintances. Venetia engrossed herself memorizing wallpaper patterns and the garland motif on the handle of her fork.

No one asked embarrassing or potentially dangerous questions. Helena did tentatively inquire into Venetia's health, pointing out that she seemed unusually lethargic. Well, hearts did not break energetically; torpor and weariness were to be expected. Venetia mumbled something about staying up reading the night before.

She was back in Fitz's brougham, the vehicle pulling away from the curb, when she saw Christian coming out from his own carriage. He wore the same slate gray overcoat that he had worn to their first morning walk and carried the same ivory-handled walking stick. But he'd lost weight—there were hollows beneath his cheeks. And faint circles under his eyes, as if he, too, had not been able to sleep at night.

The ache in her heart turned into a stabbing pain. He was here, in London. And had she risen from luncheon a minute later, they'd have run into each other.

Almost fearfully she waited for either Millie or Helena to say something. But Millie had her head bent toward her husband, listening raptly to his analysis of some household matter. And Helena was looking out the other side of the carriage, her teeth clamped over her lower lip.

No one else had seen him.

Her listlessness evaporated; she vibrated with an uncontainable energy. When the carriage turned a corner and he disappeared from view, it was all she could do to not jump out of the moving vehicle.

Such a shock, seeing him. Such an electric thrill. And such emptiness, now that he was gone again.

*H*elena stared at Venetia's departing back.

At the train station she'd looked worn. At the Savoy she'd stared, as if hypnotized, at stemware and crown molding, barely aware of the goings-on. But now, a moment after they'd walked in the front door, she was already running back out, sprouting some nonsense about having left her fan behind at the hotel.

She hadn't been carrying a fan. And even if she had, she could have dispatched someone to retrieve it for her. Helena could think of only one explanation for Venetia's strange behavior—that to this day she could not bear to be reminded of what had happened at Harvard.

And it was Helena's fault—at least in part.

"Here comes Mrs. Wilson with your new maid," said Fitz.

Her head snapped up. "When did I acquire a new maid?"

"As of yesterday, I believe. Venetia said you needed one."

The maid, who followed Mrs. Wilson into the drawing room, was Helena's age, composed and sharp-eyed. She did not look as if she would be easily bribed by offers of free afternoons. Nor did she appear likely to take off with a gentleman friend at the least encouragement. No, this one had the look of a responsible future housekeeper written all over her.

"Susie Burns, milady, miss," said Mrs. Wilson.

The maid curtsied to Millie, then to Helena.

"Miss Fitzhugh's luggage should already be in her room," said Millie to Susie. "My maid can show you where things need to go."

Before Susie could say her "Yes, mum," Cobble, the butler, walked into the room and announced, "Lord Hastings."

And in swept in the man to blame for everything.

In Helena's mind, Hastings remained the short, scrawny miscreant Fitz first brought home when they'd all been fourteen. Sometimes she conceded that he was no longer short or scrawny, but a miscreant he was and always would be.

"Where is Mrs. Easterbrook going in such a hurry? She

all but shoved me aside," said Hastings, stalking toward Millie. "And how good to see you after all this time, Lady Fitz. You look marvelously fetching."

He took both her hands and kissed the back of each by turn. Millie smiled. "Never as fetching as you, Hastings."

Helena failed to see his appeal. He was a shameless flirt, a lecher, a sloth, and—she'd found out all too late—a traitor.

He turned to her. "Miss Fitzhugh, how I have missed you while you chased bluestockings all over America. How tedious you must have found them."

"Allow me to remind you that I am just as overeducated and tedious, my lord."

"Balderdash, not you. We all know you went to Lady Margaret Hall just to be fashionable."

It was a particular talent of his that he never said more than two sentences without making her want to reach for a sharp implement.

Cobble had already vacated the drawing room. Mrs. Wilson and Susie, too, were discreetly making their departure.

"Susie, leave my luggage for the time being. Air out the gowns I did not take with me first."

One should never speak to a servant while there were guests present—it would give the impression that household staff didn't know their tasks. But Helena had counted on secreting Andrew's letters in a more secure place before someone else handled her belongings.

"Yes, miss," said Susie.

Her instruction did not escape Fitz and Millie. They exchanged a glance.

"Would you mind taking a turn with me in the garden, Miss Fitzhugh?" asked Hastings.

This was the opening she needed. "Of course. Let me change into more comfortable shoes."

If Hastings had the run of the house due to his long friendship with Fitz, then Helena need not stand on ceremony, either. She rushed upstairs to her room, sent Susie out to buy something irrelevant, unlocked her trunk, and gathered Andrew's letters. Tomorrow she would take them to her office at her publishing firm; now she locked them in her bedside drawer.

Hastings was waiting for her at the foot of the stairs when she came down again.

"Love letters," he murmured. "So gratifying to receive, so troublesome for the remainder of their natural lives."

She pretended not to hear. "Glad you could find time in your busy schedule of wenching and general wastreling to call on us, Hastings."

He offered his arm; she ignored it and walked ahead.

The Fitzhugh house backed onto a private garden shared by the adjoining houses. In a few weeks the plane trees, fully sprouted, would provide green, dappled shade. But now the leaves were tiny green nubs too shy to unfurl. Finches hopped from bare branch to bare branch, pecking at last year's seed balls. A three-tiered Italianate fountain sparkled in the sun.

"Hullo, Penny," Hastings called cheerfully.

"Hastings, old fellow," answered Lord Vere, one of their neighbors, from his perch at the edge of the fountain. "Marvelous day for October, is it not?"

"It's April, Penny."

"Is it?" Lord Vere looked befuddled. "This year's or last year's?"

"This year's, of course."

"Well," huffed Lord Vere, "I don't know what I'm doing out here in April. Everybody knows it is always raining in April. Good day, Hastings. Good day, Miss Fitzhugh."

Hastings watched Lord Vere return to his own house. "You should have said yes when he proposed last year. Were you Lady Vere, it would have been nobody's business but your own where and with whom you spend your nights."

Of course it was just like Hastings to approach the subject so baldly. "I do not marry men who do not know what month it is."

"Yet you'd gladly lie with a man who dallies with virgins?"

She ignored that jab. It was hypocrisy of the highest order for a man who slept with everything that moved to criticize one who took risks for love. "Are you happy now that you have my family in a state?"

"What would you have done in my place? If it were *your* best friend's sister teetering on the edge of ruin?"

"Save your hyperboles. I've never been anywhere near the edge of ruin. And if it were my best friend's sister, I certainly wouldn't engage in double-dealing."

Hastings raised a brow. "Allow me to refresh your memory, Miss Fitzhugh. For a kiss, I promised not to reveal the identity of your illicit lover. I did not promise that I would keep your family in the dark altogether concerning your furtive activities."

"All the same," she said, giving him her falsest smile, "you duplicitous pig."

"Admit it—you enjoyed the kiss."

"I would rather eat a live snail than endure anything of the sort again."

"Ooh," he murmured, his eyes alight with speculation. "With or without its shell?"

She flicked a dismissive finger. "Save what you think of as your wit for a more gullible woman. What do you want from me, Hastings?"

"I've never wanted anything from you, Miss Fitzhugh—I've only wished to be of service."

She snorted, this from the little snot who used to try to maneuver her into cupboards and steal kisses.

"Seeing as it was I who introduced Andrew Martin to you," he continued, "I feel a deep sense of responsibility toward your welfare. At the risk of damaging my health, I have decided to offer to see to your needs."

She'd been refraining from the moment he arrived, but she could no longer: Her eyes rolled of their own accord. "Your altruism astounds, Hastings. I am shocked you haven't been canonized yet."

"I quite share your opinion, my dear Miss Fitzhugh." He leaned in and lowered his voice. "An unmarried woman passionate enough to flout all rules and jump into a man's bed? Your needs just might cripple me."

A flush of heat rose along the column of her throat. She walked faster and made her voice frigid. "I'm touched by your willingness to sacrifice. Nevertheless I must turn down your lavish and magnanimous offer."

He kept pace. "That is unfortunate, Miss Fitzhugh. For I am a far better choice in this matter, not already being another woman's husband."

"Too bad you've nothing else to recommend you, my lord."

"As I thought, you are still completely insensible. Very well then, if you won't think of yourself, think of your beloved. His mother is not a forgiving woman and he always cringes to be thought ill by her. Imagine her reaction should she find out that he'd compromised a virgin."

Andrew was in awe and mortal dread of his mother; there was no disputing that.

"Don't fool yourself into thinking that because his mother doesn't find you objectionable, she would condone such action on his part. She wouldn't. She would crush him with her disdain."

Helena worried the inside of her cheek. "We don't plan to give ourselves away."

"I'm sure you don't, but have you taken into full consideration Mrs. Monteth's ratlike tendencies to sniff out all wrongdoing?"

Mrs. Monteth was Andrew's wife's sister, a self-righteous woman who lived to expose the faults and weaknesses of those around her.

"If you love him, leave him be." Hastings's drawl had turned steely—it still amazed her that his tone could shift so, from velvety indulgence to cold implacability. "Or, mark my word, you will make him live in misery for the rest of his life."

He bowed. "And now I'm quite finished. I bid you a good day, Miss Fitzhugh."

At the steps back into the house he turned around, an ironic smile on his lips, once again the roué. "And in case you are curious, my offer still stands."

*M*y dear boy," said the Dowager Duchess of Lexington, who had come up to London with Christian.

"I recognize that tone, Stepmama," he answered from

before the window. "You have become privy to a particularly succulent piece of gossip."

Children frolicked in the small park across the street, flying kites, feeding ducks, playing hide-and-seek. One boy managed to slip away from his governess long enough to feed an apple to the horse harnessed to a hansom cab parked by the curb.

"And a rumor of the very rarest sort, too: one concerning you."

"I see." It had been too much to hope that word wouldn't spread until he'd first had time to secure his beloved's hand.

The boy's governess scolded him and removed his hand from the horse's coat, no doubt warning him of fleas and other undesirables that were sure to be associated with such a common animal. Did the curtain covering the hansom's window flutter? The cabbie, having finished his paper, now pulled something that resembled a crumpled penny dreadful out of his coat.

"Since we arrived in London this morning, I have received not one, not two, but three separate notes concerning a torrid affair you conducted during your crossing. In plain view, no less."

At least now he could speak of her. "Yes, it's true. All of it."

Did gloved fingers grip the edges of the curtain on the hansom cab?

"Surely not all of it. Some of the rumors declare that you have married her."

He turned around. "That, no. But not for lack of trying."

The dowager duchess, who had been in the middle of

rearranging a bouquet of tulips on a console table, stilled. She, too, turned around—a pretty woman in her early forties, only thirteen years older than Christian. But instead of immediately blurting out a response, she sat down on one of his Louis XIV chairs and arranged her skirts with a deliberate thoroughness. "You proposed?"

"Yes."

"You have not said a word."

"The situation is somewhat complicated. I did not want you to worry."

"And I'd worry less when I learned it this way?"

He bowed his head to let her know that he'd heard her reproach. "My apologies, madam."

"And what, pray tell, is so complicated about the situation? When the Duke of Lexington proposes, the lucky lady accepts. That's the end of it."

If only it were that simple. "She was traveling under an assumed name."

The moment he stepped onto English soil, he'd arranged to see someone familiar with German aristocracy. The Seidlitzs were a notable Prussian clan. The Hardenbergs were Silesian nobility. But there was no Baron von Seidlitz-Hardenberg on record—and therefore not a single Baroness von Seidlitz-Hardenberg.

So much for the always minuscule chance that she had been using her real name—and could therefore be found without the whole Continent being torn apart.

The dowager duchess sucked in a sharp breath. "An assumed name?"

"I have also never seen her face."

She blinked, stunned.

"As I said, it's quite complicated."

"Really, Christian." She tapped her fingers once against the armrest of the chair. "Hundreds of properly credentialed young ladies at home and you offer your hand to someone whom you wouldn't even be able to recognize if you passed her on the street?"

"She is the one I love." That should be justification enough, but somehow it did not sound quite adequate, in the face of all the unknowns. "You will adore her—she puts me in my place."

Her Grace was unconvinced. "I'd like to meet her and judge for myself."

"I will arrange it as soon as I can convince her to accept my hand."

"And how soon can you manage that?"

"On my birthday, I hope—she has agreed to meet me for dinner at the Savoy."

The duchess rose. "You know I trust your judgment, Christian. I have trusted your judgment since we first met. But I will be remiss if I do not point out the extraordinary irregularity of the circumstances. You have put yourself at a great deal of risk here—and I do not mean your prestige or your coffer."

He deserved the warning. "I'm afraid my heart is wholly taken. I shall be miserable if I do not marry her."

"You can be just as miserable in a marriage—by then it will be too late."

"It is already too late. If I cannot have her I will have no one."

She sighed. "You are sure about this?"

"Yes."

An echo of something—fear, perhaps—rattled inside him as he gave that unequivocal answer. He'd been just as certain, upon seeing Mrs. Easterbrook for the first time, that she held the key to his happiness.

"Be careful, my love," said the dowager duchess. "Renew the offer of your hand only if she proves to be worthy of it."

He tried to lighten the conversation. "So says the woman who would have been happy to have me marry any female with a pulse."

"Only because this one has the power to injure you, my love. Only because of that."

With all the hansom cab's flaps down to hide Venetia from view, the air inside, already heavy with the odors of tobacco and gin, grew staler with each passing minute.

She couldn't care less.

The sight of her lover had turned her delirious. She couldn't reason. She couldn't think. The only thing that mattered was that she should see him again. She had no idea what she hoped to accomplish by that, but the forces driving her toward him were greater than any she could muster to keep herself away.

She'd set out from Fitz's house walking. Somewhere along the way she realized that it would take her far too long to walk to the Savoy Hotel, so she stopped and hailed a hansom cab.

Her cab reached the Savoy Hotel just as the duke climbed back into his own carriage and drove away. She followed him to his home, a very fine neoclassical structure that she despised. Perhaps if its walls were made of glass she wouldn't mind it as much. Then she might see him moving about inside, doing whatever it was that he did when he was not making her fall head over heels in love.

But she saw nothing. The governesses in the park were becoming very suspicious about the hansom cab. And it wouldn't be long now before a bobby came around and asked the cabbie what he thought he was doing loitering about outside the homes of dukes and earls.

She could not sit here indefinitely.

One more glimpse. She just wanted one more glimpse of him.

The gods were listening. A carriage emblazoned with the Lexington coat of arms drew up at the curb. A minute later, he walked out of the front door and entered the carriage.

She had her "one more glimpse." But it was like receiving a single grain of rice when she'd starved for a week.

"Follow that carriage," she instructed her cabbie. "And don't lose sight of it."

One more glimpse. Just one more when he alighted at his destination.

"Mum, you'd 'ave 'im sooner if you'd let 'im 'ave a good look at you," said the cabbie.

How she wished that were the case. "Hurry."

His carriage turned west. She thought he was headed for his club on St. James's Street, but the carriage didn't stop until it had reached Cromwell Road, right before that magnificent cathedral to the animal kingdom, the British Museum of Natural History.

Where *her* dinosaur was housed!

She threw a handful of coins at the cabbie, leaped off the hansom, and cursed her dress with its narrow skirts, which made it impossible to attempt anything remotely athletic.

He ascended the front steps and passed under the beautiful Romanesque arches into the museum. The main display in the central hall was the nearly complete skeleton—missing only three vertebrae—of a fifty-foot sperm whale. She'd never before visited the museum without stopping to admire the skeleton, but now she only looked about wildly for him.

Let him go to the west wing to amble among the birds and the fish. Or let him go upstairs. But no, presently he peeled away from the cluster of visitors gathered before the whale skeleton and headed to the east wing, where the paleontological collection was housed.

Thankfully, the gallery that greeted visitors upon first entering the east wing dealt with mammals: the great American mastodon, the perfectly preserved mammoth unearthed in Essex, the rhinoceros-like *Uintatherium*, the northern manatee, hunted to extinction toward the end of the previous century. Perhaps they were all he intended to inspect this afternoon. Or the human and primate fossils in exhibit cases that lined the southern wall. Or the extinct birds in the pavilion toward the end of the gallery—the moas were very interesting, as were the eggs of the aepyornis, a bird said to have weighed half a ton.

But he paid only cursory attention to these wonders collected from all over the world for his enjoyment and edification and made for the gallery that ran parallel to the mammalian saloon, where the reptilian remains were kept.

She still hadn't lost all hope. Several perpendicular galleries, full of marine curiosities, branched out from the Reptilia gallery. Perhaps—perhaps—

Perhaps not. He slowed, stopped before the *Pareiasaurus* skeleton from the Karoo formation of South Africa, and then leaned in to read the small plaque that gave the names of the discoverers and the donors.

Her heart thudded. Her name was on a plaque barely fifty feet away from where he stood. Although he wouldn't immediately be able to make the connection, should he find out, subsequently, that she had crossed the Atlantic at approximately the same time as he, then the coincidence would strike even him as too great, no matter how unwilling he was to think of Baroness von Seidlitz-Hardenberg and Mrs. Easterbrook as the same person.

He turned from the *Pareiasaurus*. Along the south wall of the gallery were the great sea lizards: the *Plesiosaurus* and the ichthyosaurs. Against the north wall were the cases that held the land monsters.

As if pulled by a compass, he strode toward the north wall.

*W*hy he was puttering about the premier *British* natural history museum Christian had no idea—there wasn't even a Swabian dragon on display, as far as he could recall. If anything he ought to be checking the Museum für Naturkunde in Berlin or the Institute of Paleontology and Historical Geology at the Ludwig-Maximilians-Universität in Munich.

Yet something had propelled him here. It was possible she had already arrived in London. And if she had, wouldn't she wish to avail herself of the best collection of Dinosauria in all of England?

It was a sunny, crisp day out, and the gallery was not crowded: half a dozen young men who looked to be university students; a middle-aged couple, plump and expensively dressed; and a governess with two charges whom she hushed from time to time when their voices grew too excited.

Out of an utterly irrational hope, he looked several times toward the governess. It had occurred to him that the baroness was perhaps the commonest of commoners, and therefore did not consider herself worthy of an alliance with a duke. But that was the least of his worries. What was the point of being a duke with a lineage going back eight hundred years if he couldn't marry as he wished?

The governess, a severe-looking woman in her thirties, was not amused by his attention. She gave him a hard glare and pointedly turned her attention back to her charges, pronouncing that they had better head for the fossil fish if they wanted to look at everything before it was time to go home for tea.

Her head held so high her nose pointed almost directly at the ceiling, she ushered the children out. As she did so, another woman entered the gallery from its far end. She stopped to study the flying lizards fossils on display against the wall.

His heart turned over. She wore a simple light gray jacket-and-skirt set, nothing like the romantic, softly draped dresses he'd seen on the baroness. But from the back, her height, posture, and way her clothes hung on her person—had he kept one of the baroness's dresses, it would have fit her perfectly.

The woman turned around.

The world stopped. The years fell away. And he was again the nineteen-year-old boy on the cricket grounds of Lord's, staring at her with an arrow in his heart.

Mrs. Easterbrook.

Francis Bacon once wrote, "There is no excellent beauty that hath not some strangeness in the proportion." The man must have had Mrs. Easterbrook in mind. Her nose was noticeably long. The unusual shapes of her lower lash lines made her eyes widest not at the center, but more toward the outer corners. And surely those eyes would look absolutely ridiculous were they set even a tiny fraction of an inch farther apart. And yet the effect, together with her high cheekbones and full lips, was simply stunning.

He wanted to make cast models of her. He wanted to take a set of precision calipers and measure every distance between her features. He wanted her blood and glandular fluids analyzed by the finest chemists in the world—there must be something detectibly different in her inner workings for him to respond so dramatically, as if he'd been given a drug for which science had yet to find a name.

But more than anything, he wanted to—

He yanked himself back to his senses: He was a man who had committed himself to another. The baroness might very well not reciprocate said commitment, but he expected more of himself when he gave his word.

"Nasty brutes, are they not?" said the ravishing Mrs. Easterbrook, setting her reticule down at the edge of the display case.

He glanced at the case next to him. Earlier he had been standing next to a display of giant turtles, but now he was in front of a *Cetiosaurus*. He must have drifted toward her, mesmerized.

"I happen to think they are very handsome specimens—this one, especially."

She glanced at him, her gaze a caress upon his skin. "Pah," she said. "Squat and ugly."

She stood so close they nearly touched, but her words came to him only faintly, as if muffled by fog and distance. And when he turned his head away, so that he wasn't looking directly at her, he became aware of a subtle yet decadent fragrance of jasmine.

"If you do not enjoy God's creatures, madam," he said curtly, "perhaps you ought not to visit a museum of natural history."

*W*ith that, her lover turned on his heels and left. For a brief minute, as they headed toward each other, the air had crackled with expectation. So familiar, this sensation of closing the distance between them. Any moment now, he would smile and offer her his arm. They would stand together and admire her wonderful discovery. And nothing, nothing, would ever pull them asunder again.

Then she'd noticed his expression: that of a man sleepwalking. A man bewitched, his will confiscated, his faculties forsaken.

He had not exaggerated.

Such reaction on the part of a man used to mortify her—it confirmed that she was a freak. But coming from him, she adored it. She *wanted* him to gawk at her endlessly. It didn't change the fact that he loved her for who she was.

And maybe, just maybe, she could use her looks as a lure, reel him in, and keep him close at hand until he realized that he didn't dislike her. That, in fact, he liked her thoroughly and ardently.

But then he'd recalled himself—and flinched. The

self-reproach was plain in his eyes. He thought it unforgivable that for a brief minute, he'd forgotten himself, and forgotten the baroness.

So much for hoping that he'd allow prolonged contact between them. She felt like a reaped field, her harvest gone, and nothing but a long, barren winter ahead.

Slowly she lifted her reticule, which she had set down directly atop of the plaque that read, *The fossils of the Cetiosaurus courtesy of Miss Fitzhugh of Hampton House, Oxfordshire, who unearthed the skeleton in Lyme Regis, Devon, 1883*.

She'd told him that her dinosaur was a Swabian dragon because the *Cetiosaurus* was such a quintessentially English fossil and she had not wanted to reveal her English origins. She gazed at its heavy head, its thick legs, and its stout spine, forever associated with the exhilaration of discovery and the limitless possibilities of youth.

"Madam," said a man in his early twenties at her elbow, someone she'd never met before.

"Madam, my friends and I, we row for Oxford. And we wonder—we wonder if you have any plans at all to attend the Henley Regatta?"

The beautiful Mrs. Easterbrook had struck again, apparently.

"I wish you the very best of luck, sir," she said, "but I'm afraid I shan't be there."

CHAPTER 12

*M*illie found it difficult to keep her eyes off her husband.

They'd spent the entire day together. Most of the afternoon had been taken with matters having to do with Cresswell & Graves, the tinned goods firm Millie had inherited from her father. After tea they'd discussed the improvements to be undertaken at Henley Park this year. And until the note from Venetia had come, asking them to wait for her in the study, he'd been showing her the changes he'd made to the town house during her absence.

One would think this many consecutive hours would be quite enough. But the more she looked at him, the more she wanted to look at him. It had ever been the case. Today, however, was worse than usual. Today she'd come off the train to find that he'd rid himself of the full beard he'd worn for the past two years. The impact of his unobstructed features, all those lean lines and fortuitous angles, had knocked the breath out of her.

He was Helena's twin, but he resembled Venetia in bone structure and coloring—dark hair and blue eyes. A gorgeous man, much to Millie's detriment. But if she'd fallen in love with him because he was beautiful, she'd remained in love with him because she could not imagine spending her life with anyone else.

Half an hour ago, when he'd revealed the one betterment to the town house that had not been on their list, a sparkling new commode in blue enamel with white daisies—quite the private joke between the two of them— they'd laughed so hard they'd both had to lean on the wall to stay upright. Afterward he'd smiled at her, and she'd felt as if she were above the clouds again.

But now his face was grave as he listened to her recount what had happened at the Harvard lecture, in far greater detail than she'd felt prudent setting down in the cable she'd sent to him earlier, advising him to refrain from too many questions upon Venetia's return and to be sensitive to her moods. Not that he needed such reminders from her—one could always count on Fitz to be tactful and solicitous.

"I find it curious that she is not angry," he said. "Have you noticed since you came back? She is distracted and melancholy, but she is not angry."

Millie hesitated, then shook her head. Not because he was wrong, but because she hadn't had eyes for anyone else in the hours since her return.

A knock came at the door of the study. Venetia slipped in. "Sorry it took me so long. Helena came into my room. I don't know why she is so worried about me; she really ought to worry for herself instead."

Millie looked closely at Venetia, trying to gauge whether Fitz was right. But the grimness in Venetia's expression overrode everything else.

Fitz yielded his chair. "Have a seat, Venetia."

He came to stand behind Millie's chair, his hands braced on the chair's back. She wished her posture weren't so ramrod straight. She'd love to lean back a little, and have his fingers brush against her nape.

Venetia sat down. "During the crossing, I found one of Helena's jackets among my belongings. I'm not sure when it was mistakenly packed into my trunk, but since it doesn't fit me, I left it alone. Tonight as I was getting ready for bed, I remembered the jacket, took it out of my armoire—and found this."

She placed a piece of paper on the desk, a letter. Millie picked up the letter; Fitz read over her shoulder. Her heart sank with each line.

Fitz walked away to the window.

"No signature, but he mentions his book and his mother's house by name in the letter," Millie spoke into the heavy silence. "This removes all doubts, then."

"I don't know whether I am relieved to know for certain, or disappointed beyond words," said Venetia. "I guess I still clung to the hope that we'd grossly overreacted."

Millie glanced toward her husband. He stood with his arms crossed before his chest, his face devoid of expression.

"What should we do, Fitz?" asked Venetia.

"I'll think about it," he said. "You are not looking well, Venetia. Go to bed. Have a good night's sleep. Let me worry for a change."

Millie paid closer attention to Venetia—sometimes it

took her a while to see anything besides Venetia's beauty, especially after an absence. Venetia did appear somewhat nauseated.

Venetia rose and smiled wanly. "It's the turbot from dinner. Didn't quite agree with me."

"But you hardly ate anything at dinner," Fitz pointed out.

"Should we send for a doctor?" Millie asked.

"No, please don't take the trouble!" Venetia paused, as if surprised by the emphatic nature of her answer. She softened her voice. "A little indigestion is hardly cause for alarm. I had a couple of soda tablets. I should be all right in no time."

Venetia left. Fitz took the chair she vacated. "You should be abed, too, Lady Fitz," he said to Millie. "It's late and you've had a long trip."

"Long, perhaps, but hardly strenuous." She got to her feet anyway. They'd been married long enough for her to recognize that he wanted to be alone. "Are you going out?"

"I might."

To visit a lady friend, probably. She was used to it, she told herself. And it was better this way—why tinker with a friendship as satisfying as theirs? "Good night, then."

"Good night."

He was not looking at her, but once again reading Andrew Martin's letter.

She allowed herself to gaze at him another moment before closing the door behind her.

God damn it, Fitz!" Hastings doubled over, his hands over his abdomen. "You could have ruptured my spleen."

Fitz flexed his fingers. The punch to Hastings's belly hadn't hurt, but the one to his face had. The man had a skull hard as an ingot. "You would have deserved it. You knew it was Andrew Martin, didn't you? And you didn't tell me a thing."

Hastings straightened, groaning. "How did you know?"

"I saw your faces when the two of you were taking your turn in the garden. It was plain as day you were holding something over her."

He should have taken it up with Hastings sooner, but the Cresswell & Graves decisions couldn't wait any longer. And Millie's company had been so agreeable, he'd delayed his departure from the house again and again. Incomprehensible—she was his wife; her company was his anytime he wanted.

Wincing, Hastings made his way to the coffee service that had recently been brought in. "I told you enough."

He handed a cup of coffee to Fitz. Fitz accepted the peace offering. "You let us hope, you numskull. If my sister is throwing away her future over some bastard, I don't want to spend my days praying that I'm wrong. I want to know everything beyond a shadow of a doubt so I can act."

"What are you going to do?"

"It's not as if I've a wealth of choices, do I?"

"Want me to come along?"

Fitz shook his head. "The last thing I want is to bring along one of her frustrated suitors."

"I'm not one of her suitors," said Hastings, sounding remarkably like a boy who had his hand caught in the biscuit jar. "I've never wooed her."

"Only because you are too proud."

Hastings might fool the rest of the world, but to Fitz he was an open book.

"Sod off." Hastings gingerly felt his cheek, on which

Fitz had left a nasty cut. "Why do you have to know me so well?"

"It's the only reason I like you."

"If you say anything to your sister—"

"I haven't said anything to her in thirteen years. Why would I start now?" He set aside the coffee. "I'll be off now."

"Give my respects to Martin, will you?"

"That I will do—in abundance."

enetia threw off her covers and left her bedroom. She didn't mind tossing and turning, but the ache in her breasts—an unfamiliar tenderness around the areolas—disconcerted her. She'd had her heart broken before, but this time her wretchedness had increasingly translated into miscellaneous discomforts and eruptions of bile that had nothing to do with lovesickness.

And she was so tired. Despite all the thoughts in her head swarming like locusts, she'd fallen asleep after tea. After *tea*, when she'd never napped in her entire life, and certainly not at that strange hour.

She padded down the stairs. In Fitz's study, there was an encyclopedia with an entry on fossilized footprints. Hers were in storage—God forbid Christian should find out that Mrs. Easterbrook had acquired such an object. A picture in a book was hardly the same thing, but she had no other mementos. And she needed to be reminded that he used to actively campaign for the pleasure of her company, that her continued presence in his life had mattered as much as the sun's daily climb from the eastern horizon.

But Fitz was already in the study, clad in only his

shirtsleeves, a Cresswell & Graves bottle of champagne cider and a glass by his elbow.

"Can't sleep again, Venetia?"

She took the chair opposite his. "Slept too much after tea. What are you—"

She forgot what she was about to say as she saw the small smear on the front of his shirt. "Is that blood?"

"Hastings's."

"Why do you have Hastings's blood on you?"

"Long story. Anyway, I had a tête-à-tête with Andrew Martin."

"With your fist?"

"I'd planned to, but it would have been like punching the Easter Hare."

Mr. Martin did have one of those eternally innocent faces. "So what did you do?"

"I pointed out to him the risks to Helena. That if we can find out, so can others. That if he loves her, he must stay away from her."

"You think he would?"

"He seemed contrite enough. In any case, I told him that if he gave me the least cause for suspicion, I'd remove his—pardon my language—stones." Fitz fetched another glass and poured champagne cider in both. "Now you, Venetia."

"Me?"

"Your stomach can't be upset from the turbot. I watched you: You cut the filet and moved the pieces about but you didn't eat any of it."

"Maybe it was something else."

"Maybe it is."

Why did she have the feeling that Fitz was not

speaking of another item at dinner? "I think I'll take myself back to bed."

As she reached the door, Fitz asked, "He is not married, is he?"

Without turning around, she said, "If you speak of the Duke of Lexington, I am fairly certain he is not."

"I don't mean him."

A stroke of pure genius—if she did say so herself. Now she could answer in all honesty, "Then I don't know who you mean."

*C*hristian tossed aside yet another crumpled piece of paper.

He relished writing to his beloved—a bit of his day, a thought here and there, almost as if he were speaking to her. But tonight those few lines had been impossible to write.

What could he say? *When I saw Mrs. Easterbrook, I fell instantly under her spell again. You will be pleased to know that once I remembered myself, all was well. But until then, you were the furthest thing on my mind?*

He could exclude any mention of Mrs. Easterbrook. After all, he'd visited the Savoy and discussed her with the dowager duchess—more than enough to fill a letter of moderate length. But that would be lying by omission.

It was unthinkable to lie to his beloved.

My Darling,

A test came today in the form of Mrs. Elsewhere, and I cannot say I passed: I am not as immune to her charms as I had declared. I have not done anything for which I must ask for your forgiveness, but I find it difficult to justify the direction of my thoughts.

I need you. If my weakness is exacerbated by the distance that separates us, it may be logically deduced then that your presence will fortify my every strength.

Come soon. You can easily find me.

Your devoted servant,
C.

CHAPTER 13

*M*illie sliced open the first letter in her pile of morning post.

"My dear, I have it on good authority," she said, still scanning the page, "that you broke poor Letty Smythe's heart."

Venetia and Helena had asked for breakfast to be sent up to their rooms. Millie and Fitz had the breakfast parlor to themselves, allowing for a more private conversation.

"That is a vicious and groundless rumor," answered Fitz, smiling. "I have, however, stopped sleeping with her."

"Exactly what I meant."

"Rather unfair of the rumormongers, don't you think, to always cast me in the role of the unfeeling villain? It was a pleasant interlude that ran its course."

"Does Mrs. Smythe think so?"

"Mrs. Smythe will come to agree with me."

Millie shook her head, as if they were but discussing a

misbehaving puppy. "I am not one to gloat, but I told you that you shouldn't have taken up with her."

"And I should have followed your advice."

"Thank you. May I suggest Lady Quincy? She is pretty, well-spoken, and, most important, sensible: She will not make a fool of herself when your affair ends."

"I don't think so."

"Is there something you find objectionable about Lady Quincy?"

"Nothing. But my affairs run what, three, four months? It would be disrespectful of me to come to you while I am also enjoying another lady's favor."

The pact. It was the first time in years the subject had come up. She spread a heaping spoonful of marmalade over her toast and hoped she looked as nonchalant as he did. "Oh piffle. We are an old married couple. Go ahead and have your fun. I can wait."

"I disagree," he said evenly. "Duty first."

Their gaze held. A sharp bolt of heat struck her. She looked away to the pile of letters still to be opened and picked up the one on top. "Oh well, as you wish, then," she said, slicing the envelope open with a flick of her letter knife.

At first she only pretended to read. But the words somehow leaped off the page and forced her to pay attention.

She read the letter once, twice, three times before letting it drop.

"I am afraid I have some bad news, Fitz."

*V*enetia could not remember the last time she'd vomited.

Yet just now, the smell of a slice of buttered toast, an

item that had featured daily on her plate since she first sprouted teeth, had thrown her insides into such a state of convulsion that she'd hastily retreated to the nearest water closet and there spent a wretched few minutes surrendering the contents of her stomach.

She scrubbed her mouth and washed her face. When she came out of the water closet, she nearly collided with Millie. Millie, the mildest person she knew, grabbed her by the arm and pulled her along.

"What's the matter?"

"We'll talk in your room," Millie said, opening Venetia's door.

They were greeted by the sight of Helena frantically searching Venetia's armoire.

"I gave your jacket to your maid," Venetia said. "She's probably cleaning it."

"I'd better go take a look." Helena headed toward the door. "She might not know the proper way of doing it."

"Forget your jacket for now, Helena," said Millie, closing the door. "Venetia, you might like to sit down."

Venetia did—something in Millie's voice unnerved her. "What is it?"

"Lady Avery was at the Duke of Lexington's lecture."

Venetia gripped the arms of her chair, light-headed with horror.

Helena braced a hand on Venetia's bedpost, as if she had trouble supporting her weight. "The one at Harvard?"

Which *else*?

"She was in Boston the same time we were, attending the wedding of her son's American brother-in-law," said Millie. "She returned day before yesterday. Last night she dined at her niece's place and told everyone at table what the duke had said."

And the ladies at dinner would have gone on to the night's dances and balls, the gentlemen to their clubs, and word would have spread like the bubonic plague.

The nausea came again. Except this time there was nothing left in Venetia. She clenched her teeth until it passed. "Do they all think he was speaking of me?"

"Many do."

"Do they believe him?"

"Not everyone is convinced," Millie said carefully.

That meant some were.

"He is the most eligible bachelor in the realm," continued Millie. "You are our most beautiful woman. For him to accuse you so—even the possibility of it is beyond sensational."

Venetia felt as if she were chest deep in quicksand.

Helena looked as miserable as Venetia had ever seen her. "This is all—"

She stopped short of saying this was all her fault. To do so would have been to admit that her sisters had cause to take her out of the country.

Venetia rose. "He was quite indiscreet in Boston—perhaps he thought he could afford to be, since he was far from home. But I'm sure he has since realized his error. A man such as he has no interest in brewing tempests in teapots."

"That's quite a complimentary view you take of him," said Fitz, who had come into the room to stand beside his wife.

"My opinion of him should have no bearing on my assessment of the situation. I believe he will be almost as displeased about the rumors as we are and will do nothing to add to them."

"His silence will be just as problematic," Helena pointed out. "He has to denounce the rumors as untrue."

"That will require him to lie. He will not do that for me."

"Then what?"

"This will be a test to see whether my friends are truly my friends. If they are, they will close ranks around me and not allow anyone to question either my conduct or my moral fiber."

"I will make sure my friends fall in line," said Fitz quietly.

"It is rather last-minute, but we should have no problem giving a dinner for forty tomorrow night—a rallying of the troops," added Millie.

"Good," said Venetia. "The Tremaines are hosting a ball tomorrow night. After your dinner, we will all of us attend."

"And between now and then, we should make sure to be seen as much as possible," said Helena. "And don't forget to visit your modiste. You will want to devastate everyone in your path—in the most enjoyable manner, that is."

"Yes, I believe I've just the thing," Venetia murmured.

She'd discovered during her marriage to Tony that looking perfect was often enough to convince people that she was happy. Her appearance tomorrow would leave no doubt that she was in command of every aspect of her life.

A silence fell. Millie and Fitz were certainly each thinking of the specifics of what they needed to accomplish. As for Helena, Venetia had no idea what went through Helena's mind these days. She hoped Helena wasn't again blaming herself. If anything, she was grateful for Helena's indiscretions—it had brought her the most wonderful week of her life.

"I'll be all right," she said.

Hell-bent on escape, she had not quite realized it at the time. But the worst had already happened: She had lost the man she loved.

Everything else was but ashes from the fire.

*B*ecause Christian did not frequent the London Season, Society had an exaggerated idea of the amount of time he spent gallivanting abroad. But he was rarely away more than four months out of the year. The rest of the time he looked after his inheritance.

The de Montforts had been a lucky clan. Other families just as prominent now held land and properties worth next to nothing. But the de Montforts happened upon quarries, mines, waterways, and tracts coveted by generations of builders. Directly and indirectly, through older holdings and newer ventures, Christian was responsible for the livelihoods of six hundred men and women. He educated their children and supported longtime retainers in their retirement.

His income was tremendous, but his expenses were also breathtaking. For that reason, he'd always approached meetings with his agents and solicitors with the utmost alertness. Today his attention lasted long enough to approve of a plan to petition the Shah of Persia for a concession to search for petroleum on the latter's land.

After that, he barely heard what the roomful of men had to say.

The dream had come again—Mrs. Easterbrook dressing leisurely after their lovemaking, while he gazed upon her with infinite pleasure. This time, however, when she'd turned around, she'd spoken in German—in the baroness's voice.

The worst part was that he'd awakened happy.

A knock came at the door. McAdams, the solicitor, cast a displeased eye toward it.

"Sir," said Richards, his butler, "the dowager duchess would like to see you."

Her Grace had never before asked to see him in the middle of a meeting with his men of business. Was something the matter with Mr. Kingston? He'd been in perfect health when they'd left him yesterday morning.

She was waiting for him in the drawing room and closed the door the moment he was inside. "The news is all over London, Christian. Lady Avery reports that at the lecture you gave at Harvard University, you accused Mrs. Easterbrook of killing her husbands with her greed."

Time slowed with the utterance of the word *Harvard*. The dowager duchess's lips moved at the speed of a glacier. Each additional syllable took an eon to arrive.

But he didn't need to hear the rest. He already knew. His mistake had come to deliver its costly consequences.

"Lady Avery was at the lecture herself?" He heard his own voice, detached, remote.

Her face crumpled. "Oh, Christian, please tell me it isn't true."

"I never named Mrs. Easterbrook."

"But you *were* speaking of her?"

He could not admit it, not even to the woman who had been both a mother and a sister to him. "It does not matter of whom I spoke. Rest assured I will do what I must to rectify the situation."

"What has happened to you, Christian?" Her face sagged with worry. "First a public affair and then this. This is not like you at all."

"I will take care of everything," he promised her. "I will make everything all right again."

At least on the outside.

*A*mazing how much one could do on an empty stomach when much needed to be done.

Venetia made sure she was seen everywhere: at the park, at the theater, at the latest exhibit of the British Museum. During Millie's dinner she smiled and chatted as if she hadn't a care in the world. Following dinner, she donned her armor and set out for the balls.

The armor was a ball gown of crimson velvet, cut very low and very tight. She'd had it made two Seasons ago on a whim, but she'd come to her senses and never worn it—her function at balls was that of a chaperone and a facilitator, not someone who called attention to herself. But tonight she meant for all eyes to be upon her, as she danced and laughed as if she'd never heard of America, let alone the Duke of Lexington.

By the time she arrived at the Tremaine ball, her third and last, it was well past midnight. Lady Tremaine met her at the head of the stairs and gave her an approving look.

"Brings back fond memories of when I last made a dramatic entrance—also in red velvet, if I'm not mistaken."

"You are not mistaken at all," said Lord Tremaine, who

was never far from his wife's side. "And the memories are indeed very fond."

Venetia shook her head. "You will please stop flirting in public with your wife, sir. The mind quite boggles."

Lady Tremaine laughed. "Well, in you go, Mrs. Easterbrook. They say Byron would claw his way out of his grave to rewrite 'She Walks in Beauty' if he ever saw you coming down a staircase."

Venetia possessed one of the best descents. She didn't often employ it—again, not her place as a mere chaperone—but when she did, her head tilted just so, shoulders back, arms limber, the slightest of a smile playing about her lips, both men and women had been known to drop their drinks at the sight.

Tonight the entire ballroom held its breath at her entrance, then came a scramble for places on her dance card.

But this was never about the gentlemen: A beautiful woman was always assured of *some* masculine support. Society, however, was run largely by women and for women. And women were far less forgiving of other women.

The younger girls were excited—and some, quite unnerved—by the possibility of great conflict. Some matrons regarded her with a mixture of coolness and what felt to be—she hoped she was wrong—bloodlust. They were too prudent to immediately pounce upon her and declare her a husband-killer, but they, or at least a few of them, would like to, for the sport and spectacle of it, if nothing else.

And it was they, in the end, who must declare her once again fit for Society.

At present, her allies circulated the ballroom and, subtly but firmly, let it be known that they would not stand by for her to be ostracized—that they were prepared to sever ties with the one who dared to cast the first stone.

She was grateful. But she was also a realist. If this dragged on, her reputation would diminish daily. In the end, it would not be necessary for anyone to step up and denounce her. The collective caution—and desire to not be associated with someone dubious—would be quite enough to relegate her to the fringes of Society, still received in a few households and unwelcome everywhere else.

Breathless and a little dizzy from dancing Strauss's "Wine, Women, and Song" with Lord Tremaine, she almost did not hear the announcement of the arrival of the Duke of Lexington.

The ballroom had thrummed with exiting dancers, laughing from their exertion. Now it fell as quiet as the Reading Room at the British Museum, with all eyes upon the duke, descending the grand staircase behind his stepmother—gentlemen of a party always entered a ball behind the ladies—and a man Venetia assumed to be Mr. Kingston by his side.

Lord Tremaine had been about to deliver Venetia to Fitz and Millie, but now he changed course and guided her toward his wife. The two of them flanked her—so there could be no mistake of their backing.

Christian, with his characteristic directness, headed straight for the Tremaines—and Venetia.

The air drew taut. This was not to be an overtly hostile encounter—the presence of the dowager duchess was a guarantee of civility on her stepson's part. Yet Venetia felt as if she were a novice gladiator about to be thrown into the coliseum for the first time against a seasoned combatant, with the entire audience braying for her blood.

Lord Tremaine exchanged a pleasant word with his guests, extended his welcome, and then, turning a little, as if just discovering Venetia beside him, said to the dowager duchess, "Your Grace, may I present a good friend, Mrs. Easterbrook?"

The Dowager Duchess of Lexington was very gracious, if a little struck, as people often were when first meeting Venetia.

"Mrs. Easterbrook," Lord Tremaine continued, "allow me to present His Grace the Duke of Lexington and Mr. Kingston. Gentlemen, Mrs. Easterbrook."

Venetia inclined her head. Christian looked at her the way his Norman ancestors might have scrutinized a troublesome Anglo-Saxon, and returned a cursory nod.

Well, that was it. He had allowed the introduction and would henceforth count her as an acquaintance: as open a rebuke to Lady Avery's account of events as anyone could want. He would now politely disengage himself, perhaps dance with a suitable young girl who had the favor of his stepmother, and then depart.

For a moment, it seemed that was precisely what he meant to do. But the dowager duchess placed a hand on his elbow. An unspoken message passed between them.

With a determined set to his jaw, he said, "It is expected, is it not, upon being introduced to a lady at a ball, to ask for a dance?"

Had she not ventured aboard the *Rhodesia*, she'd have taken the opportunity to let him know that their new acquaintanceship meant as little to her as it did to him.

That he, for all his title and wealth, was the last man she'd allow to put his arm about her.

But she had ventured aboard the *Rhodesia,* had spent a week falling in love with him, and every minute since thinking about him. She'd crouched in a soggy-smelling hansom for hours outside his house, like an ill-trained private investigator, just so she could see his face again.

This Venetia was not going to turn down an opportunity to dance with him, no matter how churlishly his inquiry was worded.

"The pleasure would be mine," she said.

The moment Christian saw her, the rest of the ballroom disappeared. It could have been set on fire, with beams collapsing and guests fleeing, and the only thing he'd notice would be the reflection of firelight in her eyes.

His stepmother had to nudge him before he remembered to ask her to dance.

Mrs. Easterbrook smiled at him, a smile as lovely as sunrise, as dangerous as a bullet.

More than at any point since his return, he yearned for the baroness. The world might think him mad, but to himself he never needed to justify his love for her. Everything was founded on substance. There was nothing shallow or shameful in what he felt about her.

There was everything shallow and shameful in the reactions Mrs. Easterbrook bullied from him.

The musicians struck up the first strains of "Vienna Sweets." He held out his arm, and she placed her hand on his elbow, her motion as beautiful as her person—a creature born to be heedlessly adored.

It wasn't until they were walking side by side toward the center of the ballroom—when he wasn't directly looking at her—that an odd sensation stole over him. Surely they'd never touched before, yet her fingers upon his sleeve carried a disquieting familiarity.

After the introspective opening, the waltz suddenly turned bright and cheerful. It was time to dance.

The shape of her hand in his, the feel of her back beneath his palm, the pressure of her body as he swept her into a series of turns—the sensation of familiarity only doubled, when he should be surprised that she was not as exaggeratedly voluptuous as he'd always imagined, but more lithe and willowy, reminiscent of—

No, he must not draw any similarities between them. The last thing he wanted was for his mind to start pasting Mrs. Easterbrook's features onto the baroness's still-blank face.

Then she would never live up to his expectations.

This stray, too brutally honest thought infuriated him. It did not matter to him what his beloved looked like. All the better if she looked nothing like Mrs. Easterbrook.

"Did I see Your Grace at the Natural History Museum the day before yesterday?" murmured Mrs. Easterbrook.

Some despised part of him was thrilled that she'd remember him. "You did."

It occurred to him that he'd accepted her unexpected appearance the other day as a given, as part of the trials and tribulations he must overcome before he could be reunited with the baroness. But why had she been inside the Natural History Museum at all? And wasn't it more than a little odd that the *previous* time he'd seen her, five years ago, it had been just outside the museum?

The etiquette of the waltz called for him to keep his gaze over her shoulder, but he was glad for the excuse to look at her. The déjà vu sensation of the contours of her body was becoming too strong for comfort, and his mind, never his own to control when she was around, insinuated that he'd know exactly where and how to touch to make her melt with desire.

Their eyes met. But her beauty, instead of derailing his current, highly untenable train of thoughts, only reawakened a primitive possessiveness: He wanted to lock her in his manor and allow no one to gaze upon her but himself.

She smiled again. "You enjoyed your visit, I hope."

He looked away. "I liked it well enough. And was your visit ever able to recover from the hideousness of the giant reptiles?"

"I'm afraid it never did. I don't know why I subject myself to such unpleasantness."

"Why did you, then?"

"The whims of a woman, what can I say?"

Why did he want this insipid creature? Why did he want this dance to go on and on, when he ought to be thinking of someone else?

Not too much longer now before their appointed meeting. And this time, he would not let her go again.

"How do you find London after a long absence, sir?" she murmured.

"Troublesome."

"Ah, on that we agree."

The timbre of her voice—where had he heard her speak before?

"I will call on you tomorrow afternoon, Mrs. Easterbrook," he said. "And if it is agreeable to you, we will take a ride together in the park. That should be sufficient to quash the rumors."

"And will you stop calling on me after that?"

"Naturally."

"A shame," she said. "Are Your Grace's affections engaged—elsewhere?"

Was it his imagination or had she paused deliberately before saying "elsewhere"? The word in English was nothing like its equivalent in German but somehow still managed to sound uncanny.

He looked again at her. She stared straight over his shoulder. She was slightly easier to take without the effect of her direct gaze, but still she was unbearably beautiful. The gods would have wept.

"That is none of your concern, madam."

"No, of course not, but one does hear rumors. Very prudent of you to stop calling on me once we have detracted Lady Avery. Your lady would not be too pleased were you constantly seen with me. I have, shall we say, a certain effect on men."

He hated her smugness. "My lady has nothing to worry about."

She flicked him a glance that would have made Achilles put down his shield and forsake all the glories of Troy. "If you say so, sir."

*T*hey danced the rest of the waltz without speaking. Venetia was relieved that she didn't need to go on saying things that made Mrs. Easterbrook sound the exact opposite of Baroness von Seidlitz-Hardenberg. But she missed hearing his voice, even if he now spoke an icy English instead of an affectionate German.

This was her beloved, back in her arms—a terrible miracle, but a miracle nonetheless. She found it difficult to restrain herself, to not let her left hand trace the contour of his shoulder, her right thumb caress the center of his gloved hand, or her head lean forward and rest upon him.

She wanted the dance to never end.

But all too soon, the waltz drew to a close. The dancers all around them pulled apart. The duke, too, made to separate from her. But Venetia, immersed in memories of their closeness—did not let go.

She realized her mistake after only a second. But a second was a very long time for such a faux pas. She might as well have unbuttoned her bodice; it would not have shocked him more.

And shocked he was. He regarded her with the extreme severity one reserved for those who'd trespassed against not only morality, but good taste. As if she were a common streetwalker who had marched into the ball uninvited and accosted him.

The silence, as he escorted her off the dance floor, was excruciating.

He is not here," said Hastings. "The wife's mother is ill. He has dutifully gone to Worcestershire to attend her."

Helena did not need to ask who "he" was. At first she'd been too anxious about the reception that awaited Venetia. But now that the duke had come and gone after a surprising and surprisingly effective maneuver, she'd allowed herself to scan the crowd for a sign of Andrew. His mother's family was very well connected and he could be counted on to have invitations to the more sought-after functions.

"Do you think I should be paying my addresses to Mrs. Martin, my dear Miss Fitzhugh?" he whispered. "Martin doesn't look the sort to have enough stamina to service two women. And goodness knows you could probably exhaust Casanova himself."

Again this insinuation that she must be a sufferer of nymphomania. Behind her fan, she put her lips very close to his ear. "You've no idea, my Lord Hastings, the heated yearnings that singe me at night, when I cannot have a man. My skin burns to be touched, my lips kissed, and my entire body passionately fondled."

Hastings was mute, for once. He stared at her with something halfway between amusement and arousal.

She snapped shut her fan and rapped his fingers as hard as she could, watching with great satisfaction as he choked back a yelp of pain.

"By anyone but you," she said, and turned on her heels.

For the ride in the park, Christian trotted out his grandest landau—so he could sit as far away from Mrs. Easterbrook as possible.

Which was not quite far enough to avoid the tangible pull of her beauty.

Unlike the baroness, she did not twirl her parasol, but held it perfectly steady. Her entire person was as still as Pygmalion's sculpture, cool, heartless, and nevertheless lovely enough to derange a man.

Her rose-colored afternoon dress cast a subtle blush upon her cheeks. Her eyes, in the shade cast by her cream lace parasol, were aquamarine, the exact color of the warm Mediterranean that had so enchanted the secret voluptuary in him. Her lips, soft, full, perfectly delineated, promised to taste of rose petals and willingness.

It was only when she spoke that he realized he'd already begun to mentally undress her, ripping off the silk-covered buttons of her bodice like so many currants from the stem.

"You are immersed in thought, sir. Anticipating your dinner with your lady, perhaps?"

His attention snapped to abruptly. How would she know anything of his dinner? And, an instant later, great, terrible guilt: On the eve of his much hoped-for reunion with the baroness, his mind was eagerly committing an act of infidelity.

He wanted to blame it on Mrs. Easterbrook's conduct, the way she'd held on to him at the end of their waltz: She might as well have given him the key to her house along with a wink and a blown kiss. Her intentions had smoldered in his blood ever since.

On the other hand, would he have desired her less if she'd proved herself utterly indifferent? Would it not have simply whet his appetite and made her even more coveted a prize?

"One hears talk that you have commissioned quite the grand repast for tomorrow evening at the Savoy," Mrs. Easterbrook continued.

Had she been any other woman he'd have told her in no uncertain terms to mind her own affairs. But here it was imperative that he spoke of the baroness in as warm a tone as publicly permissible.

"Yes," he said. "I look forward to a delightful evening tomorrow."

If she came.

She must. She could not desert him in his hour of need. But—the thought suddenly occurred to him—if she'd already arrived in London, would she not somehow hear of his imbroglio with Mrs. Easterbrook? And would she not interpret the public attention he was paying Mrs. Easterbrook quite the wrong way?

Mrs. Easterbrook smiled slightly. "She is a very fortunate woman, your lady."

"I am a very fortunate man, rather."

To judge her expression was like trying to gauge the variation in the sun's intensity by staring directly into it. But he thought she looked wistful. "And this is the last time I will see you, I take it?"

"Which I'm sure must be a relief to you."

She arched a brow. "You presume to know how I think?"

"Very well, then. It will be a relief to *me*."

She tilted her umbrella slightly away from her person. "There are those who like me for the way my nose sits on my face—a ridiculous reason to like someone. But it's also a fairly ridiculous reason to not like someone—as it is in your case."

"I disapprove of your character, Mrs. Easterbrook."

"You don't know my character, sir," she said decisively. "The only thing you know is my face."

CHAPTER 14

$\mathscr{C}$hristian did not give many dinners. And when he
did, the dowager duchess usually oversaw the necessary arrangements. But for this particular dinner, he
presided over every detail.

Several private dining rooms had been rejected as either
too stuffy or too floridly ornate. And when he did finally
settle on one, he had the hotel change the staid still life
painting on the wall for a seascape reminiscent of the one
in the Victoria suite. Instead of flowers, for the centerpiece
he commissioned an ice sculpture of frolicking dolphins.
He also decreed that there should be no harsh electrical
lights, but only candle flame—and not from tallows, either:
nothing but the best beeswax tapers for her.

The proposed menu he'd sent back with the direction
that it should consist of a clear consommé, a sole poached
in broth, a braised duckling, a rack of lamb broiled with

herbs, a filet of venison—and nothing else. Which had quite offended the chef, who apparently believed a romantic dinner should be conducted like a state banquet.

L'amour, he declared, wagging his finger at Lexington, must be fortified by plenty of food and plenty of flesh. Milord was already too thin himself. His night with milady might as well be two skeletons rattling in a medical laboratory!

Lexington did not yield—he had no intention of feeding his lady comatose. Finally, the Frenchman gave up on the main courses. But he would not limit himself on the desserts—none of the fresh fruit served *à nature* nonsense. There would be a charlotte russe, a *crème renversée,* a vanilla soufflé, a chocolate mousse, a pear tart, and a plum cake.

"We will still be eating at dawn," said Lexington, not without admiration for the man's dedication to his ideals.

The Frenchman kissed his fingertips. "*Et après,* you will be all the better for *l'amour,* milord."

Christian arrived half an hour early to the dinner. The table was being set as he walked into the room, crystal finger bowls, silver saltcellars, footed bowls holding grapes, figs, and cherries laid down at careful distances upon the blue damask cloth.

This wait was nothing at all of the pleasurable anticipation on the *Rhodesia.* He was normally disciplined—a gentleman did not fidget—but several times he had to stop his fingers from tapping on the windowsill. He wanted a stiff drink and a cigarette. He wanted different curtains for the room. He wanted the painting changed again.

If she would only come, all would be well.

But what if she didn't?

The tapers were lit; the glasses sparkled in the lambent light. The ice sculpture was brought in, the dolphins leaping gracefully out of frozen waves. A sixty-year-old bottle of champagne was reverently laid on the sideboard, ready to be uncorked the moment she swept into sight.

She should already have presented herself. Etiquette dictated that one arrived to dinner at least a quarter hour before the stated time, out of respect for the delicate nature of soufflés, if nothing else.

Were European customs different? He ought to know—he'd spent time on the Continent. But he couldn't think. He was in a state of mental blankness, one rung above outright panic—but only one rung.

At eight o'clock, a steward of the hotel discreetly inquired whether His Grace wished to begin serving dinner.

"Another quarter hour," he said.

When another quarter hour had passed, he gave the same instructions.

At half past eight, no one asked him anything. The hotel staff, who had hovered about for the past hour, now made themselves scarce. A bottle of whisky appeared from nowhere. As did cigarettes, matches, and a carved ivory ashtray.

She'd given her word. Was her word of so little worth to her? And if it had been her intention to break her word from the beginning, why not send him a letter and let him know?

Could something unforeseen have befallen her? What if she were lying somewhere ill and uncared for? Again, she could have written, and he'd have been at her side in a heartbeat.

But he presupposed her ability and freedom to communicate. What if she were carefully watched, once she went back to wherever it was she must go?

He gave the possibility several minutes of anguished consideration before it occurred to him how ridiculously melodramatic it was. A woman under such medieval supervision would never have been allowed to cross the Atlantic on her own, let alone conduct an affair in full view of the passengers.

The explanation for her absence had been staring him in the face all the while, but he hadn't wanted to acknowledge it: The affair meant nothing to her. He'd been the only one bewitched body and soul. For her, he'd been but a temporary source of entertainment, a way to pass the otherwise tedious hours in the middle of an ocean.

He'd been the one to press for a continuation of their affair beyond the voyage. He'd been the one to offer his heart, his hand, his every last secret. She never even gave her real name.

And, of course, never showed her face.

No, he could not doubt her. If he doubted her, he might as well doubt his ability to judge anything at all. It had to be as he'd feared, that she'd heard about Mrs. Easterbrook. God, what if she'd seen them driving together the day before? The sight of his eyes upon Mrs. Easterbrook would have refuted everything he'd told her about having put this obsession behind him.

And even if she had seen and heard nothing, did he still deserve her, he who came to the dinner with Mrs. Easterbrook's words—*You don't know my character, sir. The only thing you know is my face*—still echoing in his ears?

He'd dreamed of Mrs. Easterbrook again last night, an

even more disturbingly domestic tableau of the two of them seated before a roaring fire, he writing letters, she reading a thickish book that looked as if it had come from his library. From time to time, his dream-self would look up from his task and gaze upon her. Except, instead of the hot, unhappy surges of possessiveness that had lately plagued him, he'd felt only a simple contentment at seeing her nearby.

He'd yet to dream of the baroness.

Still he compulsively watched the carriages coming to a stop before the hotel. London's traffic was notorious at certain times of the day. A logjam, once formed, took a good, long while to clear. Perhaps she was caught in one. Perhaps she was boiling in impatience even as he sank slowly into despair. Perhaps—

Suddenly he became aware that he was no longer alone in the room. He spun around, hopes and fears incoherent in his chest.

But it was not her. It was only a uniformed porter of the hotel.

"Your Grace, a delivery for you."

For the next three seconds, he still dared to let himself hope. Perhaps she was making a grand entrance. Perhaps she would be carried in like Cleopatra, hidden in a roll of fine carpet. Perhaps—

Three porters, grunting, pulled in a handcart.

A crevasse opened before him and in fell his heart. No need to remove the tarpaulin wrapping. He recognized the stone slab by its size and weight.

She had returned his present. She would have nothing more to do with him.

* * *

*I*t was another hour before the duke left the hotel.

This time, Venetia was not waiting in a smelly hansom cab, but in a clean, elegant brougham, with tufted velvet seats, foot braziers, and tulip blossoms in bud vases mounted on brackets between the windows.

The baroness had leased the carriage. She even had her veiled hat, sitting on the seat beside her.

You still can, whispered a reckless voice inside her, as it had been whispering for the past three hours. *Go on, intercept him. Just for tonight.*

But this time he would not let her leave again. And he would not let the veil remain in place. There was no such thing as just for tonight.

Or rather, there was no such thing as tomorrow: He would throw her out the moment he saw her face and never speak to her again.

She could only watch as her lover, stone-faced, climbed into his carriage and drove away.

*T*hroughout the night, Christian swung from anger to despair and back again. In the morning, however, he summoned his carriage and returned to the hotel.

Perhaps he had been foolish. Most likely he had been beyond stupid. But he had been forthright and honorable, and he deserved better courtesy than this.

An inquiry at the hotel quickly yielded that the stone slab had arrived by courier three days before. A typewritten note had come by post the previous morning, with instructions for its delivery that evening by quarter to eight. The general manager offered his profuse apologies—there had been a change of personnel during the day and the staff of the next shift had forgotten about the stone slab until quarter to nine.

Christian asked to see the original envelope for the note. That, alas, had been discarded. But the clerk who had opened the envelope recalled very clearly that the post-mark had been from the city of London—and had been for the same day.

How likely was it that she'd come to London herself just to give him the brush-off? Not very. Still, he left instructions with a private investigator to find out whether any major hotel in London hosted a female guest of Germanic origin, between twenty-seven and thirty-five years of age, traveling alone.

He himself took the train to Southampton to speak to the proprietors of Donaldson & Sons Special Couriers. They could not tell him much: The object they'd delivered to the Savoy in London had been brought in by shipping agents from the harbor. The shipping agents' records were slightly more helpful, showing that the tablet had been unloaded from the *Campania*, a ship of the Cunard Line, which had put in at Southampton the day after the *Rhodesia*.

Christian took himself to the Cunard Line's Southampton offices and asked to see the passenger list for the *Campania* on that particular sailing. He did not recognize any names on the list, though he did learn that the *Campania* had set out from New York two days before the *Rhodesia*, but had taken nine days to cross the Atlantic due to technical problems at sea.

As he was already in Southampton, he next visited the Great Northern Line's offices and asked to see the passenger list for the *Rhodesia*. The baroness would have traveled with a maid. It should not be impossible to find out the identity of said maid.

Quite a few men disembarked at Queenstown, and not many women. Of those, most shared the men's names—wives, sisters, and daughters. And of the four who were unrelated to any men, besides the baroness herself, two were Catholic sisters and one a young girl entrusted to the sisters to escort back to her family in the old country.

Puzzled, Christian asked whether a mistake could have been made. He was advised to wait overnight: The *Rhodesia*, returning from Hamburg, was expected in port the next morning.

His night was restless, but his efforts did not go unrewarded. The next morning he spoke to the purser of the *Rhodesia* himself and learned that the Baroness von Seidlitz-Hardenberg had not purchased tickets for any domestics. Instead, while aboard the *Rhodesia*, she had engaged the service of one of the ship's stewardesses as a temporary personal maid, a girl of French origins by name of Yvette Arnaud, who of course would not have any objections to answering a few questions from His Grace the Duke of Lexington.

The stewardess appeared half an hour later, tidy and competent-looking, in the private office Lexington had been shown into. He offered her a seat and slid a guinea across the desk to her. She pocketed the coin discreetly and murmured a thank-you.

"How were you chosen by the baroness and in what capacity did you serve her?" he asked in French.

"Before the *Rhodesia* left New York City, the chambers steward said that a lady guest traveling by herself wanted the services of a maid. Several of us volunteered—there could be good tips. The steward took down our qualifications and submitted them to the baroness.

"I was a dressmaker's apprentice at one time and I said that I knew how to care for costly fabrics. But I didn't think I'd be chosen. I'd never worked as a lady's maid, and there were those among us who had and could furnish letters of character from former employers in London and Manchester."

She had been chosen because her qualifications were perfectly adequate under the circumstances—a lady who did not show her face to anyone had no need of a maid with expert coiffing skills.

But he asked the question all the same—it never hurt to hear how another mind analyzed the same data. "Why were you selected in the end?"

The girl hesitated for a few seconds. "Because I'm not English, I think."

This answer Lexington had not expected. His heart stopped. "How so?"

"Her name is German, she spoke to me in French, but her things were English."

"What things?"

"Her trunks were made by a London trunkmaker—I saw the lettering on the insides of the lids. Her boots came from a London cordwainer. And her hats—the ones that didn't have a veil on—came from a Madame Louise's on Regent Street. I know Regent Street is in London because my old employer the dressmaker hoped to one day have her own shop there."

Many English goods were acknowledged to be superior in construction and quality. It was not out of the question for a foreigner to have English-made items. But to have a wardrobe composed so overwhelmingly of English things? Wouldn't a cosmopolitan woman of the Continent spread her purchases among Paris, Vienna, and Berlin?

"What else makes you think she is English?"

"She speaks French like you, sir, with an English accent."

This was far more compelling evidence. Accents were notoriously difficult to disguise. If a native French speaker identified someone as speaking with an English accent, there wasn't much he could do but to believe her.

But if the baroness were English, her disappearing act became even more incomprehensible. He had offered marriage, for God's sake. A foreigner might not grasp the significance of it, but surely an Englishwoman understood the prestige and wealth he brought to the bargain. Even if he'd been only a quick diversion to her before then, the lure of becoming the next Duchess of Lexington should have induced her to stay.

"What else can you tell me about her?"

"She tips well—before she disembarked she gave me a hairpin with opal and seed pearls. And she has a stunning wardrobe, the most beautiful clothes I've ever seen—not as beautiful as herself, of course, but still—"

"You thought her beautiful?"

"Well, yes, she is by far the most beautiful woman I've ever seen. I told the other stewardesses that no wonder she kept herself covered—if she lifted her veil, there would be riots on the *Rhodesia*."

How many women in the world were beautiful enough

to cause riots? Not very many. And Lexington knew of only one.

"Did they believe you?"

"No, they thought I exaggerated wildly, since no one else got a look at her face. But you, sir, you know how magnificent she was. You know I do not exaggerate."

Did he? His mind, with the revulsion of a spinster hurrying past a house of ill repute, refused to contemplate Yvette Arnaud's revelations—refused to synthesize the disparate pieces of information, as a man of science ought, into one coherent explanation.

He placed one more guinea on the desk and left without another word.

*T*he urgency of the crisis and the thrill of the duke's nearness—no matter how miserable he'd made her feel at the same time—had blunted the severity of the various physical ills plaguing Venetia. Her nausea became less intense, her fatigue altogether replaced by heart-pounding dread and excitement.

But now, with the crisis averted, Venetia's body decided to remind her that it had not recovered.

Far from it.

In the morning she had to rush to the water closet twice, first when her breakfast was carried in, again when Helena, out of consideration, brought her a cup of tea with cream and sugar already added.

The first time she was able to conceal it from everyone except her maid, who'd been with her ten years and was exceedingly discreet and trustworthy. The second time, however, she was not so lucky. Helena was already instructing a footman to go fetch the doctor when Venetia over-ruled her.

Helena reluctantly agreed to wait another day to see whether a physician was truly needed. But they did not quite make it to the next day.

In the middle of the afternoon, upon finishing a batch of invitations, Venetia rose from her desk. The next thing she knew, she was lying on the Turkish carpet, with her maid frantically waving a jar of smelling salts before her.

And the doctor, alas, was already on her way.

*C*hristian dismissed the brougham that was waiting for him at Waterloo Station when he reached London. He didn't want to go back to his town house. He shouldn't have detrained from his private rail coach at all. Should have arranged for it to go all the way to Edinburgh, to put all of Britain between himself and the truth that was beginning to claw at him.

So he crossed the Thames and walked, not knowing where he was headed and not caring.

English. Beautiful.

Was it possible to un-hear those words? Damn the scientific method and its demand that no stone be left unturned. Damn his indignant self-righteousness that wouldn't rest until he'd had his answers.

He tried to scoff at himself: He was making unsupported leaps of logic. *English* and *beautiful* did not equate Mrs. Easterbrook. Besides, Mrs. Easterbrook had no purpose in life other than being beautiful. She wouldn't cover her face any more than the queen would abdicate her throne.

At some point he became aware of his hunger and walked into a tea shop, only to stop in his tracks. One entire wall of the tea shop, which catered largely to ladies, was covered with framed pictures of Society beauties.

Mrs. Easterbrook among them.

In photography, the animation and sheer dominance of her beauty was largely lost. She was but another pretty face in a sea of pretty faces, and he might not have even noticed her upon first glance had it not been for the parasol she held over her shoulder.

Dark concentric octagons upon white lace.

*M*iss Redmayne, a physician who had trained in Paris, sat down by Venetia's bed. Millie and Helena hovered on the other side.

"Miss Fitzhugh tells me you lost consciousness approximately an hour ago. And that you've been suffering abdominal ills for several days."

"That is correct."

Miss Redmayne felt Venetia's forehead and wrist. "No fever. Your pulse is fine, if a bit listless. Anything that might have precipitated the loss of consciousness?"

"I can't think of anything. I probably never recovered from the effects of the turbot."

"Did you have the turbot also, Miss Fitzhugh?"

"I did."

"Did it cause you any discomforts?"

"No, I can't say it did."

Miss Redmayne addressed herself to Millie and Helena. "Lady Fitzhugh, Miss Fitzhugh, would you give us some privacy? I might have to perform a more thorough examination."

"Of course," said Millie, sounding a little puzzled.

When she and Helena had vacated the room, Miss Redmayne indicated the bedcover. "May I?"

Without waiting for an answer, she peeled it back and pressed gently upon Venetia's abdomen.

"Hmm," she said. "Mrs. Easterbrook, when was the first day of your last menses?"

The question Venetia had been dreading. She bit her lower lip and named a date almost five weeks ago.

Miss Redmayne looked thoughtful.

"But that can't be the case," Venetia pleaded. "I can't conceive."

"The fault might very well lie with your late spouses, rather than yourself, Mrs. Easterbrook. Now if I may be so blunt, have you taken a lover since your last monthly?"

Venetia swallowed. "Yes."

"Then, as much as the diagnosis might be unwelcome for you, I'm afraid you are with child."

She'd known it, hadn't she, since the first instance of morning sickness? She'd been around other married women enough to have heard of that particular symptom. But as long as she managed to stay away from an official confirmation of her condition, she could continue to ignore what her body was trying to tell her.

No more.

"Are you certain, Miss Redmayne, that I don't have a tumor or something of the sort?"

"I'm quite sure," said Miss Redmayne. She was very sympathetic, but the authority of her tone was unmistakable.

Venetia gripped the sheets between her fingers. "How long do I have before my condition becomes visible?"

"Some women manage to conceal their condition far into the gestation with the help of special corsets and such, which we do not recommend for the harm it does to both mother and child."

A lady withdrew from Society when her pregnancy could no longer be concealed. Venetia had indeed heard of rumors of women keeping a growing belly secret until just weeks before confinement.

"But I assume that is not what you are asking," continued Miss Redmayne. "Measured from the first day of your last menses, you are considered to be in the second month of gestation. In general, you will have until the fifth or the six month before the condition becomes obvious."

At least she still had some time. "Thank you, Miss Redmayne. May I rely upon your discretion in this matter?"

Miss Redmayne inclined her head. "You may be assured of it, Mrs. Easterbrook."

*C*hristian remembered a time when the British Museum of Natural History shut its doors at four o'clock every afternoon. Would that it still did. For it was past five when he found himself before its terra-cotta facade. Had the museum already closed, he'd have come to his senses and taken flight with the speed of an antelope fleeing a lion. But the museum remained open to visitors and his feet moved of their own will past the bones of the blue whale into the east wing.

Several times he almost turned around. One time he

even came to a complete standstill, much to the annoyance of a professorial type whose path he blocked. But he could not halt the terrible momentum that eventually pushed him to move again, past the mammals, into the Reptilia gallery.

Without quite being able to articulate why, he headed directly for the *Cetiosaurus*, before which he and Mrs. Easterbrook had exchanged words—words flippant on her part and hostile on his.

When he hadn't stared at her face, he'd stared at the reticule she'd set down at the edge of the display case, because her fingers had idly played with its drawstring. The reticule itself had been pale gray brocade, embroidered with doves holding olive branches.

And where it had rested, there was a plaque.

The fossils of the Cetiosaurus courtesy of Miss Fitzhugh of Hampton House, Oxfordshire, who unearthed the skeleton in Lyme Regis, Devon, 1883.

CHAPTER 15

*O*h good," said Fitz, still scanning the letter. "Venetia is coming back to town."

Millie spread more butter on her toast. "You don't have to go, then."

For the better part of a week, Venetia had been staying in the country, recuperating from the lingering illness that she'd caught during the crossing. Fitz, who had escorted her to Oxfordshire, had become increasingly concerned she'd chosen to shut herself off from the rest of the world. He'd informed Millie, as he sat down to breakfast, that he'd be headed to the rail station within the hour.

She sneaked a look at the small mountain of letters by his elbow. He'd looked through the pile, stopped at Venetia's letter, and read it first. Now he sliced open another letter.

"Who's that from?" she asked, plastering even more butter on her toast.

"Leo Marsden."

Mr. Marsden had been in the same house as Fitz at Eton. He'd left England after the annulment of his marriage.

"Is he still in Berlin?"

"No, he's been in America since autumn last, but says he might be headed to India next."

The mere mention of India made Millie's chest tighten.

"And is that butter on toast or toast on butter?" He smiled at her. "If you like, you can serve yourself butter by the block."

So he'd noticed. She took a bite of her toast—and tasted nothing.

Fitz finished Mr. Marsden's letter, set it aside to be replied to, and shuffled through the rest of the pile. As she thought would happen, he went still.

Slowly, he turned the envelope over. There he would see the sender's name, in her bold hand, *Mrs. John Englewood, Northbrook Hotel, Delhi*. Millie kept her face down and blindly reached for something from her own heap of letters.

From the corner of her eye, she saw that he held only one sheaf of paper. The reverse side, facing her, was half blank—not a very long letter. But that Mrs. Englewood had written at all, when she'd not contacted Fitz since the day of his wedding, was a ground-shifting event.

"The Featherstones have invited us to dinner," said Millie. It seemed as if she ought to say something, keep up the pretense of normalcy. "Mrs. Brightly has set the date of her wedding to Lord Geoffrey Neels and would like us to attend. And oh, Lady Lambert is canceling her garden party: Her father passed away and she is gone into mourning."

How boring she sounded. How utterly and terrifyingly

tedious. But what could she do? Such were the things she and Fitz said to each other.

He did not even hear her. He'd reached the reverse side of the letter. And when he was done, he immediately turned it over and started from the beginning again.

She no longer bothered to be interested in anything else. He read with a fierce concentration, as if he'd gone through the letter too fast the first time and must now slowly take in every word.

And when he'd finished reading it the second time, he did not place it in the "to-reply" pile alongside Mr. Marsden's letter, but carefully—envelope and all—slipped it into the inside pocket of his day coat.

She turned her head away, back to the invitations and announcements that mattered nothing at all.

"Mrs. Englewood is returning to England," said Fitz, his tone remarkably even.

Millie glanced at him—to not give the news at least that much attention would be unnatural. "Captain Englewood has resigned his commission, then?"

Fitz reached for his coffee. "Captain Englewood is no more."

"Oh," said Millie. Mrs. Englewood was a widow. The thought clanged loudly in her head. "How did he die? He was your age, wasn't he?"

"Tropical fever—and he was five years older than me."

"I see. When did he pass away?"

"March of last year."

Millie blinked. Mrs. Englewood was not only a widow, but a widow already out of her year-and-a-day deep mourning, free to move in Society. "That was thirteen months ago. How did we not learn sooner?"

"According to her, Captain Englewood's mother had been in failing health. As she was not expected to last long, when he expired suddenly it was decided to keep the news quiet, as the death of her firstborn would cause her too much grief in her final days. But she lingered on for longer than everyone thought she would."

Millie felt a sharp pang of sympathy for Captain Englewood's mother, who no doubt hoped to see her son one last time. "They should have told her the truth. Or she'd have gone to her death thinking he couldn't spare the time to come see her."

"They did at last," said Fitz quietly. "And she passed away ten days later."

Tears stung the rim of Millie's eyes. She remembered her own mother's deathbed. Fitz had moved heaven and earth for her to return to England in time and for that she would always be grateful to him.

She took a deep breath. "When is Mrs. Englewood expected to be back?"

"In June."

A month before their eight-year pact ran out in July. "In time to have a bit of fun in London, I see. I'm sure she must be looking forward to it."

Fitz did not answer.

Millie took another bite of her toast, swallowed it with the help of a whole cup of tea, and rose. "Well, look at the time. I'd better get Helena ready. She has a fitting this morning that Venetia made me swear I would not forget."

"You barely ate anything," he pointed out.

Why must he also notice that? Why did he do these little things that gave her hope?

211

"I was already full when you came," she said. "If you will excuse me."

*C*hristian worked.

He inspected half of his holdings in person, read innumerable accounts and reports, and even did his duty as a member of the House of Lords. His peers were astonished to see him: The Dukes of Lexington had always taken a seat in the Upper House, but this particular duke, famously indifferent to politics, rarely presented himself in Parliament.

Books and letters stuffed all the remaining minutes of his waking hours.

But he needn't have been so meticulous. His mind, so long geared toward truth and rationality, now revealed itself to be quite capable of the sort of self-deception he had formerly scorned. For nearly a whole week, like a tiptoeing night burglar, he successfully skirted any and all memories and discernments that could raise the least alarm.

Then everything came crashing down. Logic was inexorable. Truth would not be denied. The evidence, having bided its time, waited for his mind to be lulled into a state of false security to mount an all-out assault on his slumbering defenses.

There was never a Baroness von Seidlitz-Hardenberg. There was only ever Mrs. Easterbrook. And he'd confided everything to her.

Everything.

No wonder she'd been so eager to depart the *Rhodesia*. She'd extracted all knowledge of his inner turbulences; there was nothing else left to learn. And no wonder she'd been so smug every time he'd encountered her since. Forevermore she'd be able to look at him and laugh, knowing just how well and truly she'd subjugated him.

Her scheme was sordid; its success, overwhelming. And he had participated wholeheartedly and loved her with everything good and worthwhile in him.

He threw the gold-embossed menus that had been printed for the dinner at the Savoy in the fire and blanketed the ashes with all the letters he'd written her, one for every day leading up to the dinner, and the last while he awaited the *Rhodesia*'s return from Hamburg. He could not quite believe it: He still wrote her after she'd reneged on her promise and given back his gift. He'd only stopped after he saw the plaque bearing her maiden name at the museum.

He prodded the burning letters with the fireplace poker. The poker was solid and heavy in his hand. He wanted to smash something with it, a great many somethings: the marble mantel, the gilt-framed mirror, the Sèvres vases. He wanted to destroy the room until nothing remained but rubble and wreckage.

But he was Christian de Montfort, the Duke of Lexington. He did not make a spectacle of his pain. He did not give in to childish rages. And he would maintain his dignity and composure, even when his heart had been dragged through a forest of knives.

A knock came at the door. Christian frowned. He'd made it clear to his staff that he was not to be disturbed. His staff was well trained and highly competent. He could only assume that there had been an emergency.

"Mrs. Easterbrook to see you, Your Grace," said Owens, the head footman.

His heart pounded violently. Come to gloat, had she?

"Did I not specify that I am not at home this afternoon?"

"You did, sir," said Owens apologetically. "But Mrs. Easterbrook, she said you'd wish to see her."

Indeed, how could anyone believe, gazing upon her radiant, hypnotic beauty, that he did not want to see her?

To reprimand Owens would be counterproductive. And for her to call on him, to acknowledge this fraud of hers, was a kindness, whether she understood it or not. Let them end their affair today with a complete rupture, everything laid out in the open, all illusions and false hopes lined up and shot.

"I will see her here," he said, "in five minutes."

He needed at least that much time to put himself together.

*V*enetia was faintly surprised Christian agreed to see her—faintly as she was not capable of feeling much else besides terror, a bloated thing with claws in her stomach and tentacles up her throat.

Her days away from London had been good for her health—a more Spartan diet had quieted her stomach and averted further episodes of morning sickness—but her mind had grown increasingly troubled as she considered her choices.

She was fortunate to possess both funds and freedom of movement. She could choose to spend autumn and winter somewhere abroad, give birth in secret, and find a good foster home for the child here in England—if, that was, she could bear to be parted from the child.

She'd thought with great seriousness of begging Fitz

and Millie for help. Millie could go away with her and then return to England pretending the child were hers. It was as good a solution as could be found under the circumstances. She trusted her brother and sister-in-law to be good parents, and she herself, as the doting aunt, could visit as often as she wanted and watch the child grow up.

Were the baby a boy, however, he'd be considered Fitz's heir. And Fitz and Millie's own firstborn son, should they have one in the future, would be robbed of his rightful inheritance. Other seemingly infertile couples had produced children after long droughts, and it would be selfish of Venetia to assume that Fitz and Millie wouldn't.

Which led her to the option of marrying, herself. Finding a suitable groom should not be an impossible task. There were other men like Mr. Easterbrook. Failing that, perhaps a widower with sons of his own, sufficiently enamored of her to not mind giving his name to someone else's child.

But her thoughts always came back to the duke. The child was his. He might not want his flesh and blood raised in another man's household. And perhaps, just perhaps, he deserved to know that he was about to become a father.

Except, for him to know, she'd have to confess everything, the prospect of which had caused her to flee as if he were Mount Vesuvius and she a hapless resident of Pompeii. How could she voluntarily face his wrath?

And yet here she was, in the anteroom of his house, her palms damp, her stomach pitching, her heart beating so hard she was nearly cross-eyed.

The footman reappeared. "This way, please, Mrs. Easterbrook."

She walked, but couldn't quite feel her feet. It was not

yet too late to turn around and take flight, reasoned the voice of her self-preservation. The duke was not going to chase her out into the streets to find out why she'd come to see him.

Run. You only believe you can do it because you have not thought this through. This confession is not some short-lived pain to be endured for half an hour. You have no idea what he is going to do. If he chooses to, he could make you miserable for the rest of your life.

The footman opened the door to a study. "Mrs. Easterbrook, sir."

Her throat tightened. She couldn't even swallow. She teetered upon the threshold—two seconds or a hundred years?—then suddenly she was inside, the footman leaving, closing the door behind her.

Almost immediately her eyes were drawn to a photograph on the mantel. She'd been too nerve-stricken to notice anything of the house, but this portrait she saw all too clearly: the young duke and his stepmother, each holding a handful of darts, standing together next to a tree.

We threw darts at a tree instead.

He had been honest and forthright. She had been everything but. And now she must suffer the consequences of her action.

The duke did not rise to greet her; he was already standing before a window. "Mrs. Easterbrook," he said without turning around, surveying the street beneath. "To what do I owe the pleasure of this visit?"

She had racked her brains over how to approach the matter, but only the simplest words emerged from her parched throat. "Your Grace, I am with child."

His head lifted abruptly. An awful silence smothered

the room. At last he said, "And what do you want me to do about it?"

"The child is yours."

"You are certain?"

His sangfroid momentarily shocked her out of her fright. He ought to be outraged, and yet here he was, acting as if the only unexpected news was her pregnancy.

"You know it was me on the *Rhodesia*? *How*?"

"Does it matter?" His tone was arctic.

She looked down at the carpet. Her actions were egregious enough. But for him to have discovered her deceit on his own somehow made everything worse. "To answer your previous question, yes, I am certain the child is yours."

"You are a wealthy woman. I imagine you have not come to ask for money."

"No, I have not."

"What do you want?"

"I—I hoped you might advise me on that."

"Why do you think I'd have advice to offer? Do I appear to be in the habit of regularly impregnating women?"

"No, of course not."

"And did you not inform me that you could not conceive?"

Did he think that she'd have deliberately misled him, in order to put herself in this untenable situation? "I did."

"How do I know you are telling the truth?"

"Concerning my erstwhile infertility? I can give you the names of the physicians who examined me."

"No, concerning your current state of health."

He meant her pregnancy. Her head spun. "You think I'd lie about it?"

She regretted it immediately: That was precisely the wrong thing to say.

He did not miss the opportunity. "You must admit, Mrs. Easterbrook, you lie about an astonishing range of things."

She took a deep breath. "I will admit that I can hardly consider myself creditable before you. But what advantage does it garner me to pretend that I am with child when I am not? The situation presents only inconvenience."

"Oh, I'm sure there is no advantage at all to carrying my child."

She had not imagined their conversation could turn in this particular direction. Was it truly so advantageous to be an unmarried woman carrying the Duke of Lexington's child?

Or was he in denial, as she had been? To accept the pregnancy as fact was to accept that there was no walking away from this affair, that its significance would reverberate in his life for the foreseeable future and beyond.

"Is there not a scientific principle that the simplest explanation tends to be the correct one?"

"And what is your simple explanation, Mrs. Easterbrook?"

"That I was stupid and did not prepare for the possibility of conception."

He turned around at last. Her heart ached. He'd become even thinner, his cheekbones prominent and sharp.

"What *did* you prepare for?"

"I beg your pardon?"

"A woman such as yourself does not cover her face without a reason. What did you mean to achieve?"

She wanted to explain her entire life leading up to his lecture at Harvard, the bouquet that had been sent to her room by mistake, and her rage-driven, slightly incoherent scheme. She wanted to tell him how he'd upended her entire plan and laid siege to her heart. And she wanted to let him know that it was the greatest mistake of her life, not revealing herself the moment she realized that she'd fallen in love.

But he would not believe a word of it. Not now. And not—she abruptly realized—ever.

Because he was a man trained to examine only facts, and the following were the indisputable facts: She had seduced him under false pretenses; she had wrested a proposal of marriage from him; she had promptly disappeared; and she had subsequently reneged on her promise to meet him again, all the while dancing with him, speaking with him, and watching him fester in his anxiety and misery.

He would not care to listen that she had changed her mind. That it had been wrenching for her to let him go— and even more so to stand before him a despised stranger. These emotions could not be scientifically tested; therefore they were nonfactors, utterly invalid and irrelevant.

She already knew this. She'd known all this from the beginning. But the pregnancy must have destroyed her common sense. Because she had come terrified but not without a sliver of hope—that she might be able to elucidate matters, to shed such a powerfully reasonable light on them that he would see her point of view.

When her love was the single most irrational and inexplicable aspect in this entire story.

"Have you anything to say for yourself?" he asked.

The coolness of his voice sent sharp pains though her. She had feared condemnation. She had never thought she'd prefer condemnation to dismissal. A condemnation was a passionate gesture, fueled by strength of feeling. A dismissal was . . . nothing at all.

She could not speak to a dismissal of love and helpless yearning. She could not speak to a dismissal of waiting outside his town house for a glimpse of him. She could not speak to a dismissal of her hopes for the future, of moving beyond this impasse and forging ahead.

Before a dismissal, and particularly one as grand and condescending as his, she had no choice but to be the Great Beauty. The Great Beauty did not have much to recommend her. But no one dismissed the Great Beauty.

"What I wanted, of course, was your heart on a plate," said the Great Beauty.

*C*hristian was cold despite the roaring fire in the grate, as cold as the trees in his garden, shivering in the rain.

"And what was the nature of your interest in my heart, exactly?"

She smiled. "I wanted to break it—I was there at your Harvard lecture."

How could cruelty ever be beautiful? Yet she was incandescent. "Because of what I'd said?"

"Precisely."

"Does that not validate my opinion of you?"

"Maybe. But you'd have a broken heart to go along with it, wouldn't you?"

A muscle twitched at the corner of his eye—at last he knew who he was dealing with. "An elegant plan," he said slowly. "A despicable one, but elegant nevertheless."

She shrugged. "Alas that I should be fertile after all. I'd much rather put you behind me once and for all."

For no reason at all he thought of the sweetness of resting his head in her lap, her fingers combing through his hair as they talked of nothing and everything. He should have left well enough alone; at least he'd have enjoyed the memories. Now he had nothing—less than nothing.

"I'm sure you would," he said, his voice uninflected.

"Well then, I have troubled you long enough," she said brightly. "Good day, sir. I will see myself out."

It was not until she was almost at the door that he recalled himself. "Not yet. We have not yet discussed what to do about the child."

She shrugged again. "The child will present no problem to a woman such as myself. I will find someone to marry me, which should be as simple as picking out a new hat. Simpler, if I may say so: These days millinery is convoluted and time-consuming. Why, last time it took me an hour to decide on all the trimmings."

Christian narrowed his eyes. "The poor dupe will be unwittingly raising someone else's bastard?"

His scowls were famously quelling. They had no effect upon Mrs. Easterbrook whatsoever.

"I can tell him if you like. Would you also like me to inform him of your identity?"

She laughed, obviously finding her own quip very funny. Her laughter was the sound of wind chimes, clear and melodious. As arrogant and callous as she was, there was not a single sensory aspect of hers that was anything less than perfection.

"I will not allow my child to be brought up in the household of anyone stupid and gullible enough to marry you."

"Well, that certainly eliminates you from contention, doesn't it? You, sir, wished to marry me, too, if I recall correctly."

She actually dared to remind him of it. Shame and anger jostled in him, both scalding hot. "I wished to marry the Baroness von Seidlitz-Hardenberg, which speaks poorly of my intelligence, but not nearly so poorly as if I had wanted to marry *you*."

She smiled, imperious, impervious. "We can stand here all day and trade insults, Your Grace. But I have appointments to keep—and new hats to select. If you do not wish your child brought up in a respectable household, do you have any better solutions to propose? Mind you, I cannot have scandals: I still have a sister to marry."

"Swear on your sister's life that you are carrying my child."

"I swear."

"Then I will marry you, for the sake of the child. But if you are lying, I will divorce you in the most public manner possible."

She looked at him a minute, her gaze limpid and unreadable. "I take it that by agreeing to marry you, I will not need to see to a wedding gown or a wedding breakfast."

"No. I will obtain a special license. We will marry before the number of witnesses as required by law. If you wish to bring members of your family, suit yourself—but I will leave mine out of this disgrace."

"And afterward? Do we go our separate ways?" Her tone was light and sarcastic.

"I will leave that to you. You may return to your own

residence or you may take up residence here. It makes no difference to me."

"How tempting. I'm sure I've never been proposed to more sweetly."

The muscle to the right of his eye leaped again.

She set her hand on the door handle. "You have a fortnight for the license, Your Grace. Afterward I'll let it be known that I am in need of a husband."

CHAPTER 16

Madam,

This is to inform you that I have the special license in hand. We will marry at ten o'clock tomorrow morning at St. Paul's Church in Onslow Square.

Yrs.,
Lexington

~

Sir,

This is to inform you that I have decided to take up residence in your house after all. Pray have it in a state of readiness for my arrival.

Sincerely,
Mrs. Easterbrook

Madam,

I will be removing to Algernon House tomorrow afternoon.

Yrs.,
Lexington

~

Sir,

Of course, a country honeymoon. I approve.

Sincerely,
Mrs. Easterbrook

P.S. In the country I require a fleet, tireless, and a mild-tempered mare and lavender-scented sheets.

enetia had kept the blue brocade gown she'd worn to marry Mr. Easterbrook, but she did not dare leave the house in something that was so obviously not a promenade dress.

She still did not quite believe that the duke would marry her. The terrible thing about having lied so overwhelmingly to him was that now she did not feel that he owed her any truth. That if he were but playing a cruel prank, she had no one to blame but herself.

She arrived at the church fifteen minutes early. He was already there in the pews, sitting with his head bowed.

At the sound of her footsteps, he slowly rose, turned

around—and frowned. He was in a morning coat, the most formal item in a gentleman's wardrobe for daytime, *the* thing to wear to one's own wedding. She, on the other hand, looked as if she'd been taking a stroll in the park and had but stopped by to satisfy her curiosity concerning the interior of the church.

"Well, I'm here," she said. "And I didn't make you wait."

His countenance darkened. Belatedly she remembered how gladly he'd waited for her on the *Rhodesia*—she was beginning to display quite a talent for saying all the wrong things.

"Let's proceed," he said coolly.

"Where are our witnesses?"

"Arranging flowers in the vestry."

The clergyman was already standing before the altar. He stared at Venetia as she approached. She recognized the signs of danger. When she'd said to the duke that she had a certain effect on men, she hadn't been exaggerating. It was not every man and it was not all the time, but when the effect happened, proposals flew like confetti and all parties involved usually ended up feeling quite mortified.

Perspiration beaded on the man's forehead. "Will you—"

"Yes, I do consent to be married to His Grace," she said hastily. "Won't you please call our witnesses?"

This didn't seem quite enough. "I know we've never met," said the clergyman, "but ma'am—"

"I'm very grateful that you can marry us on such a short notice, Reverend. Please, if there is anything we can do for your parish and for this lovely church, you must let us know."

The man cleared his throat. "I—uh—I—uh—yes, pleased to oblige, ma'am."

Venetia breathed a sigh of relief. She sneaked a peek at

the duke. His face was impassive: She might have stopped the clergyman from making a fool of himself, but the duke had guessed quite well what the man had been on the verge of doing.

And he blamed her for it.

The witnesses were called. The clergyman, having recovered his wits, now looked anywhere but at Venetia. He rushed through the prayers and asked her to repeat the vows after him.

As she followed the mumbling clergyman, she couldn't help a shudder of misery. What was she doing? Was she still clinging to some illusion that one day he might again become the lover he had been on the *Rhodesia*? And betting the rest of her life on it? Even a marriage begun in hope and goodwill could turn terrible. What hope did this union have, sealed by such antagonism and distrust?

The duke recited his vows with remarkable dispassion— Venetia had heard Fitz memorize his Latin declensions with greater feeling. Where was the man who wanted to spend every waking minute with her? Who was willing to brave every obstacle to be closer to her?

The worst thing about this forced nuptial was that they had been their true selves on the *Rhodesia*. And yet the two people tying the knot today were but their facades, the Great Beauty and the haughty, unfeeling duke.

Would she ever see his true self again? And would she ever dare let him see hers?

*H*elena was going out of her mind.

The cost of paper had gone up again. Two manuscripts she'd been waiting on continued to make her wait.

Susie, her new jailor, sat outside her office embroidering a stack of new handkerchiefs with the patience of a hundred-year-old tortoise. Yet Helena would have been all right had Andrew come for his official appointment this morning at Fitzhugh & Co., to receive the first copy, fresh off the printing press, of the second volume of his *History of East Anglia*.

Three weeks it had been since her return to England, three long, frustrating weeks, especially after she received his last letter, the day after the ball at the Tremaines's. He'd been abjectly apologetic, claiming that he'd seen the error of his ways and would no longer do anything to endanger her reputation.

Damn her reputation. Would no one think of her happiness?

Andrew's mother had fully recovered from the bout of fever that had everyone worried—Helena even saw her at a function, looking frailed but determined. He, however, continued to be absent from all social milieus. The only time she'd run into him had been on a drive with Millie, and she hadn't dared more than a smile and a nod.

And now this canceled appointment.

She paced. But that only made her more agitated. So she sat down, glanced through a batch of letters, and sliced open a manuscript package. The manuscript was for a children's book. Fitzhugh & Co. did not publish children's books, but the illustration of the two small ducks on the first page was so charming that against her will she turned the page.

And fell into an hour of pure magic.

The manuscript of a dozen stories featuring the same cast of adorable animal characters. She loved them all. But they were not arranged in quite the right order. With a few nudges and adjustments to the stories, they could be presented in a seasonal, chronological sequence. She would publish the first story on its own in September, then one book a month for the eleven months to follow. The stories would build in popularity and demand, and she would publish them in a handsome boxed set for the following Christmas.

She burst out of her inner sanctum into the reception room beyond.

"Miss Boyle, I want you to immediately send a letter to"—she glanced down at the manuscript in her hand—"Miss Evangeline South and offer her one hundred twenty pounds for the copyright of her collection. Or our usual terms of commissions. Ask her to reply at her earliest—"

Hastings was seated by the window, drinking tea.

"What are you doing here?"

"I volunteered to come and fetch you—Mrs. Easterbrook has convened a family luncheon," he answered. "You should have a telephone installed, by the way, so I needn't come all the way."

"You needn't—that is the very definition of volunteerism, is it not?" she retorted. "And why are you involved in a family luncheon?"

"I didn't say I was attending the luncheon, only that I would deliver you to Fitz's house."

"But Miss Boyle and—"

"I have ordered a basket of foodstuff from Harrods. Your employees will have a very fine luncheon. Now shall we? My carriage awaits."

As she had no good objections that could be voiced before her maid and her secretary, she finished giving directions to Miss Boyle, buttoned her jacket, and preceded him out of the door and into the carriage.

"A hundred twenty pounds for the copyright, which you will hold for at least forty-two years—that is a miserly offer, is it not?" asked Hastings as he signaled the coachman to start.

"I will have you know Miss Austen received all of one hundred ten pounds for the copyright to *Pride and Prejudice*. And that was at a time when the pound sterling was quite weak due to expenditures of the Napoleonic Wars."

"She was robbed. Will you similarly rob Miss South?"

"Miss South is free to write me with a counteroffer. She also has the option of publishing by commission, if she does not want a sizable sum up front."

Hastings grinned. "You are a shrewd woman, Miss Fitzhugh."

"Thank you, Lord Hastings."

"Which makes it even more incomprehensible what you see in Mr. Martin."

"I will tell you what I see in him, sir: an openness of spirit, a capacity for wonder, an utter lack of cynicism."

"You know what I see in him, Miss Fitzhugh?"

"No, I do not."

"Cowardice. When you first met, he wasn't even engaged."

It was just like Hastings to find the sore point in everything. "There was an expectation of long standing."

"A man should not live his life by the expectations of others."

"Not everyone lives his life solely to pursue his own pleasures."

"But you and I both do."

A year ago, she'd have categorically rejected that statement. But to do that now would make her a hypocrite. She turned her face to the window and wished again that she had pushed Andrew to defy his mother.

Her failure to do so had changed her. In many ways for the better: When she came into her inheritance, she did not hesitate a moment before using it as capital for her publishing venture—she would never let another one of her heart's desires get away from her. Once she had her arrangements in place, she'd refused to let Andrew keep his manuscript locked away. The reviews he'd received upon the publication of the first volume had him walking on air for months, thanking her profusely every time he saw her.

But at the same time, the loss of Andrew had closed an invisible door in her. The happiness they'd once shared became sacrosanct. No other man could come close to replacing him; no man ought to even try.

She wanted only what she should have had, in an ideal world.

itz whistled as he skimmed the report in his hand. Millie had never known him before he was saddled with a crumbling estate. For a man whose hopes in life had been brutally suffocated, except for one brief period, he'd conducted himself with unimpeachable dignity, burying his disappointment and devoting himself to his duties.

Not that there was anything undignified about a man whistling in the privacy of his own home—she only wished it had happened sooner. That he hadn't needed a letter from Mrs. Englewood to inspire it.

She'd thought they'd had some good times, too. The Christmas gathering had become a lovely tradition at Henley Park. Their friends eagerly anticipated their annual shooting party in August. Not to mention all the successes they'd had with Cresswell & Graves, nurturing the near-moribund firm into the brawny enterprise it was at present.

Except, none of these achievements had ever made him whistle.

Nor was it just the whistling. It was the faraway look in his eye, the secret smile on his lips. It was that his entire aspect had changed, from a conscientious married man who dealt with accounts, tenants, and bankers to an unburdened youth with only dreams and adventures on his mind.

The boy he had been, before Fate had shown its harsh hand.

And that was something Millie could never share with him, that glorious, carefree adolescence he had known before she'd arrived in his life, marking the beginning of the end.

"I hope I haven't inconvenienced everyone greatly, calling for a luncheon out of the blue."

Millie was startled out of her thoughts. Venetia sauntered into the drawing room, looking ineffably lovely. "No, of course not," Millie said. "I was already home and the company is most welcome."

Fitz tossed aside the report and grinned at his sister. "Have you missed us since breakfast or is there another reason for . . ."

He fell silent. Millie saw it at the same time: the ring on Venetia's left hand.

"Yes," said Venetia, looking down at her wedding band. "I've eloped."

Flabbergasted, Millie glanced at her husband, who looked not quite as staggered as she'd have expected him to.

"Who's the lucky chap?" he asked.

Venetia smiled. Millie couldn't tell whether it was a happy smile, exactly, but it was so dazzling it left her with little dots dancing on her retinas. "Lexington."

At last Fitz looked as shocked as Millie felt. "Interesting choice."

Helena swept into the room. "Why are we speaking of Lexington again?"

Venetia extended her left hand toward Helena. The gold band on her ring finger gleamed softly. "We are married, Lexington and I."

Helena laughed outright. When no one else joined her, her jaw dropped. "You are not serious, Venetia. You can't be."

Venetia's cheer was undampened. "Last I checked, today is not the first of April."

"But why?" Helena cried.

"When?" asked Fitz at the same time.

"This morning. The announcement will be in the papers tomorrow." Venetia smiled again. "I can't wait to see his museum."

It took Millie a moment to remember Lexington's private natural history collection and the enthusiasm Venetia had expressed for it. But that was a continent away and all playacting. Was Venetia's seeming pleasure all playacting, too?

"But why so soon?" she asked.

"And why didn't you tell us anything?" Helena was beside herself. "We could have prevented you from making this terrible decision."

Fitz frowned. "Helena, is that any way to speak to Venetia on her wedding day?"

"You weren't there," Helena said impatiently. "You didn't hear all the hateful things he said about her."

Fitz considered Venetia. His gaze dropped to her waist.

It was a quick, discreet look—had Millie not been paying close attention, she wouldn't have noticed.

"Tell me the truth now, Venetia," he said. "Did you enjoy your crossing?"

The question seemed a complete non sequitur. To Millie's surprise, Venetia flushed.

"Yes," she answered.

"And you are sure of Lexington's character?"

"Yes."

"Then congratulations."

"You can't congratulate her," Helena protested. "This is all a horrible mistake."

"Helena, you will refrain from speaking disrespectfully of our brother-in-law in my presence. If Lexington has risen enough in Venetia's esteem, then it is time you set aside your prejudices and accept her decision."

Fitz rarely stepped into the paterfamilias role, but his quiet rebuke brooked no dissent. Helena bit her lip and looked aside. The glance from Venetia was grateful and surprised.

"Will you be leaving on your honeymoon very soon, Venetia?" Fitz asked.

"Yes, this afternoon."

"Let us not stand around, then," said Fitz. "You will have a thousand details to see to between now and then. Shall we start with the luncheon?"

As gentlemen did not wear wedding bands, Christian was not immediately accosted by questions from his stepmother. But she had to know that he would not have asked to see her alone unless he had something important to say.

They both bided their time. He inquired into the comforts of the house she and Mr. Kingston had hired for the Season. She spoke of the delightful little garden that had come with. It was not until they'd come to the conclusion of the meal that the topic turned to his private life.

"Any news concerning your lady from the *Rhodesia*, my dear?"

He stirred the coffee that had been put down before him. "Stepmama, you know how I feel about those who do not keep their words."

She had sent a note the morning after asking about the dinner, and he'd told her the truth—that he'd been disappointed. He'd also said in the same note that he planned to find out the reason behind his lady's nonattendance and would let the dowager duchess know as soon as he learned anything. On this latter promise he had not quite followed through.

"Was that all it took to turn your affection? Did you not find out why she broke the appointment?"

"Yes, I did, as a matter of fact." The coffee, a very good brew, tasted far too much like the cup he'd been sipping when Mrs. Easterbrook had strode to his table that first night on the *Rhodesia*. Such an erotic charge she'd brought with her. He hadn't been able to taste black coffee since without feeling a surge of the same anticipation.

He poured a liberal amount of sugar and cream into the coffee. "Unfortunately, what I'd thought of as a life-changing event was but a game to her."

The dowager duchess pushed away the remainder of her Nesselrode pudding. "Oh, Christian. I'm so sorry."

You have no idea. "Let's speak no more of it. It's water under the bridge."

"Is it?"

The passage of time had not dulled the pain and humiliation of it. If anything, now that the shock had worn off, now that he knew exactly how she had executed her plan, every memory was an open wound.

"She used and discarded me; I've nothing more to say of her." Except he had to go on speaking of her. "I meant to tell you: I am married."

"I'm sorry, I must have heard you wrong. What did you say?"

"Mrs. Easterbrook became my wife this morning."

She stared at him, her incredulity giving way to shock as she realized he had not spoken in jest. "Why was I not told? Why was I not *there*?"

"We chose to elope."

"I don't understand the haste—or the secrecy. In the time it took to obtain a special license you could have very well informed me of your plans."

She was the closest thing he had to a mother. He had worried her and now he'd hurt her, all because he'd been too stupid to know he'd been had. "I do apologize. I hope you will forgive me."

She shook her head. "You have not offended me, my dear—I am thunderstruck. Why this cloak-and-dagger elopement? And why Mrs. Easterbrook? I was not under the impression that you were particularly fond of her."

"I am not." At least that was the truth.

"Then why marry her? You have made your choice as if wives were items on a menu, taking the fish when there is no more steak left. I'm—you have baffled me completely, Christian."

And disappointed her. She did not need to say those words, he knew. For him to exclude her from one of the most significant events of his life, and to have entered into marriage so cavalierly—or at least give the impression of having done so—he must come off as someone she scarcely knew.

He hardened his tone. "I've done my duty, Stepmama. I've married. Let us not inquire too deeply into the reasons."

She gave him a saddened but no less astute look. "Are you all right, Christian?"

"I'll be fine," he said. Then, correcting himself, "I *am* fine."

"And your wife? Does she know about your lady from the *Rhodesia*?"

He could not quite disguise his bitterness. "Doesn't everyone?"

"Does she mind?"

"I do not believe she cares at all."

"Christian—"

"I hate to be so rude, Stepmama. But my duchess"—saying the word felt like swallowing sand—"and I are departing for our honeymoon posthaste. I cannot linger."

"Christian—"

He closed his hand over hers. "I am now the most envied man in all of England. Be happy for me, Stepmama."

*C*hristian had no sooner seen off his stepmother than his butler inquired, "Earl Fitzhugh is here, Your Grace. Are you at home to him?"

Of course, his new bride's brother, here to make noises of displeasure at how unceremoniously he'd carried off the beautiful Mrs. Easterbrook. The former Mrs. Easterbrook. "I'm at home."

As Fitzhugh was shown in, he was struck by the family resemblance. What had she said? *A brother and a sister—twins—both two years younger than I am.* He should have suspected then and there—he knew very well the composition of her family. But the former Mrs. Easterbrook had been the furthest thing from his mind when she'd been lying directly beneath, beside, or on top of him.

"Will you take some cognac to toast my wedding?" he asked as he shook Fitzhugh's hand. He had no cause to be uncivil to this new brother-in-law.

"Spirits interfere with my digestion, alas. But I'll take a cup of coffee."

Christian rang for the beverage to be brought in.

"We were all taken aback," said Fitzhugh, making himself comfortable in a high-back chair. "Had no idea you'd been wooing my sister."

Neither did I, as a matter of fact. "We kept it quiet."

"I find it interesting that you said a great deal that was less than complimentary about her. Yet of the two of you, she is not the one who is angry; you are."

He didn't have the luxury of a near-perfect vengeance. "You will forgive me for not discussing personal sentiments with a virtual stranger."

"Of course I did not expect you to confide in me, sir."

The earl's eminently reasonable manner was beginning to surprise Christian.

"My sister, too, prefers to keep personal sentiments personal. But sometimes a brother sees things and draws his own conclusions. Of course, without her express permission, I am not at liberty to discuss private particulars of her life, but I will step on no one's toes in saying a few things about Mr. Easterbrook's passing."

Mr. Easterbrook, her wealthy second husband who had died alone. "What of it?"

"According to what Lady Fitzhugh has related to me, you seem to be under the misapprehension that my sister abandoned her husband on his deathbed. I was there that day. I assure you nothing could be further from the truth."

"You will have me believe she was at his bedside, holding his hand as he drew his last breath?"

"Nothing of the sort. She was downstairs, along with my wife, holding his family at bay, denying them permission, as the lady of the house, to move a single step beyond the drawing room."

"Why would she do that?"

"Because by his bedside, holding his hand, was someone Mr. Easterbrook desperately wanted to be present as he drew his last breath. His family would have removed said person and denied him his dying wish. Venetia was very loyal to Mr. Easterbrook. We all were. Lord Hastings and my younger sister were stationed on the staircase and I myself directly before the door of Mr. Easterbrook's bedchamber, in case anyone got past Venetia.

"Mr. Easterbrook's family was not pleased. Afterward, they made a concerted effort to smear my sister's good name. To protect Mr. Easterbrook even in death, she allowed it."

Christian set one finger at the midpoint of a fountain pen lying on his desk. "Mr. Townsend—are you not going to say something about him?"

"He falls under those private particulars that she will not wish me to discuss."

"Did he kill himself?"

"As I said, it is not my place."

The coffee tray arrived, but Earl Fitzhugh had already risen from his seat. "I should not take up any more of a man's time on his wedding day."

*T*hey were all so young in the photograph—except the dinosaur skeleton, which was terribly old. Helena, at fourteen, had been the tallest of them all—this was before her twin had shot up and overtaken her in height. Fitz looked as if he was trying hard not to laugh—his pictures from those years were all full of the suppressed mirth of a boy who enjoyed everything about life. Then there was Venetia, as proud as a general who had won a decisive battle, her bare hand braced—perhaps somewhat indecorously—upon the remains of the *Cetiosaurus*'s rump.

Had she been headed anywhere else, she would not have hesitated to take the photograph—she'd have packed it before anything else. But she was not sure whether she wanted it in Christian's house. He would not appreciate the reminder that he'd so enthusiastically encouraged her—the baroness—in her pursuit, or that he'd offered her a place on his next expedition.

She set the photograph facedown and turned around. Cobble, Fitz's butler, stood in the open doorway of her bedroom, waiting to speak to her.

"Yes, Cobble?"

"The Dowager Duchess of Lexington to see you, ma'am."

So the duke had informed his stepmother. One could only wonder at her reaction.

"I'll be down in the green parlor presently."

240

Time to play the Great Beauty again.

Sweeping into the green parlor, she smiled. "Your Grace, what a pleasure."

The Great Beauty had her desired effect. The dowager duchess hesitated—and squinted, as if too bright a light had been thrust into her face.

Venetia took her seat with a flourish of skirts gracefully flounced aside. "Have you come to congratulate me, ma'am? I am beyond thrilled to be married to Lexington."

This, however, had a sobering effect on the older woman. "Are you, duchess?"

Duchess. Venetia was now the Duchess of Lexington.

"I enjoy fossils, especially those from the Cretaceous Age. The duke has quite a collection of them. I am excited to visit his private museum—and to perhaps someday curate it."

This was not an answer the dowager duchess had expected. "You married him for his *fossils*?"

"Have you seen my dinosaur at the British Museum of Natural History, ma'am? A magnificent specimen. I've waited more than a decade for the chance to discover another one. By becoming Lexington's wife I will be able to go on expeditions with him, something I've wanted to do my entire adult life."

The dowager duchess's fingers dug into her skirts. "What of your bridegroom? Do you also care for him?"

Venetia was at her most charmingly flippant. "How can I not love a man who will take me fossil-hunting?"

The dowager duchess rose and walked to the Japanese screen at a corner of the parlor. A lady in a flowing kimono sat beneath a cherry tree in full bloom, her face in her hand, her melancholy as heavy as the flower-laden boughs that drooped almost to the bare ground.

Tea was brought in. Venetia poured. "Africa, I do believe, shall be our next destination. The Karoo beds are a treasure trove for reptilian remains, from what I hear. Sugar and milk, ma'am?"

The dowager duchess turned around. "Does it not matter to you that he has recently expressed some terribly unfavorable opinions of you?"

"It was certainly heartening that he came to see the light so quickly."

"Even though he is in love with someone else?"

Venetia set down the teapot and extended her hand toward the creamer. All the years of not digging for fossils had left her fingers slender and lovely. She made sure she showed them to their best advantage. "If you speak of the lady on the *Rhodesia*, I believe she has disappointed him terribly."

"And you are content to be his consolation prize?"

If only she were any kind of prize to him. "That is for me to decide, ma'am, and I've already decided."

The dowager duchess at last took her seat again. The bewildered kinswoman, however, had disappeared. The woman who faced Venetia was a lioness. "He is much more than a mere collector of fossils, duchess. He is one of the best men I've ever met, and his happiness matters intensely to me. If you want him only for his ability to take you to the Karoo beds, well, most of the year he will not be anywhere exotic or exciting. Like any other good squire, he will be looking after his land and its people. And that is what he will require of you. Are you prepared to be a good wife to him?"

Venetia felt a great tension in her draining away. Here

was someone who loved him as fiercely as she did. Someone for whom she need not play the Great Beauty.

"I'm sorry I have been so terribly flippant," she said quietly. "In truth I am heartsick."

She could see her reflection in the large mirror above the mantel. She looked very much like the kimonoed lady on the Japanese screen, burdened and forlorn.

The dowager duchess's hands locked in her lap. "Are you?"

"He hasn't changed his mind about me at all—but I've fallen in love with him."

"I see," said the dowager duchess, her tone politely incredulous.

"Yes, it's quite awful. Not to mention that he'd have preferred the lady from the ocean liner." Venetia looked the dowager duchess in the eye. "I cannot promise to make him happy. But I can promise you, unconditionally, that his well-being will always be foremost on my mind."

The dowager duchess's gaze turned thoughtful. "Those opinions he'd expressed at Harvard . . ."

"About my late husbands? He is misinformed. But I'm afraid his mind is set."

The older woman made no response. They drank their tea in silence. Elsewhere in the house Venetia's trunks were being lugged down the stairs. The brougham had already pulled up by the curb. Through the open window came her maid's voice, cautioning the menservants to have a care with her mistress's things.

"I must not impose on you any longer," said the dowager duchess, setting down her teacup.

"Would you like me to give him your regards when I

see him or would you prefer that I keep the meeting between ourselves?"

"You may give my regards to him—he must know that I would not have sat on my hands after he gave me such news."

"Of course. It's what we do for those we love."

They rose and shook hands.

"If I may give you one piece of advice," said the dowager duchess. "If you believe the duke is wrong about you, you must let him know. He can be quite formidable, but he is never closed-minded and never resentful at being corrected."

The baroness would not have hesitated; Venetia was not sure she had that sort of courage. But she nodded. "I will remember that, Your Grace."

*T*here was a reason adolescent dreams usually remained in adolescence: They were extravagant and frankly dangerous at times.

She—or rather, the possession of her—had been his adolescent dream. What did it matter that she was already married? In fantasies a husband was no barrier at all. He began to abandon the dream only after his fateful exchange with Anthony Townsend. And even then, not entirely, and not instantly.

The events he'd narrated that day at Harvard University were the stages of his own disenchantment. The incredulity of listening to Townsend, the anger brought about by his untimely death, the disillusionment at her very advantageous second marriage.

But it was not good enough for her that one man out of

ten thousand dared to criticize her. No, for his transgression he had to pay with his heart.

And now at this late date she had become his, by law and by God.

His most costly possession sat opposite him in his private rail coach, immensely and imperturbably lovely. He could not imagine that he had held her, touched her, and joined his body to hers. Her beauty was staggering, excessive, as if she were not quite flesh and blood, but an artist's conjuration, born of a bout of fevered ecstasy.

A beauty with a gravity of its own that bent light. Sunlight slanted in from only one side of the coach, yet she was most assuredly lit from all sides, an even, soft illumination such as a painter might arrange in his studio when he wished to depict an angel—or a saint who came with her own personal nimbus.

For some time she had been as still as an anatomy model; not a ruffle moved on her striped white and gold dress. But now she laid her hands upon the table that separated them and undid the first button on her glove. A blatantly immodest gesture. Or was it? They were not in public, and he, the only other person in the private coach, was her husband.

Her husband. The words, like her beauty, didn't seem real.

Slowly, almost teasingly, she parted the glove at the wrist, exposing a triangle of skin—skin he had caressed at will on the *Rhodesia*. And then, with infinite leisure, she pulled at each finger of the glove, easing the kidskin from the hand it encased. Next she removed her other glove.

It would seem only fair that she should have a defect

somewhere. Blunt fingers would be a good place to start; knobby knuckles were not too much to ask. But no, her hands were trim, the fingers long and attractively tapered. Even her knuckles were comely.

She raised those bare, winsome hands and untied the hat ribbons beneath her chin, shaking her head slightly as she removed her hat. All of a sudden it was too much. He was again struck dumb by her, unable to breathe, unable to think, unable to do anything but want—her presence tore him apart; and the only way to be made whole again was to consume her, body and soul.

The next minute he realized what had happened to him, but not before she'd caught him staring.

For a decade, I was fixated by her beauty. I wrote an entire article on the evolutionary significance of beauty as a rebuke to myself, that I, who understood the concepts so well, nevertheless could not escape the magnetic pull of one particular woman's beauty.

She knew. With surgical precision, she had peeled back his layers of defenses, until his heart lay bare before her, all its shame and yearning exposed.

He could have lived with this if only he'd kept his secret whole and buried. But she knew. *She knew.*

"Don't get too comfortable," he said. "I may yet divorce you after the child comes."

CHAPTER 17

*A*lgernon House was magnificent: the marble galleries, the soaring ceilings painted by Italian masters, the library with its collection of fifty thousand volumes, including a Gutenberg Bible and manuscripts by da Vinci.

But what Venetia fell in love with was its vast, beautiful grounds. There was a formal geometric garden anchored by an enormous fountain depicting Apollo and the Nine Muses, a sculpture garden enclosed by ivy-draped walls, and a rose garden that was just beginning to bloom, its air dense with perfume.

The house, with its venerable, weathered sandstone exterior, sat at the edge of a large rolling meadow, just as the land rose into a wooded hill. A shining ribbon of a stream meandered across the meadow, its banks dotted with willows and poplars. A herd of red deer often gathered at the stream; flocks of wild ducks came and went; and occasionally, several Holstein cows would wander into the scene to graze contentedly.

Venetia was well accustomed to the demands of running a household, but she'd never managed an establishment of such scale. Her entire first week, as much as she yearned to explore the grounds for hours upon end, she devoted herself to more pressing tasks instead, learning the house's rhythms and traditions, meeting with all the upper servants, and wrapping her hands gently but firmly around the reins of her new home.

She also wrote her family daily, describing her waking hours in great detail, so that they would not worry. Or rather, so that they could worry while knowing exactly what was going on in her new life.

In her letters she made very little mention of her new husband: There was not much to say. He spent much of his day in his study. She spent much of her day in her sitting room. The two were in very different parts of the house, and she rarely saw him except at dinner. The dining table was thirty feet long. They each sat at one end. Even without the towering epergnes running down the center of the table, she might need her opera glass to see him properly.

But sometimes, at night, she heard him come into his bedroom.

On their wedding night, after her maid had retired, she'd left her bed and opened the adjoining door a very discreet yet unmistakable crack. She wanted to sleep with him again. After all those hours alone in a private coach, with him close enough to touch and yet so far away, the memories of their nights and days on the *Rhodesia* warmed her everywhere most inappropriately. Dear God how she longed for him to make love to her again, as a humanitarian mission, if nothing else.

And then she'd waited. He'd come into the room and there had been the usual sounds of a man preparing for bed: splashes of water, plops of garments of various description landing haphazardly, the metallic click of a pocket watch set down on the nightstand.

Suddenly, silence. He'd spied the door, standing ajar in invitation. She licked her lips, wanting him to give in to his weakness, to be overcome by the temptation of her body.

Footsteps, slow and quiet. He came closer and closer to the door, so close that she could almost hear him breathing. More silence, rife with possibilities. Her heart slammed with anticipation of pleasure. Perhaps he might even speak to her afterward.

Perhaps—

The door shut with a calm, deliberate click.

She belatedly realized that without ever intending to, she'd offended him: He'd considered her invitation a nefarious attempt to consolidate her power over him. And if he'd been at all tempted, he'd now be that much more determined to stay away from her.

Still, she listened at night, not exactly with hope, but in suspense nevertheless.

But he stubbornly kept away.

*C*hristian might threaten her with a divorce, but in the meanwhile, he could not stop this marriage from taking over his life.

Confidently she'd stepped into the management of the household. It had taken his stepmother years to win over the servants, but his wife had them eating out of her hands from the very beginning. Part of it could be attributed to her beauty. His staff took absurd pride in her comeliness: *This* was how a duchess ought to look, and all the other dukes could go cry into their first-growth tea.

But she also courted them adroitly. Both his majordomo and his gardeners had long desired to bring a living vine into the dining room, to rise out of the center of the table and offer his guests the amusement of plucking fresh grapes between courses. Christian had consistently denied them the wish, citing its frivolity. She gave them the blessing to go ahead.

From her own purse, she allocated funds to Mrs. Collins to make improvements to the servants' hall. Once she learned that Richards was a connoisseur of wine, she initiated the transfer the late Mr. Easterbrook's sizable collection of vintage claret and champagne into his keeping. To Monsieur Dufresne, the chef, she promised to import a trained pig, so that he could at last hunt for truffles on the estate among the roots of its abundant oaks.

And to the lower servants, she presented new uniforms, along with gold buttons for the men and pearl hairpins for the women, which they could keep or sell as they wished. Outright bribery, in his opinion, but it certainly made her very popular. His spiffily dressed staff, buttons shining, hairpins gleaming, went about their daily tasks with a spring in the steps.

Christian took refuge in the east wing, away from all the energetic changes. The public rooms of the house were in the central block, the family rooms in the west wing. The east wing, long a lonely and somewhat deserted portion of the house, he'd turned into workrooms, an archive that doubled as a secluded study, and a private museum for his collection of fossils and specimen.

Here he dealt with the correspondence from his solicitors and agents, sorted his notes from his American expedition, and wrote his stepmother every other day to reassure her that he was settling very nicely into married life, that soon he'd have truffle with every omelet and harvest his own grapes between soup and roast.

While he was able to avoid his wife with some success during the day, there was no escaping dinner or the polite predinner chitchat she was determined to foist upon him. He didn't know how she managed it, but every night she stunned him anew with her loveliness. And he could swear each day dinner was served a quarter hour later, so that he must withstand the assault of her beauty that much longer.

The worst, of course, was at night. She left the connecting door ajar at maddeningly unpredictable intervals, sometimes two nights in a row, sometimes not for another four days. When she issued her invitations on consecutive nights, he seethed at her brazenness. When she seemed to lose interest in him, he seethed at her indifference.

He was damned if she did and damned if she didn't.

*T*he dowager duchess's advice never quite left Venetia's ear. But how did one make a man listen when he didn't want to? And when she couldn't even get him alone for more than a few minutes every day?

The third time he left his room in the middle of the night, she decided to follow him, keeping a certain distance behind. The house was hushed and still, the coppery flame of his hand candle casting vast shadows. Saints and philosophers, painted upon the ceilings of halls and passages, scowled down at her, as if they, too, did not approve of the underhanded manner with which she'd attached herself to the family.

He went into the east wing. She hadn't yet penetrated the east wing, knowing he would be displeased by her incursion. But sometimes one must encroach. Indeed, sometimes one must surround the beloved.

But whether out of cowardice or curiosity too long denied, she did not pursue him directly into his study, but instead pushed open the doors of his private museum and found the lamps.

She sighed. She'd overpraised the grounds: *This* was the most beautiful part of the house.

The museum was fifty feet long and thirty feet wide, with display cases going all around the walls. From the ceiling hung a skeleton of a Haast's eagle in midflight. The central exhibit was one of fossilized tusks, an enormous pair belonging to a mastodon, a much smaller pair probably from a dwarf *Stegodon*, and a straight tusk almost twice as long as she was tall that had once been the pride and joy of a gentleman narwhal.

"What are you doing here?"

She glanced over her shoulder. Christian stood in the doorway. She'd only belted a dressing robe over her nightgown; he was dressed more formally in a shirt and a pair of trousers. But the shirt was open at the collar. She had the strongest urge to lick the base of his throat.

He frowned. "I asked you a question."

"It's fairly evident that I am ogling—your fossils. What are *you* doing here?"

"I saw a light on and came to investigate. But I see it's only you."

He moved as if to leave.

She turned around and took a deep breath. "Wait. I want to know what exactly Mr. Townsend said to you."

His gaze swept over her, not a covetous look, but a hard, inscrutable one. "He said, 'You may yet have your wish, Your Grace. But think twice. Or you may end up like me.'"

You may yet have your wish. "Did he recognize you? He said something to me once about a Harrow player coveting me."

His jaw worked. "Yes, he recognized me. Did he kill himself?"

After all these years, the question still made her stomach clench. "Yes, with an excess of chloral. He told me that he was going to a friend's place in Scotland for shooting, but he went to London instead. Three days later, when the agent who'd let us the town house for the Season went to inspect it, he discovered Mr. Townsend in the master's room, perfectly dressed and quite dead."

"How did you know it was chloral?"

"The agent found a vial next to his hand. He kept it hidden from the police—he didn't want anyone to know that a suicide took place in the house—but later he gave it to me."

"There was no inquest?"

"Fitz was just able to prevent one. He had the police accept that Mr. Townsend died of a brain hemorrhage, and that in the confusion before his death, he wandered back into a house he knew and lay down to rest."

Christian's face was impassive. She wondered whether his mind went back to their conversations on the *Rhodesia* concerning her infelicitous marriage to Tony. "How did you find out?"

"With a visit from Scotland Yard to our house in Kent. And while the police inspector was speaking to me, the new owners of our house came to claim it—it was the first time I'd learned that the house had been sold."

She'd been stupefied by the shock of sudden eviction, the threat of an inquest, and, above all, the sheer vindictiveness of Tony's action. Helena even believed that he'd deliberately committed suicide in the manner he had to provoke police interest, to make the ordeal as ugly as possible for Venetia.

"Why did he hate you so?"

She could detect no compassion in Christian's voice— but no disdain either. "Because he believed that I'd turned him from somebody into a nobody. He'd married me to have a pretty accessory to garner himself more attention, but the pretty accessory stole all the limelight he craved and left him nothing.

"I know it makes no sense at all. I can scarcely credit it myself, a grown man resenting his wife for such a reason. But the notice I attracted maddened him—he wanted everyone's gaze squarely on himself. To that end, he resolved be become an astoundingly successful investor, so that his friends and acquaintances would stop paying mind to the wife and look to him with envy and admiration. And while he was waiting for that to happen, he'd obtain adoration from other women."

"Such as the maid he impregnated?"

"Poor Meg Munn. But maids were an unsatisfactory lot. He wanted his adulation to come from proper ladies, proper ladies who required such things as jewels before they'd admit a man to be impressive."

A hint of a volatile emotion traversed his features, but a moment later his face was again unreadable.

"When his investments turned sour one by one, he kept me in the dark. I didn't know he'd become mired in debts. I only knew the amount I was allocated to run the household kept decreasing—and I thought that was because he was mean-spirited."

Not a pretty confession, only a truthful one. "He must have believed that he'd strike gold on one of his investments. They all failed. It would have been terrifying for anyone, but for him . . . the implication that he had not been favored by God, that he could fall from grace just like any other ordinary bloke, and that he could do to nothing to stop this plunge into poverty and obscurity—he must have been in hell already."

She'd never given a full recital of the facts. Perhaps she should have years ago. Then she'd have realized much sooner that the person Tony had condemned from the beginning was himself.

And only himself.

*S*he sighed, whether from sorrow or relief Christian couldn't quite tell. What he did know was that he wished Townsend were still alive so he could bash in the man's face and break a few of his ribs besides.

She twirled the end of her robe's sash between her fingers, waiting for him to say something—or perhaps simply waiting for him to leave so she could go back to her fossils. As his gaze remained upon her, she cinched the sash rather self-consciously.

The shape of her body hadn't changed. The tightened

sash attested to a waist just as slender as it had been on the *Rhodesia*. He would not have guessed that she carried a new life within.

He hadn't been in the nursery in a while. There might still be some of his toys and books in there. And, of course, the whole of the estate was one vast playground for a child. "When will the baby be born?"

Her eyes turned wary. "Beginning of next year."

He nodded.

"I wouldn't be in such a hurry to speak to your lawyers if I were you."

He hadn't been thinking of speaking to his lawyers at all. "No?"

"Even they would think you a monster were you to orchestrate a divorce right after my confinement."

"How long do you recommend I wait, then?"

"A long time. I know what happens when a divorce is granted: The woman never gets anything. And I will not be parted from my child."

"So you will contest the divorce?"

"To my last penny. And then I'll borrow from Fitz and Millie."

"So we'll be married 'til the end of time?"

"The sooner you accept it, the sooner we are all better off." His ancestors would have appreciated her hauteur: a fit wife for a de Montfort. "Now if you'll excuse me, I must have enough rest."

He gazed at her retreating back. Foolish woman, did she not realize that he'd already accepted it from the moment he'd said "I do"?

CHAPTER 18

$\mathscr{C}$hristian had a fitful night—not that he'd known any other kind since she'd disembarked the *Rhodesia*. But after their encounter in his private museum he could only reel with shame and horror at how wrong he had been. What must she have felt, to have her character twisted and denigrated so carelessly, without the slightest regard for the truth.

In the morning he stopped by the breakfast parlor. He'd been having breakfast in his study, but he knew she usually had hers in the parlor, with the day's papers and often a copy of *Nature* by her elbow.

She was not there.

"She has gone for a walk, sir," said Richards.

"Where?" The grounds of Algernon House were vast. She could be miles away.

"She did not inform us, sir. She only said not to expect her before luncheon."

"When did she leave?"

"About two hours ago, sir."

It was not quite nine o'clock yet. If she did not come back before luncheon, she'd be out a good six hours. "You let a woman in her—"

Christian stopped himself. No one else knew of her condition yet. "Send me Gerald. Tell him to hurry."

Gerald, head groundskeeper, arrived slightly out of breath. "Your Grace?"

"Has the duchess asked you any questions about the quarry?"

"Yes, sir, she has indeed."

"When?"

"Yesterday, sir."

"Did she ask for directions?"

"She did, sir. I drew her a map. She also asked about digging implements and I told her about the cabin with all the tools in it."

"Isn't the cabin locked?"

"She asked for my key, sir, and I gave it."

Ten minutes later, Christian was on his horse, galloping toward the quarry.

The remains of the quarry consisted of a near-circular cliff with a ramp going down to the bottom. To reach the top of the ramp, he had to guide his stallion up a small hill. The sight that greeted him as he crested the knoll made him lose his breath.

Standing halfway up the earthen ramp that he'd had built years ago to facilitate access to the higher parts of the cliff was his baroness, complete with the veiled hat that had been such a part of her mystery. She stood with her back to him, studiously chipping away at a promising patch of sediment, late Triassic by the look of it. Setting down her hammer and chisel, she picked up a brush and swept away the debris around an ocher-colored protuberance. All the while she whistled, a lively aria from *Rigoletto*, her notes bright and exactly in tune, until she hit a sustained high note where she ran out of air and stuttered. This made her giggle.

At the sound of her laughter, the Ghost of Ocean Crossings Past shouldered through him, a great, muscular longing.

He did something: tightened his hands on the reins or the grip of his thighs on the flanks of his steed. The horse shifted, struck its hooves against the ground, and let out a rumbly neigh.

She looked over her shoulder. The front of the veil had been lifted over the crown of her hat; her face was dirty and smudged, her extraordinary eyes largely hidden beneath the wide brim. All the same he felt the familiar upending of his peace of mind, of the ingrained expectation that he should affect the world and those in it, but not the other way around.

He nudged his mount forward. At the bottom of the slope there was a hitching post. He tied the horse and made his way up the ramp.

"How did you find me?"

"It's not that difficult to guess which part of my estate you may wish to explore. What have you found?"

She glanced at him, seemingly surprised by his civility. "A very small skull. I am hoping it might be a juvenile dinosaur but most probably not—it's too far into the Tertiary strata."

"An amphibian, by the looks of it," he judged.

She did not quite look at him. "I'm still thrilled."

A silence spread. He didn't know what to say. For a man of science, a devotee to cold facts, he had blundered badly, allowing his action to be guided by assumption after ill-supported assumption. "You said you were there at my Harvard lecture in person," he heard himself say. "Why didn't you approach me afterward and correct my misconceptions?"

She swirled the bristles of a brush against the skull's small, sharp teeth. "I couldn't have shared the most painful details of my life with a stranger who had coldly condemned me."

No, of course not.

"So you chose to punish me instead."

She drew a deep breath. "So I chose to punish you instead."

*H*is hand tightened around his riding crop. For a moment it seemed that he was about to say something, but he only inclined his head and left: untethered his horse, rode it up the slope, and disappeared from sight.

Venetia bit her lower lip. She was still unsettled from their conversation the night before, during which she *had* shared the most painful details of her life, and he had reacted not at all.

But then he too had shared his most closely held secret and she had thrown it back in his face—with great glee, as far as he could tell.

She sat down to rest on a hardened clump of soil. After a

while, she thought of picking up the hammer and the chisel and chipping away some more at the edges of the skeleton. But her arms were sore and each whack of the hammer had jarred the socket of her arm. It had been a long time since she last dug: Then she'd been an indefatigable child who never ached anywhere; now she was a pregnant woman who didn't sleep well.

It would be wiser to be on her way back to the house. She had prepared for her outing with a flask of tea and a sandwich. The sandwich was already gone—eaten en route, as it had taken her longer than expected to find the site. The flask, too, was nearly empty—the day had warmed fast.

It would be a hot, thirsty walk home.

The sound of horse hooves and wheels. She spun around, hoping to see Christian. But it was only Wells, the gamekeeper, who'd come in a two-wheel dogcart pulled by a Clydesdale.

"Do you need a lift to the manor, mum?" said Wells.

Venetia was surprised and relieved. "Yes, I do. Thank you."

Wells carried the bucket of tools back to the shed while she climbed up to the slope to the dogcart.

"Did you happen by the quarry?" she asked, once he had helped her up to the high seat. The gamekeeper's cottage was somewhere nearby, from what Gerald had told her.

"No, mum. His Grace stopped by and asked me to wait on you. He also asked the wife to have some tea and some biscuits for you."

Wells passed her a basket covered with a large napkin. She ate a biscuit. It tasted lemony. "It's very kind of you and Mrs. Wells."

And even kinder of Christian, to arrange for transport and nourishment, before she'd even realized her needs.

All of a sudden she couldn't wait to see him again. Enough of the Great Beauty. Enough of her pride. And enough of this fretting about their impasse. He was the love of her life—it was time she treated him as such.

"Would you mind hurrying a little?" she asked Wells, who drove as if the dogcart were the state carriage during the Queen's Jubilee.

"His Grace said I was to drive slow and steady, so as to not jostle you, mum."

"That's very lovely of His Grace, but I'm not afraid of jostling. Faster, please."

The Clydesdale went from a stately trot to a more energetic trot, but Wells refused to accelerate further. Venetia waited impatiently for the manor to come into view. And when the dogcart drew up before the front steps, she thanked Wells and ran inside.

"Where is the duke?" she asked the first person she came across, who happened to be Richards.

Richards looked surprised at the question. "His Grace has departed for London."

Christian hadn't said a thing about leaving Algernon House. "Of course," she murmured, hoping she didn't look as she felt, faltering. "I meant *when* did he leave?"

"Half an hour ago, ma'am."

"Thank you, Richards," she said numbly.

She wanted to kick herself. *So I chose to punish you instead.* How could she have given that answer as if it were complete in and of itself?

So I chose to punish you instead. But my scheme disintegrated once I realized you were not the villain I believed you to be. And the greatest mistake of my life was not marrying Tony, but not telling you the truth after I fell in love.

That's what she should have said. But she was too late. He was gone, no longer even keeping up the pretense of honeymoon togetherness.

"Will you be needing anything else, ma'am?" asked Richards.

She stood irresolute.

"Ma'am?"

"You may return to your other duties, Richards."

Richards bowed and walked away. Venetia stared at his disappearing back.

"Wait!" she heard herself cry. "Ready me a carriage to take me to the rail station. I, too, am going to London."

She was not some bleating ninny who stopped at the first obstacle. He'd gone to London, not fallen off the edge of the world. She'd be there before teatime.

"Yes, ma'am. Right away, ma'am," answered Richards, something suspiciously like a smile on his face.

And she would not come back to Algernon House before she'd bared her heart.

*M*eg Munn, the maid who'd claimed to be pregnant with Townsend's child, turned out to be surprisingly easy to locate. Christian had sent out a cable before he left Derbyshire in the morning. Upon his arrival in London, McAdams, his solicitor, already had something to report.

"I spoke to Mr. Brand, the agent who'd let houses to Mr. Townsend during several London Seasons, hoping he might have some information on Mr. Townsend's staff. As it so happened, the maid Meg Munn had married Mr. Harney, one of Mr. Brand's former clerks, who is now a greengrocer in Cheapside.

"I went to Cheapside and located the establishment. Mrs. Harney told me that while she'd accepted Mr. Townsend's advances from time to time, she much preferred Harney, upon whom she also bestowed her favors. When she found herself with child, she was fairly certain it was Harney's, but she felt a little scheming would not be amiss, a way to cajole her mistress to provide a dowry for her."

"Thank you, Mr. McAdams." Not that Christian still doubted his wife. This exercise was less about proving her trustworthiness, and more—he wasn't sure what to call it. Punishment, perhaps, for himself. To see just how infinitely wrong he'd been where she was concerned. "And the duchess's fossilized footprints?"

"The paleontological artifact has been moved to Euston Station, sir. It is ready to leave when you are."

"Very good," said Christian.

He should have apologized to her in the quarry. But the words had stuck in his throat. To properly express his contrition would revisit the fact that he'd coveted her from afar these many years. And he couldn't, not before her beautiful eyes and clear gaze.

The "paleontological artifact" would have to speak for him. And by personally escorting it home, he hoped it would speak loud and clear the words he couldn't quite bring himself to utter.

A knock came at the door of his study. "Sir, I have Lady Avery and Lady Somersby calling for you," said a footman.

Lady Avery was the gossip who'd been at his Harvard lecture and then spread Christian's words all over London. Why would he want to see her and her equally worthless sister?

"I'm not at home today."

The footman withered at his tone. "I tried to inform the ladies, sir. But they would not listen to me. They said"—he swallowed—"they said that you'd regret it, sir, if you didn't hear what they had to say about the duchess."

He frowned. He could ignore any and all insinuation concerning himself, but not those concerning Venetia. *Venetia*, he repeated her name in his mind. So familiar, those syllables, the central refrain of his life.

"Show them to the drawing room."

"Yes, sir."

He strode into the drawing room five minutes later. "You are not welcome here."

"Well, well." Lady Avery smiled wolfishly. "Then we'd best state our business quickly and be on our way, ought we not?"

"We ought to indeed," echoed Lady Somersby.

"You see, sir, my sister and I take our reputations very seriously. We might be gossips, but we are reliable gossips. We do not fabricate stories and we do not disseminate news we cannot verify. At times we editorialize and offer our own interpretation of the meaning and significance of events, but we support our assertions with utmost care and we never concoct the underlying events.

"I was there at your Harvard lecture, sir, seated in the fifth row. The young man who rose to defend the good name of the beautiful women of the world is my son-in-law's cousin. I took very good notes of what you said and I knew instantly that you were speaking of the former Mrs. Easterbrook.

"As it is not my duty to protect you from your indiscretion, when I came back, I related the story faithfully and well. But you and the former Mrs. Easterbrook mounted a brilliant counteroffensive: dance, carriage ride, and elopement. Now people who have trusted my sister and me for decades have suddenly begun to question our accuracy and dependability. Our reputation is at stake here."

"That is hardly my concern," Christian said coldly.

"Of course it is not, but it is very much ours. To that extent, we redoubled our effort to prove ourselves. No doubt you will be interested to hear what we have unearthed?"

"Not at all."

As if he hadn't spoken, Lady Avery went on. "We have obtained the visitors' registry from Brooks's, for the month of August, eighteen eighty-eight. On the twenty-sixth, two days before Mr. Townsend was found dead, there were only four visitors in the evening, and you, sir, and Mr. Townsend, were among them."

A tinny, acrid taste was on Christian's tongue. Fear. Not for himself, but for his wife.

"We also have in our possession copies of the bills of sale for three jewel necklaces Mr. Townsend bought, in the weeks preceding his death. We have members of Mr. Easterbrook's family willing to swear on stacks of Bibles that at the time of his death, his wife was chatting and making merry in the parlor. And last, but not least, my son-in-law's cousin—the one who'd been at the lecture—is on his way to England: a visitor at our invitation, but also an additional eyewitness who will corroborate every last one of our claims."

"What do you want?" His voice did not shake, but he did sound desperate—at least to himself.

"You mistake us, sir. We are not blackmailers, but seekers of the truth. Granted, our truths may be trivial in your eyes, but they matter to us—as much as your pursuits matter to you and very possibly more."

"Therefore this is only a courtesy call on our part, sir," added Lady Somersby, "to let you know that we are not about to let the matter rest. We will fight for our reputation tooth and nail."

He almost laughed—*their* reputation. Except there was not the least irony in Lady Somersby's words. She meant everything she said—*they* meant everything they said. Much as he might sneer at their calling and their efforts, they took themselves with utter seriousness.

"I don't care what you say about me, but the duchess is innocent of any crimes. I will not allow you to injure her."

"Then you should not have implied that she is ruthless and greedy, sir," replied Lady Avery, perfectly at ease.

"Precisely. If you lied, you make amends. If Mr. Townsend lied, well, let the duchess make the truth known," added Lady Somersby.

"What if she has no interest in making the private particulars of her life with Mr. Townsend known to the public?"

"Then that is her choice, isn't it?"

"I went to school with Grant, Lady Somersby's nephew. The present company all know of his inclinations. Yet I've never heard either of you breathe a word of it. That tells me you do not need to speak of everything you know."

"That is different. We gossip to shed light on passions and weaknesses, not to ruin lives." Lady Avery rose.

"Mr. Townsend is already dead and the former Mrs. East-erbrook, well, she is the Duchess of Lexington—such enormous good fortune cannot be dented by a few juicy nuggets that we choose to disseminate. Come, Grace, we have importuned the duke long enough. Good day to you, sir, and we will see ourselves out."

"Wait," he said. His breaths were shallow, his heartbeat unsteady. The Lexington name could protect Venetia from ostracization, but it would not shield her from the sort of torment Lady Avery and Lady Somersby proposed to unleash: She would be forced to relive the worst moments of her life while Society feasted on her private anguish for entertainment.

"If it is true that you are truth seekers above all, and if it is true that you adhere to your own code of honor, then I am willing to offer you certain truths you will not learn elsewhere. In exchange I ask that you refrain from causing the duchess any further distress."

The women exchanged a look. "We cannot make any promises until we hear what it is you have to tell us. After all, we have toiled more than a quarter century for our reputation. We cannot overlook such a blight for a minor confession."

A minor confession. Was that what his revelation would be deemed as? There was every possibility. These were jaded women neck deep in every kind of human foible. What was to him an unbearably intimate secret might very well rank somewhere near the bottom of their scale in terms of salaciousness and titillation.

But he had no choice. His ill-considered words had been the cause of enough chagrin. No more.

The women's nostrils flared. Their gaze upon him was

that of two vultures that had waited patiently and would soon feast. He felt ill, nauseated almost, to bare his soul before such as them.

He gripped the back of the chair before him. "I fell in love with my wife ten years ago, when she was still Mrs. Townsend."

The women exchanged another look. Lady Avery sat down again.

His knuckles were white. He forced his hands to unclench. "It was—difficult. Not only because she seemed happily married, but also because my sentiments were consuming—beyond my control. Then I ran into Townsend. And he'd said what he'd said. I need not repeat how I interpreted subsequent events.

"What I did not say at the lecture was that my revulsion and outrage did little to emancipate me from my enslavement. However unwillingly, I remained in thrall to her beauty. In the ensuing years, I made sure that our paths would not cross.

"But the time had come for me to do my duty and marry. I was obliged to be in London during the Season. As my return drew near, my doubts grew. Mrs. Easterbrook's hold over me remained undiminished. If I came across her again, I was not confident that my principles would be strong enough to withstand my fixation. Years of resistance could be undone by a single encounter.

"In Sanders Theatre, my mind was in a state of unrest. I managed to get through the body of the lecture, but I betrayed myself during the questions. At the time I only thought I was reinforcing my own resolution, but I quickly realized that I'd committed a great indiscretion. I took comfort in the fact that I was more than three thousand miles from home and my American audience would not know of whom I spoke. That, as you well know, turned out not to be the case.

"Since then I've had cause to revise my opinion of my wife. I'd been very much mistaken about her. Even if I did not know what she looked like, I would still find her beautiful. I—"

The door of the drawing room opened to reveal the loveliest woman in the world, clad in a sandstone-colored traveling gown. "Christian," she said, "I know I have not been—"

She saw Lady Avery and Lady Somersby. Her eyes narrowed. Her tone turned icy. "I did not know we were at home to callers."

She was every bit the haughty duchess.

"You have met Mr. Grant, one of His Grace's dear friends from his school days, have you not, Your Grace?" Lady Somersby asked her.

"I do not believe I've had the pleasure."

"Mr. Grant happens to be my late husband's nephew—a very fine young man, and very close to myself."

She raised a very superior eyebrow. "Is he?"

"And do you know what we learned from Mr. Grant recently?" Lady Somersby went on, an infernal gleam in her eyes. "That the duke has been obsessively in love with you, ma'am, for the past ten years. In view of the turns of events of late, it is my firm opinion that he engineered this entire enterprise with the express purpose of making you his own."

Lady Avery's teacup rattled. Christian was torn between an urge to violence and a numb horror. Had he? Was this what his action had been all about? To force her to pay attention to him? To bring her into his proximity without stooping to court her?

He wanted to protest. But his tongue must have swollen to a size that not only made speech impossible, but also blocked his airway. He could not breathe.

His wife cast an incredulous glance his way. Then she faced Lady Somersby. "Explain yourself."

"You are the one woman he'd always coveted. By creating this particular tempest, His Grace easily put you in an awkward and vulnerable position, ma'am. All the better, then, to rescue you from this dilemma, no?"

"Brilliant, my dear, brilliant," murmured Lady Avery. "Now everything makes sense."

"I hate to burst this pretty bubble of self-congratulation," said Venetia, "but what dross. What rubbish. The duke had never given me a thought in his life before he spoke to Mr. Townsend—and very few since."

"I beg your pardon?" cried the gossip chroniclers together.

"Mr. Townsend had been an awful husband, but His Grace had no cause to know such a thing. Therefore one cannot blame him for taking Mr. Townsend at his word. And why, when asked a direct question, shouldn't he have used Mr. Townsend's account as a cautionary tale? After all, appearances *are* deceiving." She inhaled deeply. "Now we come to the part of the tale that you, Lady Avery, should have put together for yourself but did not: *I* was there that day at the lecture."

Lady Avery gasped. "You jest, ma'am."

"I do not. Ask anyone. Miss Fitzhugh was gathering material for an article on the graduating class of Radcliffe, and Lady Fitzhugh and I were her chaperones. You can well imagine our reaction to the duke's accusations. Miss Fitzhugh would have torched his properties had he any on the other side of the pond. But I had the better idea. I would make the duke pay with his heart. To that purpose I booked a passage on the *Rhodesia*."

Lady Somersby leaped up. "You were the duke's mysterious veiled lover?"

"I see you have guessed at long last," said Venetia with cool sarcasm. "My plans, however, went awry. The duke, I'm sure, enjoyed himself. But I was the one who fell in love. He is everything I want in a man—and much, much more, if you know what I mean."

Lady Somersby's eyes were the size of eggs. Christian's jaw dropped. His wife paid him no mind.

"I was desperately in love, but I could not approach the duke: Were we to rendezvous in London, he would demand that I remove my veil—and you can well imagine the scene that would ensue. But I followed him about, to the British Museum of Natural History, and to the Savoy Hotel where we were to dine together in honor of his birthday.

"When the scandal broke, the duke came to my aid—despite his many reservations concerning my character. He danced with me once and took me for a carriage ride in the park, but that was the entire extent of interaction he allowed between us. Our marriage came about and only came about because I found myself in a delicate condition."

Lady Avery's hand slapped against her roomy bosom. "Oh my goodness gracious me."

"Precisely. Mr. Townsend had convinced me that I could not conceive. The duke quite proved otherwise. And if you doubt me, feel free to speak with Miss Redmayne at the New Hospital for Women. Faced with such consequences, I had no choice but to approach the duke and beg him to marry me. He was understandably furious, but he did the honorable thing and made me his wife. This was why he married me, not because of some deep, dark fixation he'd carried with him for years uncounted, but because he is a man who does not let personal opinions stand in the way of obligation."

Christian was stunned. Ladies Avery and Somersby likewise so. At last, Lady Somersby said, "If you will excuse us for a moment, my sister and I must confer in private."

They took themselves to a corner of the room, behind a screen. Christian pulled his wife to the opposite corner.

"Letting them know about your condition? Are you mad?" It was not easy keeping his voice down.

"Possibly. But I can't let them go around telling everybody that you've been in love with me since forever."

"Why not?"

"Because you would have hated it. And you must choose better friends. I am extremely disappointed in Mr. Grant."

"Grant doesn't know a thing. I've not said a word to him."

"Then who could have informed those vultures? I can't believe the dowager duchess would have done something like this."

"She didn't—I've never said anything to her, either. I've never told anyone except you."

"Then—"

"*I* did. They'd dug up all sorts of evidence that Townsend and I were indeed in the same place at the same time shortly before he died and that everything else Lady Avery asserted could also be supported. They were out to prove that they had their gossip right. And I told them that if they left the past alone I'd tell them something better worth their time."

She blinked slowly, her lashes long, sooty. "Why?"

He swallowed. "I can't have you hurt again. I won't. And you, you ninny, you sweep in and undo everything I just did."

He made a throttling gesture with his hands.

She covered her mouth, then she laughed. God, how he adored her laughter.

"You do love me," she said, her voice full of wonder.

"Of course I do, you idiot. How can you think that I do not? Seen or unseen, you bring me to my knees."

"I can be on my knees sometimes, if you'd like." She giggled.

Lust jolted through him. "Be serious," he said with some difficulty. "We are in a room with two she-wolves."

"I don't care. They can't hurt me. Nor can Mr. Townsend ever again." To his shock, she wrapped her arms about him. "I love you. I love you madly. That's what I came to tell you. I couldn't help falling in love with you as soon as I got to know you. And I'm very sorry for acting the Great Beauty and hurting you."

The beauty of her words were almost beyond his comprehension. He embraced her fiercely. "I'm the one who should apologize. I started all the troubles and I was the stupidest numskull who ever lived."

Someone cleared her throat. "Your Graces," said Lady Avery, "my sister and I have come to a conclusion."

He would have told them to bugger off but his wife took charge of the situation. She disengaged herself from his arms and stepped back, but not before she rubbed her thumb along his lower lip, a gesture of blatant promise. He was instantly hot with need.

She turned toward the gossips. The smile was wiped from her face; she was once again the Great Beauty. "You will be swift about it. The duke and I have other plans for the afternoon."

Christian very nearly blushed. Lady Avery did blush, in fact.

She had to clear her throat again. "We have been conveyors of fine gossip for more than twenty-five years, my sister and I. We see so many failings and shortcomings, sometimes we forget that not everyone is selfish. You each sought not to protect yourself, but to shelter the other. And for that, we *are* willing to tolerate a stain on our otherwise spotless record. We shall not bring up Mr. Townsend's name again, and when my son-in-law's cousin arrives, I will escort him to the Continent instead of having him linger about London. In exchange, we ask that we be the first ones to inform Society of the duchess's condition, in say, four weeks' time."

Christian could not believe it. There was some humanity left in Ladies Avery and Somersby. Who knew?

His wife nodded, as if in approval. "Accepted."

The three women shook hands on their agreement. The gossip chroniclers showed themselves out. But before Christian could say anything, the dowager duchess was shown in.

"Stepmama, how did you know we are in town?"

"I gave particular instructions to your staff that I be informed as soon as you return, although"—she looked with speculation toward his wife—"I did not know the duchess has also come."

"I could not bear to be parted from my bridegroom during our honeymoon," said Christian's wife, smiling at—and thoroughly dazzling—him. "So I've chased him to London."

"I only came to take the tetrapodichnites out of storage and bring them to you."

Her smiled widened. "You were going to do that?"

"Of course."

"The tetrapo-what?" demanded his stepmother.

"Fossilized saurian footprints. My bride has a passion for prehistoric monsters."

His bride dipped her head and peered up at him from underneath her magnificent lashes. "The duke encourages it. He is going to take me on his expeditions."

The dowager duchess looked from Christian to Venetia and back again, her lips beginning to curve into a smile. "I see I've been worried over nothing. You could have told me all is well, Christian."

He could scarcely take his eyes off his Venetia. "My humblest apologies, Stepmama. I don't know what I was thinking."

The doors of the drawing room opened again, this time to admit Lord Fitzhugh, Lady Fitzhugh, Miss Fitzhugh, and Lord Hastings. Venetia gave a delighted squeal, embraced them one by one, even Lord Hastings, and performed introductions.

"And how did you know to come so quickly, Lord and Lady Fitzhugh?" asked the dowager duchess. "Did you also bribe someone on the duke's staff?"

Venetia laughed. "No indeed, ma'am. I cabled them before I left Derbyshire. There was something from my brother's town house that I wanted. But I meant only for him to send it via courier."

"As if any of us would stay behind when we know you are in town," said Miss Fitzhugh.

"It's excellent to see you, Venetia." Lord Fitzhugh placed a hand on his sister's arm. "You, too, Lexington. I see marriage agrees with the both of you."

"A very pleasant state of affairs, I must admit," said Christian, his gaze again straying toward his wife.

A look that his brother-in-law instantly comprehended. "And since you are still on your honeymoon, I believe we should make ourselves scarce. Shall we, Helena?"

Miss Fitzhugh complied reluctantly. "All right, if you say so, Fitz."

"I left Mr. Kingston in the middle of a game of chess. That would never do. I'd better head home myself," added the dowager duchess.

There was another round of hugs. Miss Fitzhugh handed her sister a wrapped package. Christian and his wife saw everyone to their carriages, then, side by side, they walked sedately up the stairs. The moment they were in his room, however, she leaped onto him and kissed him wildly.

"Shouldn't you take more care in your condition?" he managed when he surfaced for air.

"Hmm. Not yet."

He laid her down in his bed. "I am about to make love to you while you are visible. I'm not sure I'll survive the experience."

"You will." She clutched his face between her hands. "And when there is light, you can see how much I love you."

He kissed the pulse at her throat. "In that case, I could get used to it."

*A*fterward they held each other tight.

"I wanted you for my sister, you know," she murmured.

He kissed the tip of her nose. "Your sister who is in love with a married man?"

"You remember that?"

"I remember everything you said to me on the *Rhodesia*."

"Yes, that sister. My sister-in-law and I rather wistfully believed that if she'd only meet you, all would be well. So when we saw a poster for your lecture, we had to drag her to it."

He kissed her eyelashes. "How did she like me before I began to slander you?"

"I've never asked her, but *I* was quite solidly impressed. So much so that even after you'd compared me to the Great Whore of Babylon—"

"I did not."

She giggled. "So that even after you did that, I still found myself drawn to you."

"And believed me to be propositioning you even when I was not."

"You can't possibly understand—I take that back. You can very well understand what it is like to be repelled yet compelled by a person at once. I was beside myself."

"Was that what made you wild in bed?"

She snuggled closer to him. "Probably. And I was wild, wasn't I?"

"And wounded. And conflicted. And indomitable. When we were apart, I thought constantly of how you solved all your problems with your own hands—and made sure to emulate you."

"Serving as an example to the Duke of Lexington—you don't know how proud I am." She laughed as she raised herself on her elbow. "Now where is my photograph?"

"Which photograph? Is that what you wanted delivered to you?"

She nodded. "A photograph of my *Cetiosaurus*. I didn't take it with me to Algernon House just after we married because I wasn't sure whether I could ever be at home there. But this time, I was determined to take it with me no matter what. Just as I was determined to drag you kicking and screaming into my bed."

He rubbed a strand of her hair against his cheek and smiled. "Will you show me the picture?"

"I see I've dropped it by the door."

She slipped out of bed, her hair loose, her person entirely naked.

"My God, put on something."

Coquettishly she glanced over her shoulder. "So I won't look like the trollop I am?"

"So we will actually get around to the photograph. Well, too late."

He hauled her back into bed, and it was a while before either of them remembered the photograph again. This time, he left the bed to fetch it.

She opened the package and drew out the framed photograph. He studied it closely. "You look happy and confident—rather as you do now."

"It's because I feel now as I did then: that I have all my life before me and endless possibilities."

Looking at the fossil reminded him that the British Museum of Natural History was still open for the day. "If we hurry, we can have a good look at your *Cetiosaurus* in the flesh—or in the bones, rather. Then you are going to dine with me at the Savoy Hotel, to make up for what you owe me. And when we come home, I will give serious consideration to what you might do on your knees."

"Oh yes," she cried. "Yes to all three."

He helped her dress, then pulled on his own clothes. As they approached the door, beyond which they must be proper and ducal again, he pulled her close for another kiss. "I love you, mein Liebling."

She winked. "And you will love me even more by the end of tonight."

They laughed and walked arm in arm out of the house, all their lives and endless possibilities before them.

AUTHOR'S NOTE

Even though she has remarried, Christian's stepmother is referred throughout the book as the dowager duchess and addressed as "Your Grace." According to an edition of *Debrett's Peerage* from the late nineteenth century, "A Widow who remarries *loses* any title or precedence she gained by her previous marriage. From this rule there is not any exception. Society, however, from pure motives of *courtesy*, sanctions the retention of former rank, and . . . permits ladies who have remarried to be addressed as though their titled husbands were living."

Mary Anning, who lived in the first part of the nineteenth century, was a significant fossil collector and paleontologist. She is recognized by the Royal Society in 2010 as one of the ten most influential British women in the history of science. She had a more aristocratic counterpart in Barbara Hastings, Marchioness of Hastings and Baroness Grey de Ruthyn in her own right.

Read on for a sneak preview of the next
irresistible romance from Sherry Thomas

Ravishing the Heiress

Coming July 2012 from Berkley Sensation!

Fate

1888

It was love at first sight.

    Not that there was anything wrong with love at first sight, but Millicent Graves had not been raised to fall in love at all, let alone hard and fast.

She was the only surviving child of a very prosperous man who manufactured tinned goods and other preserved edibles. It had been decided, long before she could comprehend such things, that she was going to Marry Well—that via her person, the family's fortune would be united with an ancient and illustrious title.

Millie's childhood had therefore consisted of endless lessons: music, drawing, penmanship, elocution, deportment, and, when there was time left, modern languages. At ten, she successfully floated down a long flight of stairs with three books on her head. By twelve, she could exchange hours of pleasantries in French, Italian, and German. And on the day of her fourteenth birthday, Millie, not at all a natural musician, at last conquered Listz's *Douze Grandes Études*, by dint of sheer effort and determination.

That same year, with her father coming to the conclusion that she would never be a great beauty, or indeed a beauty of any kind, the search began for a highborn groom desperate enough to marry a girl whose family wealth derived from—heaven forbid—sardines.

The search came to an end twenty months later. Mr. Graves was not particularly thrilled with the choice, as the earl who agreed to take his daughter in exchange for his money had a title that was neither particularly ancient nor particularly illustrious. But the stigma attached to tinned sardines was such that even this earl demanded Mr. Graves's last penny.

And then, after months of haggling, after all the agreements had finally been drawn up and signed, the earl had the inconsideration to drop dead at the age of thirty-three. Or rather, Mr. Graves viewed his death a thoughtless affront. Millie, in the privacy of her room, wept.

She'd seen the earl only twice and had not been overjoyed with either his anemic looks or his dour temperament. But he, in his way, had had as little choice as she. The estate had come to him in terrible disrepair. His schemes of improvement had made little to no difference. And when he'd tried to land an heiress of a more exalted background, he'd failed resoundingly, likely because he'd been so unimpressive in both appearance and demeanor.

A more spirited girl might have rebelled against such an unprepossessing groom more than twice her age. A more enterprising one might have persuaded her parents to let her take her chances on the matrimonial mart for a more palatable husband. Millie was not either of those girls.

She was a quiet, serious child who understood instinctively that much was expected of her. And while it was desirable that she could play all twelve of the *Grandes Études* rather than just eleven, in the end her training was not about music—or languages, or deportment—but about discipline, control, and self-denial.

Love was never a consideration. Her opinions were never a consideration. Best that she remained detached from the process, for she was but a cog in the great machinery of Marrying Well.

That night, however, she sobbed for this man she scarcely knew, a man, who, like her, had no say in the direction of his own life.

But the great machinery of Marrying Well ground on. Two weeks after the late Earl Fitzhugh's funeral, the Graves hosted his distant cousin the new Earl Fitzhugh for dinner.

Millie knew very little of the late earl. She knew even less of the new one, except that he was only nineteen, still in his last year at Eton. His youth disturbed her somewhat— she'd been prepared to marry an older man, not someone her own age. But other than that, she dwelled on him not at all: Her marriage was a business transaction; the less personal involvement from her, the more smoothly things would run.

Unfortunately, her indifference—and her peace of mind—came to an abrupt end the moment the new earl walked in the door.

* * *

$\mathcal{M}$illie was not without thoughts of her own. She very carefully watched what she said and did, but seldom censored her mind: it was the only freedom she had.

Sometimes, as she lay in bed at night, she thought of falling in love, in the ways of a Jane Austen novel—her mother did not allow her to read the Brontës. Love, it seemed to her, was a result born of careful, shrewd observation. Miss Elizabeth Bennet, for example, did not truly consider Mr. Darcy to have the makings of a fine husband until she had seen the majesty of Pemberley, which stood for Mr. Darcy's equally majestic character.

Millie imagined herself a wealthy, independent widow, inspecting the gentlemen available to her with wry, but humane wit. And if she were fortunate enough, finding that one gentleman of character, sense, and good humor.

That seemed to her the epitome of romantic love: the quiet satisfaction of two kindred souls brought together in gentle harmony.

She was, therefore, entirely unprepared for her internal upheaval, when the new Earl Fitzhugh was shown into the family drawing room. Like a visitation of angels, there flared a bright white glow in the center of her vision. Haloed by this supernatural light stood a young man who must have folded his wings at just that moment so as to bear a passing resemblance to a mortal.

An instinctive sense of self-preservation made her immediately lower her face, before she'd quite even comprehended the geography of his features. But she was all agitation inside, a sensation that was equal parts glee and misery.

Surely a mistake had been made. The late earl could not possibly have a cousin who looked like this. Any moment now he'd be introduced as the new earl's schoolmate, or perhaps the guardian Colonel Clements's son.

"Millie, allow me to present Lord Fitzhugh. Lord Fitzhugh, my daughter."

Dear God, it was him. This mind-bogglingly handsome young man was the new Lord Fitzhugh.

She had to lift her eyes. Lord Fitzhugh returned a steady, blue gaze. They shook hands.

"Miss Graves," he said.

Her heart thrashed drunkenly. She was not accustomed to such complete and undiluted masculine attention. Her mother had always been attentive and solicitous. But her father only ever spoke to her with one eye still on his newspaper.

Lord Fitzhugh, however, was focused entirely on her, as if she were the most important person he'd ever met.

"My lord," she murmured, acutely aware of the warmth on her face, and the old-master perfection of his cheekbones.

Dinner was announced on the heels of the introductions. The earl offered his arm to Mrs. Graves and it was with great envy that Millie took Colonel Clements's arm.

She glanced at the earl. He happened to be looking her way. Their eyes held for a moment. Heat pumped through her veins. She was jittery, stunned almost.

What was the matter with her? Millicent Graves, milquetoast extraordinaire, through whose veins dripped the *lack* of passion, did not experience such strange flashes and flutters. She'd never even read a Brontë novel, for goodness's sake. Why did she suddenly feel like one of the younger Bennet girls, the ones who giggled and shrieked and had absolutely no control over themselves?

Distantly she realized that she knew nothing of the earl's character, sense, or temperament. That she was behaving in a shallow and foolish manner, putting the cart before the horse. But the chaos inside her had a life and a will of its own.

As they entered the drawing room, Mrs. Clements said, "What a lovely table. Don't you agree, Fitz?"

"I do," said the earl.

His name was George Edward Arthur Granville Fitzhugh—the family name and the title were the same. But apparently those who knew him well called him Fitz.

Fitz, her lips and teeth played with the syllable. *Fitz*.

At dinner, the earl let Colonel Clements and Mrs. Graves carry the majority of the conversation. Was he shy? Did he still obey the tenet that children should be seen and not heard? Or was he using the opportunity to assess his possible future in-laws—and his possible future wife?

Except he didn't appear to be studying her. Not that he could do so easily: a three-tier, seven-branch silver epergne, sprouting orchids, lilies, and tulips from every appendage, blocked the direct line of sight between them.

Through petals and stalks, she could make out his occasional smiles—each of which made her ears hot—directed at Mrs. Graves to his left. But he looked more often in her father's direction.

Her grandfather and her uncle had built the Graves

fortune. Her father had been young enough, when the family coffer began to fill, to be sent to Harrow. He'd acquired the expected accent, but his natural temperament was too lackluster to quite emanate the gloss of sophistication his family had hoped for.

There he sat at the head of the table, neither a ruthless risk taker like his late father, nor a charismatic, calculating entrepreneur like his late brother, but a bureaucrat, a caretaker of the riches and assets thrust upon him. Hardly the most exciting of men.

Yet he commanded the earl's attention this night.

Behind him on the wall hung a large mirror in an ornate frame, which faithfully reflected the company at table. Millie sometimes looked into the mirror and pretended that she was an outside observer documenting the intimate particulars of a private meal. But tonight she had yet to give the mirror a glance, since the earl sat at the opposite end of the table, next to her mother.

She found him in the mirror. Their eyes met.

He had not been looking at her father. Via the mirror, he'd been looking at *her*.

Mrs. Graves had been forthcoming on the mysteries of marriage—she did not want Millie ambushed by the facts of life. The not-so-pretty reality of what happened between a man and a woman behind closed doors usually had Millie regard members of the opposite sex with wariness. But his attention caused only fireworks inside her—a detonation of thrill, a blast of full-fledged happiness.

If they were married, and if they were alone . . .

She flushed.

But she already knew: She would not mind it.

Not with him.

* * *

The gentlemen had barely rejoined the ladies in the drawing room when Mrs. Graves announced that Millie would play for the gathering.

"Millicent is splendidly accomplished at the pianoforte," she said.

For once, Millie was excited about the prospect of displaying her skills—she might lack true musicality, but she did possess an ironclad technique.

Mrs. Graves turned to Lord Fitzhugh. "Do you enjoy music, sir?"

"I do, most assuredly," he answered. "May I be of some use to Miss Graves? Turn the pages for her perhaps?"

Millie braced her hand on the music rack. The bench was not very long. He'd be sitting right next to her.

"Please do," said Mrs. Graves.

And just like that, Lord Fitzhugh was at Millie's side, so close that his trousers brushed the flounces of her skirts. He smelled fresh and brisk, like an afternoon in the country. And the smile on his face as he murmured his gratitude distracted her so much that she forgot that she should be the one to thank him.

He looked away from her to the score on the music rack. "Moonlight Sonata. Do you have something lengthier?"

The question rattled—and pleased—her. "Usually one only hears the first movement of the sonata, the *adagio sostenudo*. But there are two additional movements. I can keep playing, if you'd like."

"I'd be much obliged."

A good thing she played mechanically and largely from

memory, for she could not concentrate on the notes at all. The tips of his fingers rested lightly against a corner of the score sheet. He had lovely looking hands, strong and elegant. She imagined one of his hands gripped around a cricket ball—it had been mentioned at dinner that he played for the school team. The ball he bowled would be fast as lightning. It would knock over a wicket directly and dismiss the batter to the roar of the crowd's appreciation.

"I have a request, Miss Graves," he spoke very quietly. With her playing, no one could hear him but her.

"Yes, my lord?"

"I'd like you to keep playing no matter what I say."

Her heart skipped a beat. Now it was beginning to make sense. He wanted to sit next to her so that they could hold a private conversation in a room full of their elders.

"All right. I'll keep playing," she said. "What is it that you want to say, sir?"

"I'd like to know, Miss Graves, are you being forced into marriage?"

Ten thousand hours before the pianoforte was the only thing that kept Millie from coming to an abrupt halt. Her fingers continued to pressure the correct keys; notes of various descriptions kept on sprouting. But it could have been someone in the next house playing, so dimly did the music register.

"Do I—do I give the impression of being forced, sir?" Even her voice didn't quite sound her own.

He hesitated slightly. "No, you do not."

"Why do you ask then?"

"You are sixteen."

"It isn't unheard of for a girl to marry at sixteen."

"To a man more than twice her age?"

"You make the late earl sound decrepit. He was a man in his prime."

"I am sure there are thirty-three-year-old men who make sixteen-year-olds tremble in romantic yearning, but my cousin was not one of them."

They were coming to the end of the page; he turned it just in time. She chanced a quick glance at him. He did not look at her.

"May I ask you a question, my lord?" she heard herself say.

"Please."

"Are *you* being forced to marry me?"

The words left her in a spurt, like arterial bleeding. She was afraid of his answer. Only a man who was himself being forced would wonder whether she too was under the same duress.

He was silent for some time. "Do you not find this kind of arrangement exceptionally distasteful?"

Glee and misery—she'd been bouncing between the two wildly divergent emotions. But now there was only misery left, a sodden mass of it. His tone was perfectly courteous. Yet his question was an accusation of complicity: He would not be here if she hadn't agreed.

"I—" She was playing the *adagio sostenudo* much too fast—no moonlight in her sonata, only storm-driven branches whacking at shutters. "I suppose I've had time to become inured to it: I've known my whole life that I'd have no say in the matter."

"My cousin held out for years," said the earl. "He should have done it sooner: beget an heir and leave everything to his own son. We are barely related."

He did not want to marry her, she thought dazedly, not in the very least.

This was nothing new. His predecessor had not wanted to marry her, either; she had accepted his reluctance as par for the course. Had never expected anything else, in fact. But the unwillingness of the young man next to her on the piano bench—it was as if she'd been forced to hold a block of ice in her bare hands, the chill turning into a black, burning pain.

And the mortification of it, to be so eager for someone who reciprocated none of her sentiments, who was revolted by the mere thought of taking her as a wife.

He turned the next page. "Do you never think to yourself, *I won't do it*?"

"Of course I've *thought* of it," she said, suddenly bitter after all these years of placid obedience. But she kept her voice smooth and uninflected. "And then I think a little further. Do I run away? My skills as a lady are not exactly valuable beyond the walls of this house. Do I advertise my services as a governess? I know nothing of children— nothing at all. Do I simply refuse and see whether my father loves me enough to not disown me? I'm not sure I have the courage to find out."

He rubbed the corner of a page between his fingers. "How do you stand it?"

This time there was no undertone of accusation to his question. If she wanted to, she might even detect a bleak sympathy. Which only fed her misery, that foul beast with teeth like knives.

"I keep myself busy and do not think too deeply about it," she said, in as harsh a tone as she'd ever allowed herself.

There, she was a mindless automaton who did as others instructed: getting up, going to sleep, and earning heaps of disdain from prospective husbands in between.

They said nothing more to each other, except to exchange the usual civilities at the end of her performance. Everyone applauded. Mrs. Clements said very nice things about Millie's musicianship—which Millie barely heard.

The rest of the evening lasted the length of Elizabeth's reign.

Mr. Graves, usually so phlegmatic and taciturn, engaged the earl in a lively discussion of cricket. Millie and Mrs. Graves gave their attention to Colonel Clements's army stories. Had someone looked in from the window, the company in the drawing room would appear perfectly normal, jovial even.

And yet there was enough misery present to wilt flowers and curl wallpaper. Nobody noticed the earl's distress. And nobody—except Mrs. Graves, who stole anxious looks at Millie—noticed Millie's. Was unhappiness really so invisible? Or did people simply prefer to turn away, as if from lepers?

After the guests took their leave, Mr. Graves pronounced the dinner a *succès énorme*. And he, who'd remained skeptical on the previous earl throughout, gave his ringing endorsement to the young successor. "I shall be pleased to have Lord Fitzhugh for a son-in-law."

"He hasn't proposed yet," Millie reminded him, "and he might not."

Or so she hoped. Let them find someone else for her. Anyone else.

"Oh, he will most assuredly propose," said Mr. Graves. "He has no choice."